Restless Heart

Restless Heart

Emma Lang

KENSINGTON PUBLISHING CORP.
www.kensingtonbooks.com

BRAVA BOOKS are published by

Kensington Publishing Corp.
119 West 40th Street
New York, NY 10018

All Kensington titles, imprints and distributed lines are available at special quantity discounts for bulk purchases for sales promotion, premiums, fund-raising, educational or institutional use.

Special book excerpts or customized printings can also be created to fit specific needs. For details, write or phone the office of the Kensington Special Sales Manager: Kensington Publishing Corp., 119 West 40th Street, New York, NY 10018, Attn. Special Sales Department. Phone: 1-800-221-2647.

ISBN-13: 978-0-7582-4752-0
ISBN-10: 0-7582-4752-4

First Trade Paperback Printing: February 2011

10 9 8 7 6 5 4 3 2 1

Printed in the United States of America

Chapter One

April 1873

Angeline Hunter lived a lie, each moment of each day. She endured the guilt because she had no other choice. It wasn't as if she could simply forget everything she'd escaped, or announce to the world just who she really was. No, she had made a choice and there was no going back.

She refused to feel sorry for herself; after all, she was alive and free.

Her day started before dawn in the kitchen of the Blue Plate restaurant. It was an exceptionally cold spring day and she was glad to bc in the warm kitchen making biscuits.

She put the pan of biscuits in the stove and tucked two more pieces of wood into its big belly. The first pot of coffee had just finished burbling, so she poured cool water in to settle the grounds, then sneaked a cup. As she sipped at the brew, she enjoyed a few moments of peace before the rush of the morning customers.

The back door slammed and Angeline nearly jumped out of her skin.

"Mornin', Miss Angeline."

She turned to see ten-year-old Dennis Fox step into the

kitchen with a bucket of wood for the stove. His mother, Karen, was a waitress at the restaurant. She always made sure he helped out everyone who worked at the Blue Plate. He was a good boy, a hard worker who seemed to get things done before anyone even had to ask him.

"Good morning, Dennis. Thank you for the wood. We'll definitely need it." She wrapped her hands around the ceramic mug, trying to absorb as much heat from it as she could.

"Frost was thick this morning." Dennis set the bucket beside the stove, and held his chapped hands up to the heat pouring off it.

Angeline looked out the tiny window above the sink, but the glass was fogged from the warmth of the kitchen. She lived above the restaurant in a room just large enough for a bed and a crate upended to keep a lamp nearby. Lucky for her, she didn't need to go outside in the cold most days.

Dennis set a paper-wrapped package on the table. "Somebody asked me to give you this." With a little grin, he was out the backdoor before she could ask him any questions.

She stared at the package, wondering who had given it to him and why. It had been six months since she and Lettie had arrived in the small town of Forestville. During the last year, the two of them had grown closer than most folks would ever be. They were both trying to flee the past, and they shared a secret no one must ever learn. Angeline had even dropped the last name Brown and kept the name she was born with, Hunter.

Angeline needed to make another batch of biscuit dough, but the package aroused her curiosity. Her father had always called her curiosity a sin, something to be ashamed of. That thought alone made her pick up the package and untie the twine.

She peeled the paper back and peered inside. It was a

book. Angeline stared at it, as if she couldn't believe someone had given her a book. The title read *Sense and Sensibility*. She'd never heard of it, but judging by the condition, it was brand new. Since she'd left home, she had discovered the joy of reading books, and had become a voracious reader. This was the first new book she'd ever held.

Growing up in Utah, she'd led a structured, regimented life in the Mormon church. She lived in a ward, where everyone was controlled by elders who told them what to do and how to do it. It was all based on church doctrine, but Angeline now realized just how narrow her world had been.

"What do you have there, child?" Marta Gunderson, who ran the Blue Plate with her husband, Pieter, came into the kitchen with a bowl of eggs for breakfast. She was a German immigrant who was an amazing cook and a wonderful person. Along with her husband, she had blond hair, a big heart, and made the restaurant feel like a big family. Angeline knew she'd been lucky to find a job and a home with the Gundersons.

"A book." Angeline smiled at her boss. "Dennis brought it to me wrapped in paper. He said someone had given it to him. It's a bit of a mystery."

"You don't know who gave it to you?" Marta peered at it. "That is mysterious. It looks new."

"I think it is new." Angeline felt the cover, and ran her fingers along the spine. "It's a lovely gift."

"Well, maybe you have an admirer." Marta smiled. "You're a beautiful girl, Angeline. I'm sure more than one young man in town has an eye on you, wanting to court you."

Angeline's face flushed at the mention of the young men in town. She couldn't possibly accept any man's courting her, and she couldn't tell Marta why.

"I'm not interested in young men courting me, Marta."

"Of course, you are. You should get married and have babies." Marta patted her cheek. "Love, that's what you need, child."

The book, which had been a lovely, unexpected gift, now represented the lack of possibility in her future. Angeline couldn't accept it because if Marta was right, it was a gift from a young man who was wasting his time. She set the book on the stool in the corner.

Angeline could never marry because she was already married, and there was no hope of love in her future.

The morning passed quickly with a steady stream of customers. Angeline and Marta cooked side by side as they had each day since her arrival in Forestville. It was an easy partnership, with the older woman concocting her delicious recipes at the stove while Angeline chopped vegetables and potatoes, and made all the baked goods.

By ten o'clock, they were sitting at the kitchen table drinking coffee with the waitresses, Lettie, Karen, and Alice Peters. It had become a ritual for the five of them to spend time together between meals. Pieter avoided the kitchen during those times, claiming a rooster didn't belong with the hens.

"Did you hear someone gave Angeline a gift?" Karen, a dark-haired, plump woman, who'd been widowed during the war, smiled at Angeline.

"Go on. Who gave you a gift?" Alice sat up, her brown eyes full of interest. A twenty-year-old with a pretty smile and curly brown hair, she was the favorite of most of the young men who visited the restaurant.

"I don't know." Angeline shrugged. "It doesn't matter because I can't accept it."

"What? Of course, you can. What was it?" Alice looked around the kitchen.

"It was a book, a new one too." Marta nodded sagely. "I think it's very sweet."

"Maybe it was a mistake." Angeline wanted the conversation to be over.

"Oh, I don't think it was a mistake. My Dennis told me a man stopped him outside the restaurant and specifically told him to give the package to Angeline, the blond angel in the kitchen."

Cold fear crept into her stomach. She lived in fear that her past would catch up with her one day. After Karen's mention of the man who gave Dennis the package, Angeline's instincts were screaming for her to run, to leave Forestville. Immediately.

She got to her feet, unable to sit there any longer. Perhaps one day she might find a place where she could be safe from Josiah, but it obviously wasn't in Forestville.

"Don't be afraid, Angeline. You look as white as a sheet." Karen patted her hand. "It was Samuel Carver, the man who does carpentry work around town. He eats here every day and has taken a shine to you."

Samuel Carver. She didn't even know who he was.

"Who is he?" Angeline was proud of the fact her voice didn't shake.

"His father runs the newspaper. Samuel was just a young man when the war started and he enlisted." Marta shook her head. "Poor boy looked like a skeleton in rags when he came back."

Angeline, despite her initial fear, was caught up in Samuel's story. "What happened?"

"He left an eager boy of eighteen, came back a man much older than twenty-two. Now he's quiet, standoffish even. He bought some supplies here and there until he had himself a set of tools; he works with wood, fixing things, making furniture." Marta patted Angeline's hand. "It took a few years, but now it looks like he's set his sights on a pretty girl to court."

"I don't want him to court me." She turned toward the sink, eager to change the subject. Even if the man was a longtime resident, a man with ambition, she wanted nothing to do with him.

"If she doesn't want attention from a man, then we need to respect that." Lettie met her gaze, understanding clear in her brown eyes. The two of them had a secret no one knew about.

"Well, give the man a chance, Angeline." Karen slurped her coffee noisily, a habit that annoyed even her friends. "He's actually quite handsome."

"Yes, he is handsome for a half-breed. His mama was an Indian, you know. But he does have good hair and teeth, which are important. Plus his father educated him, so he's a smart half-breed." Alice sat prim and proper at the table, speaking of Samuel as if he were a horse up for auction. "It wouldn't be so bad to have him as a beau, since you don't have any family and all."

Half-breed? Angeline didn't even know what that meant, but from Alice's snide tone, it couldn't be good. Honestly, it didn't matter if this man was rich and had a big house, she didn't want to have anything to do with any man. Ever.

"None of that matters to me. I don't want to have a beau. I'd like to be left alone." Angeline washed her mug by rote, not really seeing it. She was desperately trying to keep her memories locked away, but the darkness pulsed behind the locked door within her.

Be strong.

"Oh, Angeline, you can't mean that. No one wants to work here unless they have to." Karen sounded sad and angry at the same time. "I would take him if he wasn't younger than me."

"You can't be that choosy, you know. The men in this area aren't all finds," Alice joined in. "And like I said, for a half-breed he's—"

"Enough." Lettie rose, her chair scraping across the floor. "Let her be. She doesn't want a beau, a sweetheart, or gifts. Perhaps you all need to mind your business."

The silence in the kitchen was palpable, charged with emotion Angeline didn't want to deal with. She wiped her hands on her apron and stepped out the backdoor for fresh air. It didn't matter if it was frigid outside; she couldn't bear to be in there another moment.

Samuel Carver leaned over the old printing press and tried to pry the paper from its maw. Damn thing was older than Methuselah and regularly ate the precious newsprint. If he had some money, he'd buy replacement parts for his father, but publishing a newspaper brought in only enough to scrape by.

Without warning, the paper came free and Samuel careened backward with it clutched in his hand. He landed against the table behind him with a thud. Sam closed his eyes and counted to ten, his hand massaging his bruised back.

"Are you all right?" His father stood there with a cup of coffee, his salt-and-pepper hair in disarray, glasses perched on his forehead. His bright blue eyes were full of concern, and for the first time that morning, lucid and focused.

"I'm fine, just fighting with the monster again this morning." Sam held up the crumpled paper in his fist. "Ate more newsprint already today."

"Sorry. I went to get coffee and it was running just fine." Michael Carver had a brilliant mind; he'd been an excellent teacher, writer, and father. But something had started stealing bits and pieces of that mind, leaving him with holes in his memory and his abilities. Sam had hidden his father's decline from most everyone, but eventually they would know.

It was becoming more and more difficult to keep up the pretense every day without making his father panic or get insulted. Sam was exhausted from the effort and the malfunctioning press notched his frustration level even higher.

He took a deep breath and thought about something else as he readied the machine to begin printing again. That something else was inevitably Angeline Hunter.

It had been six months since she'd arrived in Forestville and a day hadn't gone by that he didn't think about her. She was exquisite to look at, in face and form. He'd never felt that kind of reaction from a woman before, no matter how beautiful. No, there was something else, some kind of instant connection.

Unfortunately, she hardly even knew he existed. At least she hadn't until this morning, when he had impulsively handed Dennis a book to give her. Now she probably thought Sam was odd. However, he'd often seen her sitting on the back steps of the restaurant reading a book in the late day's light. The halo of the sunset surrounded her, making her ethereal in his eyes.

Sam had been struck by what he could only term infatuation. She had already made an impression on him, but the sight of her reading had brought his fascination to a different level.

Now he thought of her every day with an almost embarrassing frequency. Sam wasn't given to flights of fancy or poetic rambling, but there was something about the woman that called to him at an elemental level. He'd given the book to her on impulse. It had cost him quite a bit of money he could hardly afford. He wasn't sure yet if he regretted the impulse.

Sam loaded more paper into the printing press and started it running again. This time, thanks be to whatever forces were at work, the press did not jam. It hummed along as if it wasn't the most confounded machine on the planet.

He sat down with a sigh at the old scarred desk in the corner. The desk was something his father had found abandoned by a wagon train heading to Oregon twenty years earlier. The roll top had long since stopped functioning. It was still solid though, and served its intended purpose, even if it was as ugly as the printing press.

Life in Forestville was somewhat boring, truth be told, and most of his father's stories on the one-page sheet related to happenings outside of town. Information he received from other sources was infinitely more interesting.

Sam sometimes wondered why he stayed there, what kept him in the small town, or even what had brought him back after the war. It was hard to understand himself, much less to articulate to someone else.

Life was predictable in Forestville and it was that sameness he craved. After witnessing the evil that men do, the sweetness of his hometown was a salve to his wounded soul. And now there was Angeline.

He needed to get to work on his next job, a fence at the Widow Primrose's house, but his mind kept wandering to the restaurant. Perhaps if he spoke to Angeline, it might help tamp down some of his imaginings. Of course, that meant any fantasies he'd built up around her would be put to the test. She might be completely different than he expected.

Sam stared down at his ink-stained hands, at the scars and calluses. He might not be a gentleman, or be able to provide anything aside from conversation, but she might like him. What did he have to lose? It was noontime, so he would have dinner at the Blue Plate.

Decision made, Sam rose from the desk and headed outside to wash his hands. He could at least try to get the ink off his fingers.

He hoped she liked the book.

Angeline was off-center and jittery. She dropped a plate, put too much salt in the meat, and forgot to put vegetables on no less than two orders. Marta kept looking at her as if she was a stranger, and Karen had completely lost patience with her.

"You need to stop this right now." Lettie frowned at her. "You're calling attention to yourself."

Angeline looked up at her friend, the only person in the world who would ever know what she'd gone through. "I can't help it."

"Yes, you can. Nothing bad has happened to us in Forestville, but that doesn't mean it won't. If you keep this up, you won't have a job for long. No man is worth giving up what you've fought tooth and nail for." Lettie's brown gaze was steady, familiar. With a nod, she went back out into the restaurant with two plates to serve, leaving Angeline with her thoughts.

Lettie's words helped Angeline come down from the ledge she was teetering on. She'd never had someone admire her from afar, and since she'd left Tolson, Utah, she had never felt safe. Ever. Just because she and Lettie hadn't seen anyone following them didn't mean no one was.

She understood this Samuel Carver was someone who had lived in Forestville all his life. He was harmless, according to everyone who worked at the Blue Plate, even Pieter. Yet she was still unaccountably nervous about the entire affair.

Angeline decided to give the book back to him. It wouldn't be right to keep it, especially considering how nervous it made her. She had rarely received gifts in her life; she could count them on one hand. They had all been from her sister, Eliza, given in secret since their father did not believe in gifts. He was a church elder, a man who was strict and severe, never allowing his daughters even an inch of room to be individuals. They learned early on to obey him or suffer a beating with a switch, or his belt. They celebrated nothing and worshipped every day. It was a gray, dreary, colorless existence.

Angeline still marveled at the colors of the world around her now that she had her eyes open.

"Don't forget to slice the bread." Marta set a ham slice on a plate. Her reminder was surprising since Angeline rarely forgot to do anything.

With an embarrassed smile, Angeline sliced the next loaf of bread quickly, placing two steaming pieces on the plate. She added carrots just in time for Alice to come in with a big smile on her face.

"Your beau is here."

Angeline stopped in mid-motion. "Excuse me?"

"Your beau is here. Samuel Carver is here for dinner and I would swear he's spiffed up for it." Alice grinned widely. "He's ordered the ham and potatoes, with apple pie. Do you want to serve him?"

"No, I do not." Angeline felt her nervousness returning and silently cursed Alice for her silly enthusiasm.

"Oh, why not? He asked for you." She waggled her eyebrows. "He might not be rich, but he sure is sweet." With a cheeky grin, she took the plate and left the kitchen.

"You might as well talk to him. Don't listen to Alice prattle on about him being a half-breed. He's a good boy, no matter who his mother was." Marta put ham on another plate. This time it was for Samuel Carver. "If you hide in here, it will make it worse."

Angeline knew she was right. The longer she hemmed and hawed about the gift and the man, the worse it would be. She needed to tell him there could be no future between them.

With a firm spine, she put potatoes on the plate to accompany the ham and nodded to Marta. "I'll be right back."

Angeline stepped into the restaurant and looked around. There were a number of people at tables, but she had no idea what the man looked like. Alice's silly description meant nothing except that he was a man. As if she'd conjured the waitress, Alice appeared next to a man sitting in front of the bay window. She pointed and winked at Angeline.

Now she really was uncomfortable because Alice had no tact or consideration for other people. The man looked up and saw Angeline standing there.

The ground shifted beneath her.

His hair was the color of midnight, so dark it was nearly blue-black. It hung straight to his shoulders, too long to be fashionable. The ends curled up slightly as if a breeze had come through and ruffled it. His shoulders were wide, but not overly so.

He had an intense stare that made goose bumps crawl over her skin. His eyes were also darker than pitch, black pools that seemed to be bottomless. To her surprise, his skin was lightly tanned, with tiny laugh lines around his eyes and mouth. He could be any age, but she knew him to be twenty-nine. He had the demeanor of a man who had seen too much in his short life.

The bright blue of his shirt contrasted so much with the rest of him, she had to blink to absorb it all. He was a striking man, not classically handsome but fascinating.

Angeline did not ever remembering seeing him before, which wasn't surprising because she worked in the kitchen most days.

She managed to swallow, somehow, before she stepped toward his table with her heart firmly lodged in her throat. He watched her with wide eyes, unsmiling and unthreatening. She couldn't have explained it to anyone, but Marta had been right—Samuel Carver was no threat to her.

"Good afternoon, Miss Hunter." His voice had a lilt to it, one she'd never heard before. It was like warm honey on a piece of toast.

Angeline thought perhaps she would be embarrassed by her reaction, but she wasn't. "Good afternoon, Mr. Carver." At least she set the plate down on the table without dropping it.

He smiled. "I hope you're enjoying the book."

She licked her lips and managed a small smile. "I've never had a new book before. I-I wanted to say thank you, but it's much too extravagant for me to accept."

There, that sounded reasonable and intelligent. He, however, shook his head.

"I can't take it back."

"Please, it must have cost you a lot of money." She put her hands in her apron pockets and clenched them into fists, her right hand pressed up against the book. "It's not appropriate for me to accept it."

He hadn't even glanced at the plate. His gaze was locked on hers. "I know it was forward of me, but I saw you reading on the back steps one day. You seemed to be at peace with a book in your hands."

Angeline unwillingly nodded. "Yes, that's exactly it. It's almost as if the books give me peace."

This time when he smiled, she found herself smiling back. The situation had gotten complicated in less than five minutes.

"I feel the same way about books. So please accept the gift from a fellow reader. It's nothing more."

She was torn between what she had to do and what she wanted to do. Angeline could not become attached or involved with any man, regardless of her silly heart's reaction to him. It didn't make it any easier to conjure up every other reason why she needed to keep her distance from him.

Angeline wanted to sit down and talk to him. Horrified by her reaction to this stranger, this man who seemed to be able to see into the depths of her soul, she backed away.

"I have to go back to the kitchen and work."

"Of course. It was wonderful to meet you." This time he looked hesitant, almost as if he was shy.

Angeline knew she really should not accept the book, but it remained firmly in her apron pocket as she stepped back toward the kitchen. She felt his stare as she retreated, knowing he watched her from the table by the window.

Her heart skipped a beat.

Chapter Two

Angeline sat on the corner of her bed and stared at the book. The morning chill hung in the air as the lamplight filled the room with warm shadows. She caressed the spine and cover, ashamed of her enchantment with it, but thrilled to have it in her hands.

She hadn't yet opened it, afraid if she cracked the spine, Samuel could not sell the book back to whomever he'd bought it from. Angeline couldn't keep it, she knew that, but she pretended for a little while that she could. It was an extravagant gift, meant for a woman who could give a man something in exchange. She was not that woman and would never be.

Samuel was not what she'd expected. He was handsome, mesmerizing even, with his dark hair and eyes. Yet her attraction to him was much more than that; it was as if she already knew him. That's what scared her the most—she could not be with him, yet now that she'd met him, she was drawn to him. In fact, she'd even dreamed of him the night before.

She could only remember fragments of the dream, but when she thought of Samuel, she felt warm inside. Surprisingly, she hoped he would be there for breakfast so she could see him. Perhaps she'd built up a fantasy about him that couldn't possibly come true. Or perhaps she'd find that he was even more than she imagined.

Angeline brought the book to her face and inhaled. The sharp scent of paper and ink tickled her nose, tempting her to open it, to indulge in the pleasure of reading it. She closed her eyes and breathed in again, her fingers tightening on the cover.

If only she could keep it.

With a sigh, she set the book on the bed and rose. It was time to go to work. The sun was nearly up, which meant she was already late getting the biscuits made.

As she walked out the door, she looked back at the book lying on the bed so innocently. Angeline should have handed it back to Samuel the day before, or at least dropped it by his house in the afternoon. All she could do now was wonder why she had not.

Samuel woke abruptly, covered in sweat and breathing as if he'd run from one end of town to the other. After taking deep gulps of air to chase away the shadows riding his back, he took a sip from the glass of water on the stand next to the bed. He'd discovered soon after returning home from the war that if he didn't pour the water in the glass before bed, his hands shook too much to do it after he woke.

The room was awash in the gray light of dawn, cold enough that he could almost see his breath. He needed to get up and stoke the fire, but he couldn't yet because of his wounded leg. The muscles were constantly sore, but now he was in pain, and a great deal of it. It was a reminder of the war he could not forget, no matter how hard he tried. The blood, the pain, the very image of the bayonet slashing open his thigh replayed itself almost daily. Another "gift" from his time as a soldier.

After a few minutes of vigorous rubbing, the pain receded

enough that he could finally get up. Sam rose and walked to the window. He pressed his forehead against the cold glass.

Something had happened in his dream. He couldn't quite remember what, but he knew it had to do with Angeline. She had been in danger and he was desperate to help her. They'd exchanged a few dozen words and now he was dreaming about her?

What the hell was that all about?

Sam was afraid he was becoming obsessed with the blonde. Jesus, he'd bought her a gift before he'd even heard her speak a word. How loco was that? His fellow soldiers would have teased him mercilessly about being a lovesick fool.

They might not have been too far off the mark either.

He managed to shake off the uneasy feeling that plagued him, but just barely. She had secrets behind her blue eyes, deep ones he craved to know more about, even if he wouldn't admit it to anyone else. For six months she'd lived and worked at the restaurant, without anyone really getting to know her.

Sam just wanted to stop being obsessed with her. It was causing him to lose sleep, spend plenty of time pleasuring himself, and countless minutes wondering what she was doing, thinking, planning. He was a fool and he knew it.

She hardly knew he existed.

None of that changed his feelings though. He craved her presence like the earth craved the rain. She was mysterious, alluring, and he was attracted to her as he'd never been to anyone before. Perhaps if he kissed her it would break the spell she seemed to weave around him without even trying.

Sam cleaned up and dressed, telling himself he was hungry for breakfast and not hungry for Angeline. Oh, how he lied.

The morning air was a light caress on his face as he walked toward the Blue Plate. A low mist hovered over the ground as he walked through town. The sun peeked over the horizon, not yet strong enough to burn off the chill in the air. Spring was coming, finally, judging by the fact the dew had not frozen.

If spring was just around the corner, it meant he would get more work and maybe his father could sell the newspaper business. He was having more bad days than good and Sam knew it was only a matter of time before his father would have to be watched all the time. For that, Sam needed money. He'd have less cash to spend at the restaurant, not to mention less time.

When he arrived at the Blue Plate, instead of heading inside to eat, he found himself walking around to the back. To the spot where he'd first seen Angeline reading on the steps back in October. A lifetime ago it seemed. He didn't know what compelled him to walk back there, but when he did, he found Angeline without a coat, gathering wood from the pile.

"Angel, what are you doing? You'll freeze to death." He took the wood from her as she stared at him, her nose red from the cold.

His arm brushed her breast, earning a surprised yelp from her and an instant hard-on from him. Her scent washed over him, feeding his arousal, making him nearly careen out of control.

He leaned toward her, the wood forgotten, the coolness of the air a distant memory. She licked her lips, the nip in the air making them a darker pink. Sam moved as if in a daze, his body buzzing with only one goal.

Kissing Angeline.

His blood thrummed through his body and he swore the air between them crackled as he came within an inch of being pressed up against her. She sucked in a short breath, her blue gaze as wide as the sky above.

Against his will, with his mind screaming for him to stop, Sam leaned forward and kissed her. Oh, God, her lips were softer than anything he'd ever felt in his life. She tasted of coffee, of woman, of an angel's sweetness. He brushed her lips again, their breaths mingling in the cold air in a small poof of whiteness.

Sam groaned and stepped back, this time it was his body howling in agony. His cock was hammering against the buttons that held it back.

What the hell had he just done?

Angeline shivered and licked her lips again. "What did you call me?"

Sam stopped, completely flummoxed by her question. He expected her to slap him, kick him in the balls, or at least turn and leave him standing there like the idiot he was. "I don't know. What did I call you?"

"You called me Angel." She shook her head slowly. "Believe me, I am no angel, Samuel."

He needed to apologize, but didn't know how. Sam wasn't used to the softer things in life. A warrior at heart, he could hardly bear not taking this woman to his bed. He wanted her with the heat of a thousand suns.

"You look angelic to me. And please, call me Sam."

Was that the best he could do? *Moron.*

"Don't let the outside fool you. Nothing about me is angelic." She backed up toward the stairs and stumbled.

Sam grabbed her by the elbow and she gasped; her gaze again slammed to his. He wanted to gasp too. Touching her sent a jolt through him unequaled in his life. It was as if a bolt of lightning had come down from the clear sky and struck them. Every hair on his body stood on end.

Her mouth opened and she scrambled to her feet, apparently eager to stop touching him. Sam rubbed his hands together to prevent himself from reaching for her again.

He didn't necessarily believe in the gods or the spiritual teachings of his mother. Yet, the gods in their wisdom had obviously made this woman to be his other half, his mate. There could be no other explanation.

"I have to get back to work. Marta will be wondering what happened to me." Her voice was strong, but he heard a slight tremble nonetheless.

"Let me bring in the wood for you."

She hesitated and Sam didn't blame her. "All right, come in then, Sam."

His name on her lips sent a shiver through him that had nothing to do with the cold, and everything to do with the arousal already coursing through him. He filled his arms with wood and stepped into the warm kitchen. Marta stood before the stove, frying bacon. When she spotted him, her brows went up.

"You don't look much like Daniel." She chuckled. "Thank you for helping Angeline. I'm not sure where that boy has gotten to."

Sam put the wood in the bucket beside the stove. "More?" He directed the question to Marta, unable to look at his angel without dropping to his knees to beg for one hour in her bed.

Completely fucking loco.

"Another armful would be perfect. Thank you, Sam." She winked at him and inclined her head toward Angeline, who was currently scrubbing her hands in the wooden sink.

Sam wanted to press himself against her, feel the softness of her ass as it cradled his hardness. He wanted to cup her breasts and pinch her nipples until they budded beneath his fingers.

If he wasn't careful he might embarrass himself in front of Marta, and then Pieter would try to kick his ass. Shaking off the urgency of his apparently uncontrollable lust for Angeline, Sam went back out into the cold. He sucked in a lungful of crisp air, then filled his arms one more time with wood.

This time when he came back in the kitchen, only Marta was there. Disappointment tasted like ash on his tongue.

"Oh, don't be discouraged, young man. She's got no family to speak of, except for Lettie, and I think she's a cousin or an aunt. There's no one to protect that girl, and I think someone has hurt her already." Marta shook a wooden spoon at him. "You behave yourself and no more sneaking kisses."

Unbelievably, Sam's cheeks heated. "I didn't sneak."

"No, but you took without asking. She's a bit flustered, but lucky for you, not angry. I'd say it's a good start, even if you did flub the first kiss." Marta nodded sagely. "Mark my words, she's never shown a speck of interest in a man before. You, Samuel Carver, are just what she needs."

Sam grinned at her prediction. If she was right, then he had a chance even if he did make a mistake. However, the kiss itself was no mistake. He'd spend many a moment reliving the feel of her lips against his.

It would only get better from here.

Angeline splashed water on her face and told herself to relax. She could hardly believe she'd stood there and let him kiss her. Not once, but twice.

And she'd enjoyed every second of it.

She gripped the washstand with both hands as the water dripped from her face into the basin. Her entire body trembled with the aftermath of the kisses, but mostly from when he'd touched her. She'd never felt anything like it, even when she'd kissed Jonathan Morton, the man she'd once dreamed of marrying. Her life had taken a right turn since then, and the sweet infatuation she had had with the young man was long gone, destroyed by the secret she now bore: She was a married woman.

Yes, her marriage as third wife to Josiah Brown had crushed every dream she'd ever had, and the horror that followed was worse than any nightmare she could have imagined. A shudder snaked down her spine as the dark memories crept across her mind. She wanted so badly to forget, to erase the memories of his cold hands and hard fists. She shivered and hugged herself. She could not let the ghosts of her past ruin the present.

Now here she was in a situation she'd never expected, never wanted. She was drawn to Samuel Carver, to his dark visage, his intensity, and even his warm, soft lips. Her body heated all over again and she splashed more water on her face.

She needed to talk to someone who could help her figure out why she had such a strong reaction to a man she barely knew. And especially why she let him kiss her and silently encouraged him to. Her sister, Eliza, would know, but she was off with her man somewhere and couldn't help.

Angeline dried her face and fixed her hair, tucking the stray strands into the braid hanging down her back. She knew the person she should talk to was Lettie, the only woman who knew what Angeline had gone through, what had sent them both running into the night.

She'd never expected someone like Samuel, nor what his presence did to her equilibrium. What she needed to do now was pretend nothing had happened. That thought made a chuckle burst from her throat—it would be easier to tell the sun not to rise.

The rest of the afternoon passed quickly and Angeline was too busy to think about Samuel, or his kisses. She didn't catch her breath until nearly eight o'clock, after the supper crowds had finally thinned.

"I'll be back in a few minutes, child. I need to check to make sure Pieter ate." Marta left Angeline alone in the kitchen to clean up.

After putting on water to heat so she could finish the dishes, she poked her head out of the kitchen door and waited until Lettie noticed her. Angeline motioned her friend into the kitchen, eager to talk. She wrung her hands as she paced the kitchen until finally Lettie came in.

"What do you need?" The brunette was a bit abrupt, although never rude. She just didn't do what she called "wasting time" talking.

"I need to talk to you," Angeline blurted. "About a man."

Lettie's brows went up. "A man? What man?"

"Samuel Carver, the one who gave me the book." Angeline touched the book, still firmly tucked into her apron. "He kissed me."

"He did what? Did he force you?" Lettie sounded so fierce, Angeline was nearly afraid for Samuel.

"No, nothing like that. I, uh, I let him kiss me. And, well, I liked it." Angeline's cheeks heated as she confessed what was really bothering her. "After Josiah, I didn't think, I mean, I never thought I'd want someone to kiss me."

Lettie took her hands. "You are too young to have that monster's memory on your skin. I'm sorry you had to go through that."

Angeline managed a shaky smile, although inside she wanted to cry. It hadn't been her choice, of course. Her father followed the teachings of the church of Latter Day Saints, and she was taught to obey no matter what. She didn't have the wherewithal to refuse an order to marry a man who had offered for her. She'd always wished she'd had Eliza's spirit, but instead Angeline had been the obedient daughter, never knowing she would nearly give her life for her obedience.

Eliza had left home with nothing but her courage and her books to follow a hired gun sent by Josiah to track down his runaway wives. Angeline was alive only because of her sister and her amazing bravery. Eliza had stayed with the bounty hunter to ensure Angeline's survival.

"I'm sorry you did too. That man deserves no woman in his bed." Angeline's voice trembled with fury. Although she was terrified of Josiah, if he was there she would strike him with anything she could lay her hands on. He'd taken away her future, her innocence, and her trust.

"Truer words were never spoken." Lettie didn't smile much, which was understandable considering she'd lived under Josiah's rule for five years.

Angeline's eyes pricked with tears. "I'm confused, Lettie. I don't know what to do. The first time I saw Sam, I felt strange, as if it wasn't really me talking to him. And then today when he kissed me, when he touched my hand, I had never felt such a thing."

Lettie led her to the table and they sat down. "What did you feel?" She seemed genuinely interested, as if she herself had never experienced such attraction either.

"It was like a thousand fireflies had landed inside me, their heat and flutters warming me until I felt hot. His lips were so soft, softer than flower petals." Angeline had never considered herself a poet, but the words simply flowed from her, as if they'd been trapped there since her encounter with Samuel. "I didn't understand what was happening and my reaction scared me."

Lettie sighed. "I remember that feeling, the trembling in your stomach, the tingles on your skin."

"Yes, that's it, exactly." Angeline frowned. "You didn't feel that with . . ."

"No, absolutely not." Lettie shook her head so hard, her hair nearly came out of its bun. "I felt nothing but disgust and fear with Josiah. No, it was another man, my first love, Robert. We waited to get married until I was twenty-three, but by then his parents had already arranged for him to marry an eighteen-year-old girl."

"I'm sorry, Lettie. I didn't know." Angeline saw the sadness beneath the anger. Lettie might be a bit caustic on the outside, but it was a wall she'd built to protect herself from the terrible dark things in the world.

"It was seven years ago, a lifetime it seems. I never forgot the feeling of kissing Robert though." Lettie looked infinitely sad. "I knew he was the only man for me, but he has three children and a wife now. Sometimes I avoided going to church so I wouldn't have to see them together."

Angeline heard the pain in her voice and gripped her friend's hands. "Oh, Lettie, there must be someone else out there for you."

"I doubt that." Lettie's left brow rose. "We're both stuck in a situation of our own doing, trapped by the shadow of a man who refuses to let us go."

The reminder made Angeline's stomach twist. Lettie was right, of course. They would never be free of Josiah Brown until he died. Although he was fifty, he was in excellent health judging by the strength in his hands and fists.

She wanted Lettie to tell her what to do, to reassure Angeline her needs were normal, and to follow her instincts. Yet deep down, she knew it wouldn't happen. Lettie knew the risks they took every day and having a relationship with a man was simply out of the question.

Angeline's heart squeezed so hard, tears pricked her eyes.

Chapter Three

It became a game of sorts. Sam would say hello and Angeline would respond. Then she'd walk away before he could take the conversation any further. For the last two weeks, he'd been frustrated, aroused, and intrigued.

He could see in her eyes she was interested, yet she held herself back, turning away. Still, she met his gaze when he walked into the restaurant. Every time he saw her blue eyes, he immediately thought of their kiss, the sheer bliss of those stolen moments in the cold morning air.

Not to mention the dreams he was having about her every night. For Christ's sake, he hadn't come on his sheets since he was thirteen years old. He'd had to wash them twice over the last week. Thank God, his father hadn't noticed. He was busy with the paper, or so lost in his own world, he wouldn't have seen a train coming through their living room.

Sam had to talk to her, had to make her understand he meant her no harm. He couldn't continue this way or he'd fall over from exhaustion. Even the Widow Primrose had noticed how distracted he'd been. For God's sake, he'd nearly nailed his thumb to the fence he'd been building for her.

It was embarrassing as hell.

"You like that blond girl, eh?"

Sam turned to find an old man peering up at him. He was a grizzled old coot with the dirtiest clothes Sam had ever seen. He'd often seen the man hanging around behind the restaurant, digging in the scraps.

"That's none of your business, old-timer."

"It's my business all right." The old man poked at his shoulder with one bony, dirty finger. "I look after those girls at the Blue Plate for Pieter. He gives me free vittles, but even if he didn't, I'd watch over them."

Sam didn't know what to make of the man. "How long have you been looking out for them?"

"Oh, roundabout five years." The old man's breath gusted past Sam and yesterday's onions right along with it.

Sam eased back away from him, a hammer firmly gripped in his hand. "That so? Do they know about it?" He had no idea what loco notions the stranger had in his head, but he wasn't about to take any chances.

"Miss Marta does and Karen. That Alice—" He scrunched up his nearly toothless mouth. "She's mean enough I don't talk much to her, but the blond angel, she's something different."

Sam narrowed his gaze. "You'd best not bother any of those ladies." The last thing he wanted to do was get into a scuffle with an old man who was hard on his luck.

"I don't bother them none. I just keep an eye on them is all." The man looked insulted. "I just wanna make sure the angel is safe."

Sam frowned at him. "What's your name, old-timer?"

"Jessup. I used to work in the mines back in the day, but I got me a bum arm so mostly now I look out for folks." He sounded as if he believed every word he said.

"What do you want with me, Jessup?" Sam needed to focus on work, not on a crazy old man.

"I seen you watching the angel." Jessup eyed him up and down.

"She's not your daughter or anything to you," Sam snapped. "What I do is none of your business."

"She's an angel, that's what she is. I don't want no devil making her cry."

"Cry? Who made her cry?" Sam's own protective instincts surged forward.

"Well, now, I don't rightly know who, but I seen her crying once or twice." Jessup scratched his bald pate. "It was a bit ago, mebbe a month or so."

"That was before I gave her, well, before I met her." Sam didn't want to admit to the man he'd been watching her since the moment she arrived in Forestville. It was only in the last few weeks he'd found the courage to speak to her. Fool that he was, he thought her too good for him, like the angel Jessup believed her to be. She was human just like him, if ethereal in face and form.

Jessup peered at him. "So you like the blond angel?"

Sam could have lied, but he didn't. "Yep, I do." He sighed and tapped the hammer against his palm. "Now all I have to do is convince her she likes me." He managed a smile.

"I can help you with that."

A spark of hope lit up inside Sam, although he was definitely dubious. "You can help me."

"Yep, sure can." Jessup grinned, showing his two front teeth. "The angel needs a good man to help her stop crying. I think you're the right man."

Sam didn't know if the man was completely loco or if he could really help, but it was worth taking a risk. God knew he wasn't doing a very good job of convincing her he was the right man.

"What can you do?"

Jessup smiled even wider. "You just wait and see."

Angeline wanted to talk to Sam, but she didn't know how to approach him. He said good morning to her or good afternoon, and smiled. Each time he did it, she wanted to sit with him, to find out more about him.

But she didn't.

She was a coward and she knew it. Life had taught her not to trust men and she'd learned her lesson well. Much as she'd enjoyed his kiss, and the book which she'd devoured in only two nights, Sam was still a stranger and a man. Angeline was completely unsure of what do to.

It had been two weeks since the kiss, since her world had turned sideways and all she could do was hang on. Two weeks of speaking to him without really talking. It was a beautiful morning and she happily agreed to go to the general store to pick up baking soda for Marta. The morning rush was over and there was still at least an hour before the dinner crowd began arriving. Since the bread for dinner was rising, Angeline was free to try to clear her head.

Her worn boots made a dull *thunk* on the wooden sidewalk as she made her way to the store. She'd had the boots for years and they pinched at the toe, not to mention the sole was nearly worn through. Although she'd love to be able to purchase a new pair, it was an extravagance her small salary could not endure. Angeline knew how to do without.

"Good morning, Miss Angeline."

She turned to find Jessup, the old man who charmed her with his toothless grin and offers of help. "Good morning, Mr. Jessup."

"Oh, I done told you, it's just Jessup. I ain't no mister." He smelled decidedly ripe and she took a surreptitious step back to avoid the smell. It wouldn't be polite to tell him how much he needed a bath with soap.

"Well then, good morning, Jessup." She smiled and started to walk on.

Until he spoke again.

"I seen Sam Carver talking to you. Is he bothering you?"

If only he knew how much, but it wasn't the kind of bother he was talking about.

"No, he's not bothering me. Mr. Carver is a gentleman, Jessup."

Except, of course, when he kissed her behind the restaurant, those sweet, hot kisses she couldn't get out of her mind.

"Then he has my permission to court you."

She turned to look back at him, her mind racing with the possibilities of exactly what Jessup was talking about.

"Pardon me?"

The old man hooked his thumbs in his suspenders and rocked back and forth on his heels. "Seeing as how you don't got no family in Forestville, and I don't got a family to look after, I figure we should look after each other."

Strangely enough, his logic made sense to her. It was her heart, however, that stuttered at the thought that this stranger, a man who'd barely known her for six months, would be willing to be her surrogate family. It took a moment for her to find her voice.

"Jessup, that's very kind of you. I'm not sure what to say." And she didn't. In her family, there were rules to be followed, chores to be done, but no room for this type of connection. How could she feel kinder toward a man she hardly knew than her own father?

"Oh, you don't gotta say nothing." He snapped his suspenders. "Now I seen Sam moping around and I seen you moping around. It seems to me you ought to get to courting, so there's no more moping."

It was as simple as that to Jessup. Stop fighting the urge to be together and simply be together. She wanted to so badly, her fists clenched around her small reticule. It would be so easy to give in, but it wouldn't be fair to Sam. There could be no future for them other than broken hearts and empty promises.

"I don't think I can do that." She swallowed the lump of regret. "Mr. Carver should find another girl to court."

"What if he doesn't want another girl to court?" Sam's deep voice came from behind her, startling her so, she must've jumped a foot in the air.

Angeline closed her eyes and counted to five before she answered. "Then he's set himself up for heartbreak."

She felt him step up behind her, his scent and the heat from his body washing over her.

"I'm willing to take that risk. Are you?"

What could she say? "Oh, by the way I'm married." Although, in the eyes of the law, she had lived in sin as third wife to a church elder with hard fists and a nasty disposition. The truth was simply too horrible to speak.

His hands closed around her shoulders and her entire body sighed with relief. This was apparently what she'd been needing and wanting, his touch, his very presence in her life. Angeline didn't know what connected her to him, but she knew it was strong.

"I don't know, Mr. Carver." Her voice was so soft, she hardly heard it.

"I asked you to call me Sam."

He turned her around to face him, but she didn't look up. Instead, she focused on the red-and-black plaid shirt stretched across the broad expanse of his chest. She was embarrassed to note there were no chest hairs poking up through the neck of his shirt. That made her wonder just how smooth his chest was, and then a low thrum began deep inside her.

Sam put his finger on her chin and raised her face until she met his gaze. His dark eyes were just as fascinating as she remembered, and up close, they were riveting.

"I can't stop thinking about you, awake or asleep. I almost hammered my own hand this morning. If you don't say yes to my courting you, I'm liable to do something really stupid."

His thumb brushed her lips and a shiver snaked straight down her spine. "Please."

"You'd best say yes, Miss Angeline, so's I can be on my way."

She'd forgotten about Jessup. Sam smiled, the corners of his eyes crinkling.

"Angel, say yes." His husky tone skimmed across her skin.

Angeline should say no, should step out of his reach and go to the store. She knew it, but she also knew she wasn't going to.

"Yes."

A loud whoop sounded from behind her as Sam leaned down to brush his lips against hers again. Tingles turned into something more at the touch. Angeline knew she'd made a choice, but whether it was the right one remained to be seen.

You should have told him about Josiah.

She pushed away the guilty voice inside her and focused on the incredible man in front of her. He cupped her cheek and his eyes darkened.

"You're so beautiful, sometimes I wonder if you really are an angel. I could stare at you for hours and never get tired of the view. And your skin is softer than a rose petal." He almost looked embarrassed at what came out of his mouth.

Angeline, on the other hand, was touched by his words. There weren't too many compliments doled out in her family. Vanity was discouraged, as was celebrating individuality. She knew she wasn't unattractive, but she never thought of herself as beautiful. Until Sam told her so on a dusty street in Forestville, Wyoming, on a sunny morning.

"Thank you." Her voice was husky with emotion and it was her turn to be embarrassed.

"You're welcome. Now can I escort you to wherever you're going?"

Angeline wondered what people would say, but then

pushed aside the thought. This wasn't Tolson and every move she made wasn't catalogued in the good and bad columns of life. Walking arm in arm with Sam would simply be enjoyable.

"Yes, please. I'm going to the store to buy baking soda for Marta."

Sam looked over her head. "Thanks, Jessup. You can be on your way." He met her gaze again. "I'll look after Miss Angeline now."

The sound of his voice made her want to curl up in front of a fire next to him. To wake up in the morning to that husky, sexy voice. To hear him whisper in her ear again. Oh, so many wishes and wants—Angeline had definitely gone far beyond what had been considered acceptable in Tolson.

She was living life for herself, and no one else. It felt pretty damn good too.

He held out his arm and she slipped hers into the crook of his elbow. His strength was obvious in the firmness of his muscles and the confident way he patted her hand. They walked arm in arm down the sidewalk, and that's when Angeline noticed something.

Sam walked with a limp.

In all the times she'd been with him, he'd been sitting or standing near her. She'd never been close enough to realize he had a hitch in his step. Angeline wanted to ask him what injury caused the problem, but didn't want to be rude just after accepting his offer to court her.

The limp made his stride match hers, even though his legs were longer. It was as if whatever had happened to his leg made him slow down long enough for her to catch up. Angeline smiled at the thought, earning a few smiles in return from folks walking down the street.

By the time they reached the store, she wanted to keep going, to walk for hours with Sam beside her, but Marta was waiting. Angeline had to get the baking soda back to her or the dinner meal would be affected. Something like regret swept her as they walked into the store.

"I just need to get baking soda, so it will take only a minute or two."

Sam held the door open for her. "Take your time. I finished Widow Primrose's fence with Jessup's help so I'm free until this afternoon."

"Jessup's help?" She didn't know the old man had any skills as a carpenter.

Sam looked sheepish. "Well, he came to talk to me about you like he was your pa or something. Wanted to make sure my intentions were honorable. After he found out I was looking to court you, he helped me finish the fence so I could ask you."

Angeline's heart fluttered. Again, the insight and thoughtfulness of a man most people ignored was humbling. Jessup was a very good person, and from now on she would be sure he didn't have to eat scraps for meals. She'd make sure he got a plate of hot food every night. After all, they were family now.

Sam courted her each day for a month. He would arrive for breakfast at the restaurant and ask for Angeline at his table. It got to the point that young Alice wouldn't even say hello to him anymore. She'd simply walk into the kitchen, then come back out with Angeline behind her.

The sight of the woman he was rapidly falling in love with would send his heart racing and his cock pulsing. She would smile shyly at him and ask him what he wanted to order.

Each day he brought her a gift: a rock, a seed pod, a beautiful flower, a leaf, or even a pinecone. She accepted each gift with grace, and sometimes she was even as fascinated as he by the piece of nature.

Sam wanted her to be at peace with the world around her. His mother had taught him when there was an imbalance, when a living being did not embrace the earth, then peace could not be achieved.

Angeline had no peace. He could see that she was struggling daily to fight whatever imbalance was in her soul. Sam promised himself he'd help her find that balance and peace.

The gifts were small pieces of the world outside the restaurant, the place she'd hidden from since her arrival in Forestville. He could count on one hand how many times she'd left the restaurant. The walk to the store when he'd finally convinced her to let him court her was only the fifth time.

Five was obviously a special number, one he kept in mind with each gift. So he brought her five of each piece of nature. With each gift, he saw the shadows in her blue eyes begin to recede.

Day by day, she was finding peace. Sam would ask her a question after he gave her the gift, something to find out a bit more about her.

He knew her favorite color was blue, that she loved to read, that her little finger was crooked, that one ear was higher than the other, and that she blushed when he complimented her. That told him Angeline had never had much praise or recognition for who she was.

Sam didn't want to overwhelm her with daily compliments, so he saved them to give her when she seemed the saddest. That was the one thing he had to battle most fiercely—the sadness in her soul.

It was a Friday morning, early enough that the sun was just skimming across the ground, raising a mist of warmth from the cool earth. He had found a fossil of a leaf when he was digging the new outhouse at the hotel. Not that he'd tell her where he'd found it—digging a new shithole wasn't his idea of a topic for discussion while courting.

However the fossil was special, as unique as Angeline. He kept it tucked into his hand while his thumb ran over the indentations in the soft stone.

As he stepped into the restaurant, his heart thumped madly. He was about to ask Angeline to do something other than talk to him. She could say no, which given Sam's limited experience with women, would be devastating.

Alice rolled her eyes when she saw him. "Do you ever stay home for breakfast?"

Sam was tense enough that her snide comment made his temper rise. "Is there some reason why you're always ornery around me?"

"She's jealous." Karen, the older waitress with the little boy, looked at Alice with one brow raised. "None of her gaggle of beaus has courted her so, ah, regularly."

"I am not jealous of an orphan with a half-breed courting her." Alice sneered. "I just get sick of fetching Angeline from the kitchen every morning."

Sam endured the insult with the stoicism he had developed over the course of his life. That didn't mean it didn't sting.

"You're green-eyed jealous." Karen laughed as Alice's face flushed.

"Shut your mouth, Karen. At least I don't tumble into the sheets with every man who smiles at me." Alice stomped out the front door, leaving an uncomfortable silence and an embarrassed audience.

Karen flapped her hand as she averted her gaze from Sam. "Pay her no never mind. She's young and full of vinegar."

Sam wanted to offer her sympathy for the young woman's comment, but figured she would rather he ignore it. He chose to simply nod at her and then walk toward the kitchen. Toward Angeline. Away from the insults young Alice had decided to heap upon him for no apparent reason.

He rubbed the fossil in his hand as he stepped into the kitchen. Angeline glanced up from cranking the handle on the coffee grinder. Her surprise gave way to a shy smile.

Sam felt immediately better.

"Good morning, Angel."

"Good morning, Sam."

"Hello to you too, Mr. Carver." Marta chuckled from the stove as she laid bacon into a frying pan; the sizzle and aroma filled the kitchen.

"Good morning, Marta." Sam smiled at the older woman. "It smells wonderful in here."

"Where is Alice? She usually comes to get our Angeline." Marta wiped her hands on her apron.

"She, uh, had to step outside for a minute."

Marta frowned. "Step outside? I ain't never known her to step outside unless the building was afire." She peered at Sam's face and he felt her looking through him like a mother who always knew when her child lied. "She has a mean mouth, I know that. Don't listen to what she says if she was using her sharp tongue on you."

"Don't worry, Marta, I'll be fine." He turned to Angeline, who was now frowning too.

"What did she say to you?"

"Nothing I want to talk about." He glanced at the coffee grounds. "I don't suppose you have any coffee brewed already?"

She didn't smile, but did nod. "I can bring some out to your table. With your eggs, bacon, and biscuits."

Sam took her hand and kissed the back. "You remember what I like for breakfast."

"How could she not? You've been ordering the same doggone thing for a month." Marta harrumphed from the stove.

Angeline's mouth twitched. "Two eggs over easy, three biscuits, and four pieces of bacon with black coffee."

Sam laughed and kissed her hand again. "You really are my angel."

Their gazes locked and a pulse snapped between them. Every small hair on his body rose to attention, as did a flush on her cheeks. The connection was so strong, all it took was a simple touch and one look.

He turned her hand over and put the fossil on her palm. "Today's gift. It's special, just like you are."

Marta made some kind of noise, but wisely kept quiet. Sam appreciated that, although he wished he and Angeline were alone.

Angeline turned the small fossil over in her hand, peering at it, running her finger along the ridges of the leaf pattern.

"What is it?"

"It's called a fossil. Thousands of years ago, a leaf fell in the mud and it was buried beneath rocks and dirt. The leaf didn't survive, but it left an echo of what it was behind." He watched the wonder spread across her face.

"Thousands of years ago? I could never imagine something like this survived for so long."

"It was protected by the dirt and rocks, cocooned in the layers above it." He imagined himself as the dirt and rocks and Angeline as the delicate fossil to protect.

"This is too precious to give me as a gift." She held it out to him, her face a mask of self-sacrifice. "I can't accept it."

"You accepted the book."

"That was different. I, um, wanted to read it," she confessed. "In fact, I've read it four times already."

That was news to him. Since he'd given her the book, nearly two months ago, she hadn't mentioned it once. Now to hear she had been reading it over and over, well, that made him feel even bolder.

"Then you can accept the fossil. I found it while I was digging a, uh, for a job." He still wouldn't admit he had found it while digging a new outhouse.

"Are you sure?" Her blue eyes were full of delight.

"Never more sure of anything in my life."

She finally smiled again. "Thank you, Sam."

"You're welcome, Angel." He regretfully let go of her hand. "I'd like to ask you to take a walk with me today, after dinner is over. Down to the lake and back."

She looked startled, as if she hadn't expected him to ask her to go anywhere, ever. "A walk?"

"Oh, say yes, Angeline. He's been faithfully courting you for a month and ain't asked you for nothing but eggs." Marta threw up her hands. "I was beginning to think he wasn't ever gonna ask."

Angeline met his gaze, asking him without words if he would keep her safe, from even himself. He answered her with a wide grin.

"Miss Angeline Hunter, would you do me the honor of accompanying me on a walk to the lake at three this afternoon?"

She giggled, sounding more like a young woman than she ever had. To his surprise, she curtseyed. "I would be honored, Mr. Samuel Carver."

He whooped and danced around the table, quickly sending a prayer of thanks to the gods around them. Sam was finally getting through her shell, through the wall that kept her away from everyone and everything.

The fossil really was special.

Sam couldn't believe she'd said yes. It was warming up outside. Spring was starting to spread its wings. He planned to walk down to the lake with her, steal her away for a couple of hours from the kitchen she spent so much time in.

He peered at his reflection in the looking glass and frowned. The scar on his eyebrow made his eyes uneven, but there was nothing he could do about it. He'd suffered worse than the wound on his face, much worse.

"What are you doing?" His father stood in the doorway, a smear of newsprint on his wrinkled cheek.

"I'm getting ready to go courting." Sam couldn't help the grin that spread across his face.

"Courting?" His father scratched his nose. "What woman in her right mind wants a crippled husband?"

Sam's stomach flipped while his heart flopped. He didn't know what would possess his father to be so cruel.

"I mean, Sparrow doesn't want you. I'm the one she loves." His father spoke of his mother as if she were the one being courted. It made the sting of his words less painful, but not by much.

"Pa, I'm Sam, your son, remember? I'm courting Angeline. She works in the kitchen at the Blue Plate." Sam tried to swallow the lump in his throat, but it was firmly lodged in place.

"The Blue Plate? Isn't that the place Marta and Pieter want to open?" His father looked so confused, his brows nearly touched.

Sam smiled shakily. "Yes, it's Marta and Pieter's restaurant. Why don't I get you settled in your room for a nap?"

As he led his father to his room, he realized the older man's shirt was inside out and, at the same time, he smelled something suspiciously like urine. It was acrid enough to make Sam's eyes water.

He spied an overfull chamber pot beneath the bed and realized he hadn't been keeping an eye on his father's hygiene. No doubt he'd simply forgotten to empty it. For a week.

Sam held his breath as his father lay down. When the older man was tucked beneath the blanket, Sam blinked away the sting of tears in his eyes. This was obviously a bad day for his father, one of the worst so far. It brought the entire situation to a head—this was a problem Sam would have to face.

First, though, he'd empty the chamber pot and clean up a bit. By the time he finished, he looked at the clock on the mantel and found he was half an hour late to meet Angeline.

"Shit."

Sam ran out of the house, his mind in a turmoil over what to do about his father. He wondered how he would explain to Angeline why he was late without revealing his father's secret. Then he wondered if she'd understand.

No one waited outside the restaurant, so he stepped in to find Angeline sitting at a table by herself. Her gaze was full of questions and some disappointment. Sam sighed and ran a hand down his face.

"I'm sorry, Angel. I meant to be here on time, but something happened with my father." He tried to think of a delicate way to tell her, but his emotions were still running too high.

"Your father? He runs the newspaper, doesn't he? Is he all right?" She rose to her feet, still looking distant and unsure. Sam noticed her blue dress was tattered at the edges, often mended if he wasn't mistaken. He told himself he'd make sure she got a new dress as soon as he could afford one.

"Yes, he's fine. His name is Michael. He used to be the school teacher in town, then he took over the newspaper about five years ago." Sam remembered how excited his father had been about the paper, especially after he'd been replaced at school by a younger, cheaper teacher.

"What happened?"

Sam swallowed. "Pa had an accident with the printing press. It was a huge mess."

Liar.

The smile he managed to find was nothing short of pitiful.

"Can we still go for a walk?" He needed to have some sunshine, some sweetness. The dark shadows in his life were sometimes overwhelming. Time with Angeline was the only lightness he had.

"Of course. I'd like some fresh air." She picked up a brown shawl and wrapped it around her shoulders.

Sam held out his arm and thankfully she took it. Just having her beside him, touching him, was enough to ease the strangling sensation he'd felt since his father's comments had cut him so deeply.

The sun greeted them as they walked outside and Sam sucked in a deep breath. Angeline's sweet scent entered him, washing through him, and leaving behind the feeling that he'd been in a cleansing rain.

"How far is the lake?"

"Not too far. Just past the livery, there's a copse of cottonwood trees and then the lake. It's small, but pretty deep. When I was a boy I used to go swimming with my mother there. She taught me how to stay afloat." He smiled at the memory, both sweet and painful when he realized she had been gone for ten years already. Sam missed her, but knew she was part of the earth now, as nurturing as she had been in life.

"You swam in a lake with your mother?" She sounded amazed. "She taught you?"

Sam wondered just what kind of parents Angeline had endured. "Yes, she did. My mother was half-Shoshone."

He wondered if Angeline would walk away from him now she knew he was what many people called a half-breed. His father had loved his mother deeply, and Sam had known love from both his parents. He'd never known what true hate was until he left their care to take on the world two thousand miles east.

That thought was for another day, so he pushed it aside.

"What is 'Shoshone'?"

"It's an Indian tribe that lives mostly in Idaho. That's where my parents met." He smiled at the story his mother used to tell of how his father got chased up a tree by a cougar and she'd rescued him. It never failed to make her laugh and his father bluster about how the cat was bigger than a horse.

"An Indian tribe. Oh, that's what Alice meant." Angeline turned to look at him. "She mentioned your heritage, so I guess that's where you get the dark hair and eyes?"

She sounded sincere and incredibly innocent. Sam found those qualities unique and so appealing he didn't know how to react. All his life he'd been treated differently, as if there were something wrong with him because his mother had been Indian. Angeline had none of that prejudice and he couldn't help wondering why.

"Yes, Indians have dark hair and eyes." He tried to think of a way to ask her without sounding like an idiot. "You haven't heard of Indians?"

She shook her head. "I grew up in a, um, very secluded community. We didn't really have much contact outside of the ward, I mean, the town." She sounded as if she regretted every word that had popped out of her mouth.

Sam didn't know what a *ward* was, but it didn't sound like a fun place to live. Considering how uncomfortable she seemed, he decided not to push too far, especially on their first outing together.

The cool air was warmed by the sun as they walked side by side down the street. He ignored the looks from people who stared at them, embarrassed to wonder if they were staring at him or at her, or maybe even both of them.

When they reached the end of the sidewalk, he breathed a sigh of relief to be away from the prying eyes of the people of Forestville. Sam was accepted in town, but not necessarily into people's homes. Even though he was only one-quarter Indian, his black hair and eyes set him apart from everyone else. He didn't want Angeline to feel the sting of his social status, but if she didn't understand prejudice against Indians at all, he had no idea how to explain it to her.

They walked another ten minutes until they arrived at the copse of cottonwoods. He immediately felt better, more relaxed. The lake shimmered in the afternoon sun like floating crystals. The sight made him shade his eyes and slow his pace.

Angeline sucked in a breath. "It's lovely." Her voice was hushed.

"In the summer, the grass is thick beneath your feet, the sun warm on your face, and the water cool on your skin."

She shivered. "I imagine you must love it here. I know I would." She sighed.

Sam looked at her, stunned by the change in Angeline. Inside the restaurant she was beautiful, but out in the bosom of nature, she was simply exquisite. Her long hair shone like spun gold, wisps blowing softly in the breeze. Her normally pale complexion had already become rosy, making her look healthier, more alive. Her blue eyes sparkled as she gazed around her.

She belonged outside, surrounded by nature. The spirits of the earth, sky, and water gave her the gift of life, of that he was certain. Angeline was a creature of nature, not one who belonged in a hot kitchen. He wished he could build her a home out here, where she could live in harmony with everything around her.

She turned and smiled at him, her gaze so full of unrestrained joy, it was his turn to catch his breath. His body surged with heat, with attraction, and the purest connection he'd ever felt.

He stepped toward her, closing the gap between them until mere inches separated them. Sam took her hands in his and pulled her flush against him. Her eyes widened but not with fear, rather with excitement.

"Will you kiss me again, Sam?"

He managed a smile, although every nerve in his body snapped to attention. "I want to, Angel. I can't imagine ever wanting something more."

She rose on her tiptoes and pressed her lips to his, with a clumsiness that only made him want her more. Sam accepted her gift, the kiss of a woman to a man. It was brief, barely a brushing of mouths, but it made him burn for her with a fire he hadn't expected.

He blew out a shaky breath as their gazes met. An answering fire burned in her beautiful blue eyes.

This time he pulled her against him until he couldn't tell where he ended and she began. They were one being, sharing space, breath, and themselves. As his mouth descended on hers, she closed her eyes again and he kissed her.

This was not like the sweet kiss she'd just bestowed on him, or even the gentle kisses they'd exchanged before. No, this was something very different: elemental, passionate, consuming. Her lips were soft and unsure, moving against his. He taught her how to kiss, to move with him. Sam showed her how much he wanted her, kissing and licking her lips from one end to the other.

Angeline sighed when he nibbled at her lower lip, giving him the opportunity to dive into her mouth. She froze, almost in fear. Sam gentled his touch, gently lapping at her tongue until she began to melt against him once more. She made tentative movements, the sweet heat of her mouth promising so much more.

Sam shook with the force of his arousal, needing so much more. He hardened, pulsing hard and fast against her soft belly. He felt her stiffening again and pulled back from the precipice he teetered on.

Angeline made a soft sound in her throat as he forced himself to break contact with her. Their breaths came in short bursts. Sam's heart was beating so hard, it threatened to burst from his chest.

They stared at each other and Sam saw the same confusion he felt reflected in her gaze.

"What just happened?" she blurted.

Sam shook with the power of their connection. He'd never expected to find something so raw with someone he'd just gotten to know. However, he couldn't fight what was clearly happening.

"It appears we were supposed to go courting."

She frowned. "I don't even know what that means. Sam, I feel funny inside, like I can't catch my breath."

He took her hand. "Me too."

"Sam, I'm scared." She pulled away from his touch. "I want to go back."

Sam took her hand again, and it felt clammy and cool. "Then we'll go back. I don't want you to be scared, Angel." He kissed the back of her hand. They started walking back toward town. "I would never hurt you."

Angeline nodded. "I know that, somehow I know that. I-I'm scared because I never felt this way. Kissing isn't supposed to do that."

He stopped to look at her. "What do you mean?"

She looked around, flushed and flustered. "Kissing is supposed to be a chore, endured because that's what men like. It-it's not supposed to make me all warm i-in places I can't mention."

Sam suddenly felt something other than arousal. Pure fury pushed it aside. "Who hurt you, Angel?"

She shook her head. "Nobody." Her gaze fell to the ground, as if she couldn't bear to look at him.

"That's the first time you've lied to me."

"Sam, this is a bad idea. I don't th-think we can court anymore." Tears glistened in her eyes and she stepped away from him. "I won't let you make me do it either."

Sam let his arms fall to his sides. "I won't make you do anything."

She started to walk away from him when he spoke again.

"But I think I'm already in love with you."

Angeline sucked in an audible breath and stopped, pebbles tinkling around her boots. "What?"

Sam closed his eyes and leapt off the cliff. What did he have to lose?

"I think I fell in love with you the moment I saw you reading on the steps in the sunset. It was as if something compelled me to come around the corner and find you." He had to make her understand, to stop her from walking away. Sam had a feeling if she did, there wouldn't be another chance to say what he needed to. "I don't know if you believe in fate, but everything in my life has led me to you. Then when we kissed, I felt whole. It feels like love to me."

Angeline turned and he saw tears streaming down her beautiful face. His heart constricted at the idea he'd made her weep.

"Angel, I—"

She leapt into his embrace and hugged him so tightly, he forgot to breathe. Sam held on tight, knowing he had the rest of his life in his arms.

Chapter Four

Angeline peered at her reflection in the spoon. It was Sunday and she was going to see Sam at his house, meet his father, and have dinner. She was used to spending Sundays on her knees in prayer or in service. Now she'd be spending it with the man who'd shown her what it meant to be loved.

She didn't know if she loved Sam or not, but everything she felt when she was with him was so different, it was definitely more than anything she'd ever known. At the very least, she was falling in love with him. He was smart, considerate, and downright fascinating. It made her relationship with Jonathan appear shallow and fleeting.

If her sister, Eliza, were there, Angeline would ask her what it all meant, but she was on her own. Courting in the real world was so different from the Mormon way, she was like a blind man feeling her way around a dark room. Lettie didn't approve and made no secret of it.

Angeline was completely out of her element, and yet she'd never been so happy. Every moment she spent with Sam was like a gift, a treasure to put away in her heart. Oh, she wasn't fool enough to believe there wasn't anything bad in the world of courting. Being with Josiah had taught her too much about the evil that men do.

Perhaps she was just ignoring that darkness. Maybe she wanted to because of how Sam made her feel. Even her nipples ached when he kissed her. Not to mention that secret place a woman guarded from everyone but her husband. It was his to do with as he pleased, no matter what she wanted.

Angeline refused to live like that anymore. She wanted to make the decisions about her own body. Thank God, Lettie had left Tolson with her, had taken the chance of leaving their husband and his invisible prison. There was no comparison between Josiah and Sam other than the fact they were both male. She wouldn't call Josiah a man, however. He was a coward and a bully. Every morning the sun rose, she watched the beauty in front of her and felt blessed to be away from the darkness of Josiah's house.

Now she was going to Sam's home to meet his father and perhaps take another step toward a normal life. If she could even figure out what normal was supposed to be. Now that she'd been away from the church ward for eight months, she realized that what she'd been taught was completely different from the rest of the world.

Whatever it was she had with Sam, it defied everything she knew. Although she was scared out of her mind, for once in her life, she was going to follow her heart. She hadn't done that a year earlier when Josiah offered for her, and she'd wanted to wait for Jonathan, the young man she believed she loved. Instead, she obeyed her father.

Not anymore.

"What are you doing?" Lettie's voice was hard.

Angeline didn't turn to look at her standing in the doorway. "I'm going to meet Sam's father and have supper with them." She was proud her voice was firm and decisive.

"Didn't you learn your lesson? Courting and spending time with folks is a good way to get yourself killed." Lettie shut the door and stepped into the small room. "No matter how good he makes you feel inside, you're putting yourself in danger."

Lettie's brown eyes were serious, but within their depths, Angeline also saw concern. They had been through a lot together, and although they didn't act it most of the time, the two of them had a bond no one could ever break.

"Sam is no danger to me."

"Yes, he is. He's dangerous to your heart. You've been mooning over him for two months, ever since he gave you that cursed book." Lettie picked up the book in question and shook it at her, then tossed it on the bed. "Don't throw away everything you've gained for one man's kisses. It isn't worth it. You've just risked everything to escape from that kind of servitude." Her voice was high-pitched and nearly desperate now.

Angeline took her friend's hands and was shocked to find them shaking. "Lettie, I won't throw anything away. I'm just, well, following my heart."

Lettie's eyes grew suspiciously wet. "That's what I'm afraid of. A heart shouldn't do anything but beat and keep you alive. If you follow your heart, you're going to regret it." By the tone in her voice, she had done just that.

Angeline was shocked to realize someone had hurt Lettie before Josiah. Perhaps it was Robert she spoke of, but whoever it was had damaged her heart badly enough that the pain still echoed years later.

"Whoever hurt you should be whipped."

Lettie appeared a bit flushed. "Ain't nobody to whip."

"What happened?"

"Nothing worth talking about." Lettie flapped her hand in dismissal. "I was a stupid fool and it's done."

"No, not a fool. It's called being human. You might want to try it some time." Angeline was pleased to see the corners of Lettie's mouth kick up in a grin.

"I'll think about it."

They grinned at each other at the familiar phrase. It was something they'd repeated to each other during the long journey east, when they were scared out of their minds, waiting for Josiah to appear, to drag them back. One night they huddled behind rocks in the Utah night with only the stars and each other for company. Side by side, they'd survived by sheer willpower alone.

Lettie was stronger than Angeline. She was the one who kept them going when Angeline wanted to give up. Lettie pushed and pushed, made them talk about the most inane topics just to keep their minds engaged. Whenever Lettie would encourage Angeline to talk about something new, she'd groan and snap, "I'll think about it."

It had become a familiar phrase, something they repeated to each other like a battle cry. It made them both stronger, tougher, able to handle any challenge that came their way.

"I'm not changing my mind about this." Angeline had the greatest respect for Lettie, but Sam's courtship was too important to give up. "I can't."

The older woman frowned. "You're a fool then."

"So be it. It won't be the first time." Angeline hugged Lettie quickly, then moved away. "Thank you for caring, for worrying about me. Not many people are left in the world to do that."

"That's the truth if I ever heard it. It's you and me, Angeline. No matter what man catches your eye." Lettie turned and walked toward the door. She was bitter at the age of thirty, too bitter for someone so young.

Angeline wished something or someone good would happen to her friend, just as Sam had happened to her. Life hadn't been kind to Lettie, and it was time that changed. Perhaps Angeline would find a way to make that happen.

Putting aside thoughts of her friend, she focused on getting ready for dinner. After pronouncing herself as presentable as she would get, Angeline put on her shawl, the one item she owned that had belonged to her mother, and walked downstairs.

Telling herself she wasn't a coward, she went out the kitchen door so no one would see her leave. It wasn't that she was embarrassed to be going to Sam's house. Rather she was embarrassed at how little she knew of courting, of relationships between men and women.

She would be nineteen in the fall, yet what she knew of men could fit in a thimble. Even though she had been married, she was ignorant of such a simple thing as how to kiss. Sam had taught her quite a bit by the lake. It was wonderful, and made her feel tingly from head to foot.

She couldn't wait to do it again. Or perhaps more.

The sky was slate gray with clouds, but no rain fell. Perhaps it would hold off until later and she could walk to Sam's house without getting soaked. She was so preoccupied with the threat of bad weather, the five-minute walk seemed instantaneous. She stood in front of the house staring at the sign FORESTVILLE NEWS, which was faded and peeling.

Angeline hadn't told Sam she'd never read a newspaper. Never knew about them until she had left Tolson. Truthfully, she was hoping to see some of the inner workings of the office. She had become a regular reader of books, and perhaps if she understood the newspaper, she would read that too.

She raised her hand to knock when the door swung open. An older man stood there with a tin cup in one hand, a black smear on his cheek, and his glasses perched on his balding pate.

"Can I help you?"

"Mr. Carver. My name is Angeline Hunter. I'm here to see Sam." At least she didn't sound like an uneducated fool.

"Sam?"

She frowned. "Sam Carver. Your son?"

"Pa, it's okay. She's my friend." Sam appeared beside his

father, his face a tight mask of reined-in emotions. "Let's get you back inside."

He met Angeline's gaze and she was shocked to see disappointment, fear, and a plea for understanding. Something was obviously wrong with his father.

"I don't remember that woman. Is she here to see Sparrow?"

"No, she's here to see me." Sam apologized to her with a glance and then turned to lead his father back into the room.

She stepped inside and closed the door. The smell of paper hit her first, then there was something else, likely ink or perhaps the machinery used to print the newspapers. Although she wanted to explore more, she followed Sam and his father into another room.

The kitchen was not in good shape, barely functional, with a tiny pot-bellied stove, a battered coffeepot, a battered wood sink, and a few tin plates on a crooked shelf next to a dirty window. It was definitely a man's house without much of a woman's touch.

"I'll be right back." Sam smiled sadly. "Can you wait here for me?"

Angeline nodded and he gave her a grateful glance before he led his father out of the kitchen. While she waited for Sam, she wandered back into the open area where the machinery was. It was rather nosy of her, but she couldn't help herself. Her curiosity just wouldn't be quiet.

The machine was enormous, covered with particles of paper and smears of ink. It had a maw that looked dangerous enough to bite off a hand. She had no idea how how the machine worked and hoped Sam would explain it to her.

Her boots made a path through the dust and tiny paper bits on the floor. She made her way to an old desk in the corner. It was a large wooden desk with lots of cubbies and small drawers. Judging by the scratches, it was well used and rather old.

Various papers littered the top, some with notes in a man's handwriting, others with numbers like arithmetic problems. She smiled as she noticed a note that read, "Tell Sam to order newsprint."

It was a peek into the life of a man she never would have met if she hadn't left Tolson. He was a journalist, a man who would not have found a place in the ward, who would have been shunned for what he did. She was glad to have met him, even if he seemed to be a bit confused.

"I'm sorry, Angel." Sam's voice startled her and she dropped the note back on the desk.

She turned to find him in the doorway, his expression full of shadows and secrets.

"Nothing for you to be sorry about. I did notice there's nothing cooking. I thought we were having supper?" She didn't understand what was going on with his father, but Sam had invited her for a meal, her first outside of the restaurant since she'd arrived in Forestville.

"I meant to cook, I did, but Pa is having a bad day. He's been having a lot of bad days." He walked up beside her and smiled sadly. "You, however, make my day brighter by just being here."

Her heart sped up and she felt herself leaning toward him, eager to be near him, to feel the rush of his presence. He stepped closer and she didn't move back. She felt his body heat reach out to hers. Her breath began to come in gasps as he leaned in toward her. She knew he was going to kiss her—she wanted him to. Angeline had never wanted anything more than to feel Sam's lips on hers again.

"I'm going to kiss you." His husky voice grazed her ear, sending a shiver up her spine.

"Please," was all she said, all she could say.

He cupped her cheek and gently pulled her mouth toward his. Lips brushed once, then twice. She shivered, goose bumps racing down her skin. He was gentle, so gentle she hardly knew what to do. She knew he wouldn't hurt her, but she didn't know how to act with a man.

"Are you afraid?"

"No, just nervous." She was distressed to hear her voice shaking. The last thing Angeline wanted was to appear weak.

"You've been with a man before?" His hand slid up and down her arm softly, leaving a trail of heat in its wake.

"Yes." Her knowledge of mating had initially come from the animals around home, and then from the animal she'd married. This, however, was so different she was unsure of herself.

The only thing she did know was that this time she didn't want to be a passive participant. Angeline wanted to use her body the way she wanted, not the way someone else wanted. He led her out of the workroom and into a bedroom. The snick of the door closing echoed in her ears. He leaned toward her, pulling her close.

"Does that feel good?" he whispered in her ear, his breath hot and moist against her. His tongue reached out to lick her lobe and she jumped. He froze in place until she laughed.

"I'm sorry. You tickled me."

His laugh was low and rumbly, echoing through her chest. She was beginning to warm up so quickly, soon she'd have her clothes off before he had a chance to take them off.

Well then, why shouldn't she?

Angeline stepped away from him, her body already crying out from losing contact with his. She reached for the buttons on her shirtwaist and actually heard him swallow.

"What are you doing?"

"What I want to do." She didn't explain further, didn't want to really. Angeline felt her own power surging through her. This time it would be her choice.

The cool night air hit her skin as she slid off first her shirtwaist, then her skirt. The one sad petticoat followed, leaving only her chemise between her naked skin and Sam's touch.

Angeline shivered, but it wasn't from the cold. The very idea of him touching her was so appealing, her body reacted before he even came close. She chuckled at the thought of how different this was, then pushed away all her preconceived notions along with her chemise.

She stood there nude, her body there for him to see in the soft light coming through the curtains. He held out his hands and waited, allowing her to take the next step. Angeline's heart tumbled a bit at the gesture. Sam was definitely the kind of man she could fall in love with, and not just a young girl's love, but a deep and abiding love she would feel in her bones as well as her heart.

Angeline stepped closer and took his hands in hers, then placed them on her breasts. The nipples hardened instantly at the touch of his callused palms. She gasped at the contact as it sent a bolt of pure arousal straight to her core.

"Angel, you're so beautiful, so damn soft." His voice was full of need, echoing her own.

"Kiss me, Sam."

"No need to tell me twice." He lowered his head and pulled her against him.

The combination of her naked skin and his rough clothing made for a delicious friction. His lips were gentle, nipping at hers until she gave herself fully to the kiss. He had sensed her hesitation and waited. Angeline was ready for him, more than ready. She needed him to touch her all over.

Her tongue snuck out to lick his lips, then darted back into her mouth. She was an amateur, but she learned quickly. He moaned low in his throat and soon his mouth was open, his tongue repeating the same gesture. Hot, wet heat slid between them as she opened her mouth to his questing tongue. Soon they were mimicking the act of sex, plunging into each other's mouths in a timeless dance.

She felt his cock harden against her belly and, to her surprise, she wasn't afraid. Sam was so different from Josiah, patient and gentle. Angeline wanted to mate with him and become one with the dark-haired, dark-eyed man who called to her heart.

"You're still dressed." She sounded winded, which in a way she was. Her heart raced, her breath was shallow, and her entire body was pulsing with the need for more.

He chuckled and stepped back, a shudder wracking his body. She realized not only did she wield power, but her kisses, her very body, held sway over his. It was a defining moment for her. Angeline reached out and started unbuttoning his shirt.

She did it because she wanted to, because she wanted to show Sam she wasn't afraid, that she wanted to be joined with him. Although he allowed her to undress him, she felt the coiled strength within him just waiting for release. He was hard all over, muscles and sinew stretched over bone in a symphony of male beauty.

His chest was very nearly hairless with flat, copper-colored nipples. She ran her hands down his chest and his entire body hardened.

"Jesus, Angel, that, uh, feels good." He was panting by the time she finished unbuttoning his trousers and slid them down. His union suit dangled from his waist, held up by the erection beneath them like a tent. She pulled until it pooled around his feet. His cock was very large, nestled between his legs with a set of nicely rounded balls.

It was the final test for her.

Angeline reached for him, finally throwing aside all memory of the horrors of her marriage. Sam was much more than just the man she was kissing. Her hand closed around his staff and a shudder rippled through his body. He was silk over steel, hard and so incredibly soft at the same time.

"I don't think I can take much of that," he choked out. "You—ah, damn, that feels good."

Angeline felt her own body reacting to simply touching

his. He was a full-grown man in her power, and she felt free to do as she pleased. She leaned forward and brushed her nipples against his chest.

He grinned and pulled her flush against him. They were both completely nude and she gasped as she touched him from head to foot, skin to skin. He was hot and hard all over, such a contrast to her own body. Angeline breathed in his scent and that of their combined arousal—a heady combination.

"Angel," he whispered against her ear. "I want to make love to you."

Angeline opened her wings and leapt. "Yes, please."

He led her to the bed, kissing her as they walked. Fierce kisses designed to make her want more, and they were working. By the time they got to the bed, she felt as if her body was on fire.

Angeline lay back and opened her legs. His gaze widened as he drank in the entire sight of her.

"Like a goddess come to life."

She was sure she didn't look like a goddess, but with his words, he made her feel like one. He lowered himself until he was hovering directly over her.

"Are you sure about this, Angel?"

She reached down and stroked his cock. It jumped against her hand, leaving a trail of sweet wetness. Angeline brought him to her entrance, letting him feel how wet she was, how much she wanted him, wanted this.

"Never been more sure of anything."

"Good, because I think I'd die if we stopped."

His staff slid in slowly, its passage made easy by the moist heat of her core. Inch by inch, he pressed forward. There was no pain, no discomfort, nothing but a feeling of being stretched and tingles of pleasure. Angeline pulled at his back to make him go faster.

"Patience, honey. I want to feel every second of this, of you, of us. God, you feel like heaven."

He fully sheathed himself inside her and paused. She felt his body shaking, knowing she was trembling as well. It was as if someone had made them to fit together, a perfect match.

It felt simply astonishing to have him, so large and hard, inside her. She throbbed around him, clenching and unclenching, wanting and needing more.

"Please, Sam, please." She didn't know what she was asking for but she needed it now.

Sam heard her and started moving. With each pass, his speed increased as did Angeline's tingles. They spread out from her center in waves, making her restless with need. The tingles reached her nipples, which ached with pleasure as they rubbed against his chest with each thrust.

Angeline felt something inside her coil tighter and tighter. She scratched at his back, not understanding what was happening. He responded by moving faster and harder, the sound of their choppy breaths loud in the quiet room.

"Sam, I need. Please."

She didn't know what to do, but she knew she needed something. And only he could give it to her. Angeline knew she'd lose control if she didn't find what she sought.

"Hang on, Angel."

Sam lifted himself up onto one arm and reached between them. His thumb landed on her hooded button and he started flicking it. Angeline almost bucked him off with the force of her reaction.

It was amazing to think that small piece of flesh could be manipulated to bring her such ecstasy. He flicked faster, the rhythm matching that of his cock as it slid in and out of her.

Angeline stopped breathing as a wave of something she could only call rapture overwhelmed her. She wanted to scream, shout, roar at the heavens as the most perfect pleasure washed through her. She whispered his name, or she could have yelled it.

There was nothing but Sam and their joining, and the intensity of it. He jerked and plunged so deep inside her, he touched her womb. Angeline dug her hands into the bed, pushing up against him as the waves ebbed through her. Her eyes saw nothing but Sam, her heart knew nothing but Sam, and her body was now one with Sam's.

She didn't even realize she was crying until he lay beside her and wiped her cheeks.

"Don't cry, Angel."

Angeline smiled at him. "Why not? I just experienced the most perfect moment in my life and I found it with you."

Sam pulled her into his arms and they lay together, heart to heart, as Angeline wept into his shoulder. She'd never felt such peace and contentment before Sam. He was the other half she'd been seeking all her life.

Angeline was in love.

Chapter Five

Jonathan Morton rode into the small town of Forestville with a weariness he'd never felt. His journey was nearly over and he couldn't be happier. Only a few more weeks and he'd be back in Tolson, free to marry Angeline and start the rest of his life. It was the reason he pushed himself and his horse so hard.

He missed her.

Jonathan hadn't written to Angeline, knowing the letters wouldn't reach her anyway. Her father, Silas, had a firm hand and did not allow his daughters any freedom whatsoever, and that included choice of a husband.

Her sister, Eliza, was a different girl, odd but smart and likeable. But Angeline, she made his heart turn into a thundering horse whenever she smiled. He'd enjoyed his missionary trip immensely, but couldn't wait to get back to Tolson. To Angeline.

He stopped in front of the hotel and dismounted, his legs shaking with exhaustion. He'd driven himself and his horse hard the last month as he rode back from Oklahoma to Utah. The sun was just setting, casting an orange glow on everything.

At first, he thought he was seeing things, but no, his eyes

weren't playing tricks on him. Right there, walking toward him, was Angeline, arm in arm with an Indian.

His heart fell to his feet, then bounced back up again to hit his pride dead on. Jonathan was no coward, but the shock of seeing her was enough to make him speechless. As he watched, they approached a building with a sign that read THE BLUE PLATE, likely a restaurant.

The Indian leaned down and kissed her, making Jonathan's blood boil in his veins. He stepped toward them, ready to defend her honor, to stop the bastard from soiling the woman who was to be his bride.

"She's not yours anymore."

Jonathan turned to find Lettie Brown standing on the sidewalk. She looked the same as always, brown and drab, with the weight of world on her shoulders. It took him a moment to realize Lettie was there in Forestville too, hundreds of miles from home.

Perhaps he was dreaming. Why would both of them be so far from the ward? Lettie was married to Josiah Brown, a church elder and a stern man who tolerated no deviation from what he considered to be the truth. Then there was Silas Hunter, a man who would never allow his precious daughter to travel away from Tolson and most especially would not tolerate her kissing an Indian in the street.

"Lettie?"

"Yes, Jonathan."

"Am I dreaming?" He touched his dusty face, wondering if he'd find a fever or some other cause for the strange visions.

"No, you're not." Lettie stepped toward him, her arms crossed and a fierce scowl on her face.

"Why are you here? And for that matter, how did you get here?" Jonathan was full of questions, but those two were the ones he simply had to know.

"We're here because this is where we stopped, and God

apparently thought it great fun to bring you here as well." Lettie moved close enough so he could see the sheer fury in her eyes. "I'm here because I got tired of Josiah's iron fists and the sting of his whip. I'm here because I wanted to live my life without cowering every day, wondering what infraction I might commit to warrant a beating. I'm here because *I* chose to be here and there's not a damn thing that bastard can do about it."

Jonathan knew Josiah was mean, but he'd had no idea how bad it was being married to the man. A whip? Lord have mercy on Lettie and all she'd been through. He couldn't even think of a single thing to say.

"You'd best forget what and who you saw here." Lettie's statement sounded like a warning.

"But what about Angeline?" His heart stuttered at the thought of never seeing her beautiful face again. He loved her and wanted her for his first and only wife.

Lettie shook her head. "You lost her a year ago. A few months after you left, Josiah turned his gaze on her. She became his wife last August."

All the blood drained from Jonathan's face and he staggered beneath the weight of that awful news. "You lie."

"I wish I did. That girl, that woman, is one of the strongest people I've ever met. She did as she was bid and for her obedience she lived with that monster for two months." Lettie's stern expression softened. "Angeline might look as if she would break easily, but she has a backbone of steel. If it weren't for her, I'd be dead." Her voice caught on the last word and she sucked in a shaky breath.

Jonathan felt as if someone had kicked him square in the chest. His heart clenched so tightly he almost stopped breathing. Josiah had taken Angeline to wife? Josiah knew how much she and Jonathan loved each other. How could he? To know his beautiful Angeline had lain beneath the old man made his stomach turn.

"You ran."

"No, we took our freedom and left. Josiah doesn't give up what he covets though. He's already sent one killer after us." Lettie narrowed her gaze. "If you tell him where you saw us, she's as good as dead. The only reason Angeline's alive is because of Eliza. She followed the bounty hunter sent to kill us and stopped him when he had a gun to Angeline's head. Do you understand what I'm telling you? Josiah tried to have us killed because we left the prison he called marriage."

Jonathan managed to make it to the steps of the hotel before he vomited in the bushes. What Lettie had told him couldn't possibly be true. Yet it appeared the two women were there in a small town in Wyoming, unprotected and alone. He took a handkerchief from his pocket and wiped his mouth while he shook like a newborn calf.

When he straightened up, Lettie was standing by his horse. Waiting.

"I must speak to her."

"I don't think that's a good idea. She's been on her own for nearly a year. Angeline is not the same girl you knew."

A year?

"I still need to speak to her. Lettie, please, I love her. I can't simply walk away and never see her again." Jonathan couldn't believe he was begging. "Please."

"In the morning then. Get yourself cleaned up and get some sleep. Your clothes could use a good brushing too." Lettie gestured to the building behind him. "The hotel is a nice one. You'll find everything you need."

He wasn't happy with waiting to speak to her, but judging by the expression on Lettie's face, he had no choice. She might just shoot him down if he tried to speak to Angeline before the morning. Lettie was one tough, cool, unmovable force.

"Fine then, in the morning." He stood, not surprised to feel weak in the knees. "Where should I meet you?"

"Come to the restaurant across the street at six. I'll be waiting for you and take you to Angeline." Lettie stepped forward until she was mere inches from his face. "I'm warning you, Jonathan Morton, I will do everything I must to protect her and myself. Do you understand me?"

He didn't miss the threat, that was for sure. "Yes, Lettie. I understand. Don't worry, I won't betray you."

She stared at him a few moments longer, then turned. "See you at six tomorrow."

With that, she walked away, leaving Jonathan standing on the steps of the hotel, confused and heartbroken. He wondered if he'd even be able to sleep.

Angeline dreamed of Sam, of his hands, his mouth, his dark eyes. She woke with her entire body humming with need. She had never experienced such a thing, and was therefore frustrated beyond measure to not understand how to relieve it, other than being with Sam again.

She splashed cold water on her face, which helped a little, but not much. Her nipples actually ached and when she took off her nightrail, the cool morning air made them pucker even harder. She looked down at the rosy nipples and touched them with her fingertips. A pure bolt of lightning shot down her body directly between her legs.

Angeline gasped at the sensation, so she touched them again, this time with thumb and forefinger. It felt even better, easing the ache within her. She closed her eyes and imagined it was Sam touching her. His callused skin caressing hers.

A knock at the door startled her, breaking the spell of imagining what might happen.

"What?"

"Good morning to you too." Lettie sounded like her usual chipper self. "Get downstairs, it's nearly five and you haven't started the biscuits yet."

Angeline stuck out her tongue at the closed door. "I'll be right there."

She was confused and excited by everything that had happened with Sam the night before. If she was smart she'd talk to someone about what she was feeling, but Angeline didn't feel comfortable telling anyone. It was so personal.

Was this how lovemaking was supposed to feel? If so, she realized what Josiah had forced on her was simply against nature. Sam had showed her that a man could be gentle, respectful, and still find pleasure, as well as give it.

Angeline dressed quickly, her mind still buzzing with questions she didn't have answers to. Lettie waited for her at the bottom of the stairs, her foot tapping and a scowl on her face.

"You know people might think your face has a permanent frown." Angeline was pleased to see Lettie's mouth twitch.

"Get in the kitchen and bake." The older woman ushered her through the kitchen door.

Marta was absent so Angeline and Lettie stoked the fires, readying the oven for baking breakfast. It was an easy partnership, one they'd cultivated over the last year. Some folks never saw past the gruff exterior Lettie showed the world. She was really an emotional person, capable of great courage and deep friendship. Angeline never could have made it on her own without Lettie by her side. She was closer to Angeline than her own sister, Eliza.

"I have something to tell you and you're not going to like it." Lettie set the flour canister on the table.

Angeline didn't like the tone in her friend's voice. It made the hairs on the back of her neck stand up. "What is it?"

"Yesterday afternoon I saw you with that man, Samuel Carver." Lettie met her gaze. "He kissed you right on the street. You need to be more careful than that. I thought you understood the danger of getting involved with someone."

Angeline felt her cheeks heat. "I like him, Lettie. A lot."

That particular fact made her feel both guilty and wonderful. "I won't stop seeing him because you think I won't be safe. I can't. Sam is a part of me now."

"More than Jonathan?" Lettie stared at her.

Angeline swallowed. "Yes, much more."

"I'm going to tell you something and you've got to promise not to have a fit of the vapors."

"What? Vapors?" Angeline's heart thumped hard. "Tell me what's going on."

"Someone else saw you with Sam."

"We were on the street, Lettie. Anyone could have seen—"

Lettie grabbed her by the shoulders. "Listen to me, Angeline, it was Jonathan. He's here in Forestville. He *saw* you and Sam."

At first Angeline could not grasp what Lettie had said. It couldn't possibly be true. "Jonathan. My Jonathan?"

"Not anymore. He's just Jonathan Morton." Lettie's reminder stung.

"What is he doing here? Why is he here?" Angeline's throat grew tight as she tried to understand what was happening.

"As luck would have it, he was on his way home and just happened to stop in Forestville." Lettie shook her head. "It appears we are the butt of another of God's jokes. If Jonathan tells Josiah—"

For the first time, Angeline saw a crack in Lettie's armor and real fear shone in her face.

Angeline took Lettie's cold hands in her own. "I'll talk to him, tell him why we left Tolson. He'll understand. He just can't betray us."

"Never doubt the evil a man is capable of, no matter how good you think he is." Lettie's voice rang with bitterness.

Everything Angeline had hoped for, everything she dreamed about with Sam was about to come crumbling down around her. If Jonathan knew, that meant the Mormon church would know soon. He was a good man, a devoted brother, and would choose loyalty to God over his loyalty to an old love.

"Is he still here in Forestville?"

Lettie nodded. "I told him to stay at the hotel last night and be here at six this morning."

It was at least a start. Angeline knew she could try to convince him to keep their secret. They had loved each other, or at least she'd thought it was love. Now she knew it was a deep friendship that had grown into infatuation, nothing more. What she was already feeling for Sam was stronger than any of her emotions for Jonathan.

"Then I'll see him at six and find a way to convince him to keep his silence." Angeline was surprised by how firm she sounded.

She would convince Jonathan to keep their secret.

The next thirty minutes went by quickly, too quickly. Angeline wiped her hands on the towel to get rid of the flour, then looked toward the door to the dining area. Lettie gave her a quick hug and kissed her forehead. It was the most affection she'd ever received from her. It made Angeline's throat grow tight and she had to swallow three times before she felt more in control.

She took a deep breath and opened the door. At first, she didn't see anyone, then she stepped into the room. Jonathan stood at the door, a stark expression on his face. He was so familiar, so dear to her, affection for him washed over her. There he was, a poignant reminder of the life she could have had.

Her heart kicked into a gallop and suddenly everything was too real. The stress of the last eight months washed over her and a sob exploded from her throat. In seconds, Jonathan was there, pulling her into his arms. She leaned into him, his scent familiar and comforting.

"Shh, it's okay Angeline. It's okay. I'm here now," Jonathan crooned. "Don't cry."

Angeline was so very tempted to simply let Jonathan take care of her, to give him control and take the burden off her shoulders. It would be easy.

A year ago, she might have done just that. Yet Angeline was not the same person she had been then. She was stronger, smarter, and more confident. She didn't need a man to take care of her; she could take care of herself.

Angeline extricated herself from his embrace and stepped back. Jonathan reached for her, but she held up her hands to stop him. She refused to allow herself to fall into the habit of letting a man take care of her.

"Jonathan, it's good to see you." She managed a shaky smile.

"Angeline, I can't believe you're here. Lettie told me the strangest story, but I just didn't believe it." Jonathan sounded hurt. "What happened?

"Josiah offered for me and my father accepted." It sounded so simple, yet it was anything but. "I was raised to obey, Jonathan, so I did." She shrugged away the pain, not wanting to relive it again. There were some things she'd never tell anyone.

"How could you marry him? I don't understand, Angeline." Jonathan frowned. "Why didn't you go to the church elders, try to find a way to wait for me?"

She shook her head. "My father made an agreement with Josiah, not you. He saw potential to advance his position in the church. He is no fool and had no qualms about getting rid of at least one daughter with an advantageous marriage."

His gaze was hurt and confused. "Then why did you leave your husband? If it was such an advantageous marriage, how could you leave?"

"I tried to be a good wife, but there was nothing I could do to make him a good husband." She took a deep breath, knowing that she was pushing her relationship with Jonathan by asking for his silence. "Jonathan, I have to ask you not to tell anyone you saw us."

His mouth dropped open. "You want me to simply forget I saw you, forget you are married, forget you were on the street kissing an Indian?" He sounded desperate.

She took his hands in hers; they were cold and clammy, trembling. Angeline knew he was hurting, but she had to make him understand that if he didn't do as she asked, she'd be hurting worse, or perhaps dead. Jonathan was her friend and she had to rely on that friendship.

"Jonathan, you are very special to me. We grew up side by side; you've been my best friend all my life. I need you to trust me, to believe I had no choice but to find another path in life." She squeezed his hands. "Please, Jonathan, please."

"Angeline, I would do anything for you. I'd kill for you. I'd die for you. But I can't forget what I saw. And I can hardly believe what I'm hearing." He pulled away from her and sat down heavily. "I love you, Angeline. I wanted to marry you, have babies, and grow old with you."

Angeline sat in the chair beside him. "I did too, but it didn't work out that way. Josiah has already snatched that opportunity from us and we can never get it back. That door is closed and locked for us."

Jonathan banged the table with his fist. "I can't just leave. What if I stay here with you? I can help take care of you."

"You can't stay here. Your life is in Tolson, your faith is there."

"So is yours."

"No, it's not. It will never be again either. There's nothing for me in Tolson but pain and death."

He scoffed. "You're being dramatic. I'm sure Josiah would punish you, but death? You can't mean that."

Angeline couldn't begin to tell Jonathan how frightened she'd been for her life, the terror of having a man put a gun to her head, and of never knowing when she went to sleep if she'd wake up again. He couldn't possibly understand unless he'd been with her the last nine months.

"He's already sent one man to kill me. He'll likely send more until he gets what he wants."

"I don't believe it. Josiah might be a bit stern, but he's not a murderer. He's a well-respected brother."

Angeline's anger bubbled up, something she had never allowed before her flight to freedom. "You don't believe *me*. Then let me show you what your well-respected brother did." She reached for the button on her blouse.

"What are you doing?"

She ignored his protestations and finished unbuttoning her blouse, then turned and pulled it down from her shoulders. His gasp told her the lash scars on her back were visible. Each mark was an inch of agony, a piece of her soul ripped from her.

Tears stung her eyes, but she blinked them away and put her shirt back on. Her hands trembled so badly, she could hardly manage the buttons. By the time she turned around to face him, she had regained control of her emotions.

Jonathan looked pale and stricken. "Josiah did that to you?"

"That's only a small bit of what he did to me." Angeline shuddered, remembering the perversity Josiah enjoyed in his bed with implements of pain and even multiple partners. She swallowed hard and pushed aside the darkness. "I will not go back to him, even if it means dying."

"I don't think it needs to come to that. Angeline, I had no idea." He shook his head, his eyes full of sympathy. "I'm so sorry."

She sat back down and clenched her hands together so he wouldn't see how badly she was shaking. It was too important to keep her focus on what awaited her in the future instead of on the past.

"You've nothing to be sorry for. I told you we will always be friends. You have always been a part of my life, but my future isn't with you." She was pleased to see resignation on his face rather than disbelief.

"I think I believe that now." Jonathan ran his hands down his face. "I almost want to believe this last day was a dream, or a nightmare anyway."

Angeline managed a smile. "Unfortunately it's not. I am glad to see you, but you must promise me you'll not tell anyone you saw us."

"I won't tell anyone, but in return I'd like to come see you again." He still appeared as though he was having trouble accepting the fact she was no longer his.

"I don't think that's a good idea."

He leaned forward and touched her clasped hands. "Please, Angeline. As you said, we've been a part of each other's lives for so long, I can't just never see you again."

Angeline felt her refusal wavering and had to put some distance between them. She walked toward the big window and looked out into the street. The sunrise painted the buildings pink and orange, its beauty reminding her the world was not always full of dark corners and shadows.

"I won't change my mind. It's got to be this way. As glad as I am to see you, I have to say good-bye, Jonathan."

He sighed and she heard the scrape of his shoes on the wood floor. "Good-bye, Angeline."

She waited for him to come near her, but instead she heard the *snick* of the door closing. Then through the window, she saw his solitary figure disappearing down the road toward the livery.

Her heart hiccupped as the final piece of the girl she was walked out of her life. Now she could only look forward. Toward Sam. Toward happiness.

"Are you all right?"

Angeline didn't turn around to look at Lettie. She didn't want her friend to chastise her for crying, for regretting the fact her life had taken such a hard right turn. It was difficult enough to accept the fact she could never go back, never see anyone from Tolson again. So very hard.

"No, but I will be."

Lettie squeezed her shoulder. "No matter what happens, Angeline, you've done the right thing."

A small sob crept up her throat. Angeline shook her head and didn't turn around. This time she would endure the pain on her own. She had to say good-bye in her heart to the man she had held dear nearly all her life.

"Good morning, Angel." Sam peeked his head into the kitchen.

Angeline smiled shyly at him. "Good morning, Sam."

She looked so beautiful, so tempting, covered with flour and biscuit dough. Damn, he really was going loco if flour was sexy.

Someone pushed him into the kitchen from the dining room. He stumbled in, almost falling on his head. Pieter stood in the doorway. His blond hair was peppered with gray to match his bushy eyebrows, which were currently in a deep scowl.

"What are you doing in here, Carver?" Pieter's accent had faded but not entirely. He sounded as if he said "doink" which tickled Sam, though he didn't feel it prudent to say so.

"Flirting with Angeline."

At the stove, Marta barked a laugh. "He's honest, Pieter. You must give him that."

"Ha, I give him nothing. This girl has no father so I look after her." He gestured to the door. "You buy breakfast or you leave restaurant."

Angeline stared at Pieter, her expression one of disbelief.

Sam again wondered who had hurt her so badly that she would be shocked by someone's kindness. The same thing had happened with Jessup.

"I'll buy breakfast. I just wanted to say good morning to the most wonderful biscuit baker in the world." He winked at Angeline and was pleased to see her blush. Her creamy cheeks flushed an adorable shade of pink.

"Bah! Off with you, young man. She works, does not have time for your foolishness." Pieter escorted him out to the dining room without much force behind his hands.

Sam was heartened to see the older couple taking care of her since there was no one else to do it. Except for Jessup, of course, and he was a character too. Angeline inspired people to love her, to want to help her, and take care of her.

"What do you plan on doing with our Angeline, Samuel?" Pieter crossed his arms over his chest and rocked back on his heels.

"I plan on marrying her." The words just exploded from his mouth, although he hadn't planned on it. In fact, the thought had only been a whisper in his mind. Obviously, his heart had already made up its mind.

"Yah, that's good. She needs a good strong man." Pieter glanced at Sam's leg. "You were a soldier, but you work with wood now, yes?"

Sam resisted the urge to rub his wounded leg. It was bad enough the older man was pointing out he wasn't perfect. "Yes, I am a carpenter and I also make furniture."

"Good, good. You live with your father, yes?"

It started to feel as if Sam were being interviewed by Angeline's father, rather than her boss. However, he was happy to give an accounting of himself. Pieter and Marta had never had any children and Sam was pleased to see how much they cared for Angeline.

"Yes, I do. He publishes the newspaper." Sam wasn't about to tell Pieter just how little his father did with the newspaper. Most of the time, Sam did eighty percent of the work.

"Yah, is good newspaper." Pieter nodded sagely. "I will let you court her, but you may not hurt her." He shook his finger at Sam. "She is a good girl, so you must be a gentleman and do things right and proper."

If Pieter only knew what Sam and Angeline had already done. Sam wisely kept that information to himself.

"Thank you, Pieter. I will be a gentleman and I will never, ever hurt her." Sam planned on doing nothing but loving her, keeping her safe, and spending his life doing it.

After peering at Sam for another minute, Pieter apparently was satisfied, and he patted his round belly. "Good, good. Now you eat breakfast." He spotted Alice nearby and called to her as he walked back into the kitchen. "Alice, take Samuel's order so he can eat."

Alice, the brown, curly-headed waitress, had always treated him as if he were beneath her. She was the last person Sam wanted as his waitress, but he sat down at the table and waited. It was just another day in town, where folks thought what they wanted about him for no other reason than his heritage was different.

With an exaggerated sigh, Alice approached his table. "Do you need a menu?"

"No, I'll have two fried eggs, four pieces of bacon, three biscuits, and black coffee. Please." He tried to find a smile, but from the expression on the young woman's face, she wouldn't accept it anyway.

"Be right up." She followed Pieter into the kitchen, leaving Sam with his thoughts.

And they were all about Angeline.

Angeline finished the last batch of biscuits and put them in the oven. Marta kept smiling at her, making her feel foolish.

She didn't want to be courted by Sam, but she couldn't stop it. Her heart was already his.

How could she continue though? She had to tell him about Josiah and soon. Then there was Jonathan. Someone had probably seen him with her or Lettie. He'd seen Angeline with Sam. There were so many secrets between them, it was like having ashes in her mouth that she couldn't spit out.

If she told him the truth, Sam might decide she wasn't the right woman for him. That would leave her on her own again, but it would ease her conscience. Yet she would be so completely and utterly alone. Her heart would be shattered, again. Angeline was caught in a situation of her own making, one she was both miserable and ecstatic to be in.

She loved Sam, and each day that feeling grew stronger. There was no doubt in her mind he was the salve to her soul that she needed to live. If she told him about Josiah, she could lose that and him.

Her stomach clenched hard at the thought. Pieter walked back into the kitchen, looking as if he were very satisfied with himself.

"Pieter, what did you do?" Marta leveled a disapproving gaze at him. "Did you chase Samuel from the building?"

"No, I did not. I talked to him man to man. Angeline doesn't have a papa to look out for her, so is my job instead." He grinned at her. "Samuel is a good man, an honest man. He will make good husband."

Angeline tried to catch her breath as emotions pummeled her. Pieter and Marta, a couple she only knew eight months, who had taken her in as their employee, were now treating her as their daughter. Just as Jessup had pledged his protection, these lovely people were doing the same. It was so very different from what she expected, from what she had experienced in her life. There was such genuine goodness in the world and it resided in these wonderful folks.

Pieter kissed Marta loudly on the cheek and she giggled.

With a chuckle, he went out the backdoor just in time for Alice to come breezing into the kitchen, a look of distaste on her face.

"Your beau is out there looking for breakfast again." She pointed at her. "I don't want to serve him. You get him eggs, bacon, biscuits, and coffee."

"Alice! You are being rude." Marta pointed a wooden spoon at her. "Samuel is a customer and you are a waitress. Angeline is a cook and does not serve customers. You do."

"I don't want to. He looks at me with those black eyes and it's creepy." Alice shuddered.

Angeline wanted to slap her.

"He is not creepy."

Alice rolled her eyes. "Then you bring him his breakfast. I've got real customers out there." She left the kitchen, leaving a wake of negative energy in the whirl of all the positive.

Unfortunately, that was all it took to pull Angeline back into the pit of worry. She had to make a choice very soon before she was so far into a relationship with Sam, she would destroy them both with her lies.

"That Alice, she is young and foolish." Marta cracked two eggs into the hot frying pan, the sizzling loud in the quiet kitchen. "I think sometimes she should not be serving people when she's not nice to them."

"She just doesn't understand him. People have to be taught to hate." Angeline knew that firsthand.

Marta's gaze snapped to hers. "You are right, child. People do have to be taught to hate."

Angeline didn't respond because she didn't know how. Instead, she got a plate and started putting together Sam's breakfast. This, at least, she could do for him.

It was late, likely near midnight. Angeline couldn't sleep and the book she was reading was making her cross-eyed. Karen generously lent her books whenever Angeline asked.

She'd been fortunate enough that her late husband had left her quite a collection.

Angeline had missed supper and her stomach kept rumbling. With too many things on her mind, and an empty belly, she headed downstairs to get something to eat.

With only a candle to light her way, she tiptoed through the quiet restaurant and into the kitchen. She knew there'd be some leftover bread and honey to quiet her growling stomach. As she pulled the jar of honey from the pantry shelf, she heard a shuffling sound in the restaurant.

Angeline's instincts roared to life and she set the jar down without a sound, then blew out the candle. She didn't know whether or not to be afraid, but she did know to be careful.

She closed her eyes and listened, waiting for another noise. Within seconds, she heard it again, only this time it was louder. Angeline crept to the kitchen door with her heart in her throat and opened it just a crack. As she peered out into the restaurant, she strained to see whatever it was that was making the noises.

Whatever or whoever it was, they were farther away than she'd thought. Likely on the stairs or in the hallway leading to the storage room at the front of the building.

Angeline was trapped. She would either have to hide in the kitchen until whoever it was went away or find out who was creeping around at midnight, so she could eat and go to bed.

The old Angeline might have hidden, but the new and improved version wasn't about to. Marta and Pieter had become family to her and she wouldn't let anyone threaten them or their livelihood. She looked around the kitchen and spotted the rolling pin made of marble. It was solid enough to cause damage without being too heavy for her to carry.

As she left the kitchen on bare feet, the rolling pin was firmly held in her hand. She walked slowly toward the sound of the shuffling, her curiosity peaking the closer she got. Then she heard it.

A moan.

Angeline stopped, completely flummoxed. She couldn't decide if it was a moan of pleasure or pain. If the former, then she needed to go back upstairs immediately. If the latter, then she needed to wield her rolling pin.

She stepped closer still and peeked around the corner. Near the door to the storage room beneath the stairs, she saw two shadowy figures lit only by the dim moonlight coming in from the front door behind her.

Angeline squinted, but could only see that one was shorter than the other. She was about to give up trying to figure out if someone was in trouble when she heard what was distinctly a slap.

She tightened her grip on the rolling pin and stepped into the hallway. Her stance was wide and her protective instincts screaming.

"Let her go."

The two figures stopped moving and turned toward her.

"You heard me. Let her go. Now."

"Angeline, please help me." Alice's voice was full of panic.

"Who the fuck are you?" The man's voice was rough, gravelly, as if he'd eaten a mouthful of pebbles.

Angeline got goose bumps just hearing it, but she couldn't back down. "I'll split your skull open if you don't let her go and leave here right now."

"She's a cock teaser is what she is." The taller shadow pushed the short one toward the floor and Alice landed with a thump and a cry of pain.

"And you're an abusive bully. Don't make me tell you again. Get out." Angeline slapped the rolling pin on her hand, the smack loud in the quiet hallway.

"What are you going to do?"

"I told you. I'll split your skull open, then tell the sheriff you broke in and tried to attack Alice. Everyone will believe the angel." For once, she was using her "angelic" demeanor to her advantage.

The man scoffed. "You don't sound angelic to me."

Angeline smiled. "You have no idea who I am or what I'm capable of. Don't doubt me when I tell you I will do everything I can to protect Alice." She slapped the rolling pin again.

"Didn't want no cock teaser anyway. I just wanted a good fuck." He walked toward her and Angeline backed up to her left, letting the man know she was still there, still armed.

"You can find that at the saloon, I believe. Miss Daisy and her girls are there for a good fuck." Angeline heard Alice gasp and ignored her. It felt good to use naughty words and feel the power of them as she shocked herself and her audience.

"Who the hell are you?"

"Nobody you want to tangle with. Now get out." She watched him slink toward the door, her eyes straining in the dark to see just where he was.

It was a good thing she was alert because he moved so suddenly she had only seconds to react. The man lunged at her and she brought the rolling pin down on his head. The crack resounded through the air and she stumbled backward from the force of the impact. The man dropped to the floor with a thud and lay still.

Angeline was breathing so hard she was getting lightheaded. Alice appeared beside her, staring up with wide brown eyes.

"Angeline, I think you killed him."

"If I did, then he had it coming. That man was hurting you and he tried to hurt me." Normally Angeline would have run for help, but she was determined to finish this situation on her own. "Now let's check on your errant beau."

"He's not my beau. He's just a man I met yesterday who was nice to me. One of the cowboys passing through town who was handsome." Alice's voice cracked. "Why do I always let myself be wooed by a pair of pretty eyes?"

"Stop feeling sorry for yourself and help me." Angeline rolled the man over and checked to be sure he was breathing. At least she hadn't killed him. "Go get the lantern from the kitchen and a tablecloth."

Alice ran to the kitchen and reappeared seconds later with a tablecloth clutched in one hand and the unlit lantern in the other. Angeline sighed and took the lantern from her.

"Now go get a match to light it."

Alice pulled one from her pocket and Angeline smiled at her. It was the first time the two of them had connected and, strangely enough, it was over the prone body of an unsuitable suitor.

Angeline lit the lantern, then adjusted the wick so they could see better. The cowboy was handsome, with sandy blond hair and a strong jaw. He was also huge. No wonder Alice couldn't fight him off. Angeline swallowed the lump in her throat at the possibility of what the man would have done to Alice if she hadn't conked him on the head.

She laid out the tablecloth beside the man on the floor. "Now let's roll him onto it."

The two of them managed to get him onto the tablecloth with a lot of effort. Angeline was panting and sweating by the time she was done. She glanced down and realized she was only wearing her nightrail.

"I'm going to get my coat; then we're going to drag him outside."

Alice's eyes widened. "We're going to do what?"

"You heard me. We're going to drag him into the mud where he belongs. Then we'll wake up the sheriff." Angeline wanted the cowboy to know exactly who had bested him and whom not to bother again.

By the time she got downstairs, Alice had slid the man all the way to the front door on her own. Angeline gaped at her.

"You're stronger than you look."

"So are you. Now let's get this man out of here before I get too scared to help." Alice, despite her brave words, was trembling beside Angelinc.

Within minutes they'd dragged the man out onto the porch, down the stairs—although he'd moaned as each step made his head bounce—and into the street.

Angeline wiped her brow on her coat sleeve. "Now we need Sheriff Booth and some rope."

"I'll get the sheriff." Alice took off running down the street, her petticoats flying around her in the darkness like a flag.

Angeline went back inside to the kitchen and found twine. She cut off a length and hurried back outside. By the time Alice came back with the sheriff, the man was tied up like a turkey and snoring like a saw.

"Miss Angeline, what's going on?" Sheriff Booth was a good man, one she trusted.

"This man was attacking Alice, so I hit him on the head with a rolling pin. We dragged him out here and tied him up for you." Angeline rose, the stress of the night's activities making exhaustion wind its way around her. "He's a big man so I'd suggest a horse or wagon to transport him to jail."

"Well, then, that's a right fine idea," the sheriff said. Angeline realized that over the course of the last eight months, she'd made friends in Forestville. It made her feel proud to be a part of the town.

"I'll go get the wagon and one of the deputies to help me." He turned to Alice, who was standing there hugging herself. "You all right, Miss Alice?"

"I am now thanks to Angeline." Her voice, normally snide and sometimes spiteful, was soft and defeated.

"Why don't you girls go on inside and lock up. I'll take care of this fella for you."

Angeline took Alice's arm and led her up the steps, locking

the door behind them. Her hunger forgotten, she walked up the stairs with the older girl still at her side. When they reached the three identical bedrooms where Angeline, Lettie, and Alice slept, she let go of the girl's arm.

"Alice, are you all right?"

It took a few moments, but she finally responded. "No, I'm not. I w-was really afraid down there for the first time. I flirt a lot with men and I let them kiss me, sometimes more. I know it's dangerous, but with my parents gone in the fire, I don't have anyone else. The men make me feel good, special."

Angeline's heart pinched at the idea that this beautiful young woman was lonely enough to look for affection from strangers. "You are special, but sometimes you keep other people away, people who do care about you. If you'd spend time with us, perhaps you wouldn't need to feel good with these men."

Alice nodded. "I was just lonely."

Regardless of whether or not the girl pushed her away, Angeline pulled her into a quick hug. Alice was like a limp rag in her arms.

"Me too."

"You too? Even with Lettie and that Sam fawning all over you?"

Angeline shook her head. "I've been lonely most of my life. I have Lettie, but she keeps to herself with me as much as she does with all of you. I don't have anyone besides myself. My sister lives far away; in fact, I don't know where she lives."

"I didn't know that. I thought you were so happy and had so many folks fawning on you." Alice cleared her throat. "I was jealous."

Angeline sighed. "You've nothing to be jealous about. I found Sam because I wasn't looking for him. If you spend more time taking care of yourself, being with your family here at the Blue Plate, maybe you'll find what makes you happy."

Alice cocked her head to the right. "You know, that sounds like a fine idea."

"Good, now let's go to bed before Pieter and Marta find out what we did." Angeline leaned down and quickly hugged Alice again. This time she received a hug in return. "Good night."

"Good night, Angeline, and thank you. For everything." Alice's voice was thick with emotion. For the first time since they'd met, Angeline was seeing the true person that lurked beneath the persona Alice showed the world.

"You're welcome." Angeline went back into her room, completely exhausted, and climbed into bed. This time she fell right to sleep, content with the help she'd given Alice. It wasn't often that Angeline was able to be the one doing the rescuing. Truthfully, it felt nice—no, it felt wonderful. She'd done something good.

Chapter Six

Sam stood in the kitchen, rubbing his gritty eyes and waiting for the coffee to boil. He yawned so hard, his jaw cracked loudly in the quiet kitchen. It had been a long night, full of dreams and dark figures. He couldn't quite remember exactly what he dreamed of, but he knew it was different from his normal dreams.

Most days his subconscious returned to the war, to the painful memories he tried so hard to forget. The repetitive nature of his dreams meant he could not escape them.

However, since he'd met Angeline, his dreams had slowly started to change. Instead of dreams of blood and pain, they were full of unknown threats and fear.

He didn't know what to make of them and that bothered him more than not sleeping. Sam was off center and out of control with his obsession over Angeline. What he needed to do was marry her; then she'd be the first thing he saw every day and the last thing he saw before he went to sleep at night. Perhaps then he wouldn't have bad dreams.

The coffee was finally ready and he could hardly wait to pour a cup. It wasn't dawn yet, so the dark, hot brew was much needed. He closed his eyes and sipped it slowly. The heat slid down his throat like nectar. He might be a terrible cook but, damn, he made good coffee.

A knock at the door made the coffee splash on his hand.

"Shit." He set the cup down on the counter and shook his hand against the pain.

With a frown, he went to the front door. He didn't know who would be at the newspaper office at five in the morning, but the knock didn't bode well. Sam walked as fast as his stiff leg could carry him and by the time he made it to the door, whoever was on the other side was pounding like a hammer on it.

"I'm coming, I'm coming." Sam had the awful notion something had happened to Angeline. His heart froze at the thought.

He yanked open the door to find Jessup on the front stoop. The old man's nose was red as a beet and crusty with mucus. He stared hard at Sam, his expression as serious as the blackness of the night behind him.

"Jessup, what are you doing here?"

"I seen your pa." Jessup wiped his nose on an equally dirty sleeve. "He was out yonder by the lake in just his union suit. I tried to run him down but that man is fast as a greased pig."

Sam's fear about Angeline turned to ice-cold terror at the thought his father was out in the cold morning alone. "Where is he now?"

"Dunno. It's dark and I lost sight of him. I ran right over here to get you." Jessup looked genuinely concerned.

"Let me get my trousers on." Ignoring the pain in his leg, Sam sprinted up the stairs to his room and yanked on his clothes. Guilt washed over him, filling him with remorse for not making sure his father was safe. Sam knew his pa was suffering, that his brain was losing bits and pieces of itself.

Now he was out in nearly freezing temperatures with no

clothes and maybe even no shoes. Sam tried to tamp down his panic, but it bubbled through him as if he'd eaten poison.

Sam's leg was screaming by the time he made it back downstairs. The front door was wide open and Jessup was gone. Sam cursed and yanked on his boots so hard, he lost his balance and fell backward into the wall.

Stars exploded behind his eyes as he gasped at the pain. Tears stung his eyes as he finished pulling on his boots a bit more slowly.

"Sam?"

Angeline's voice cut through his fog of self-pity and fear. He glanced up to find her in the doorway, her eyes wide with concern. She wore her blue dress with the buttons done up wrong, a shawl around her shoulders, and her blond hair in a cloud as if she'd just risen from bed.

Sam thought she'd never looked more beautiful.

"Jessup came and got me. He said you were in trouble." She stepped into the house and held out her hand to him. "Let's go find your father."

Without asking any questions, she simply accepted that he needed help and came to his side. If he needed proof their connection was strong, it was right there in front of him.

He got to his feet and took her hand. "My father is down by the lake. We'll need light."

"Jessup has a lantern. He's waiting for us."

He couldn't begin to express enough gratitude to his friends for their help. God only knew what he'd done right to deserve it, but he was not about to question it.

As they walked out the door together, the wind immediately cut into his face. He held his hat down with one hand and walked toward the light at the end of the street. It had to be Jessup, the crazy old man who had suddenly become his guardian angel. It was frigid, cold enough to make his hands numb by the time they'd walked the half mile to the edge of the lake.

Jessup was nearly dancing in place. " 'Bout time you got here. I'm freezing my balls off."

Angeline made a choking sound.

"Jessup, just tell me where you saw him." Sam peered through the darkness, trying to see a shadow that moved, a glint of anything.

There was no moon, nothing shining down to guide them, other than the lantern clutched in Jessup's hand. Sam took it from him and started walking around the edge of the lake. The leaves and fallen sticks, long since dead from the previous fall, crunched beneath their feet. In the darkness the buds of spring were not visible.

The lake lapped gently to the right, guiding them along the shore. They walked single file with ten feet between them, Sam at the head of the column.

"Pa!"

"Mr. Carver!"

"Crazy old man!"

Sam cursed at Jessup. "That's the pot calling the kettle black."

"Exactly. I know loco when I see it. 'Sides you won't care if'n we find him."

Sam couldn't argue with that logic. They pushed on, slowing down to check behind each boulder, each tree. Sam's feet grew numb, and he knew his father must be completely frozen. The fact that Angeline was plodding along behind him made him love her all the more.

"Pa! Where are you?"

A noise from the left made Sam stop so suddenly, Angeline ran into him. Her soft breasts pushed into his back and a small "Oof" popped from her mouth.

"Did you hear that?"

The three of them stopped, the only sound their harsh breathing. Then Sam heard it again. A soft cry, like a child.

His leg was dragging behind him as Sam headed toward the sound. Angeline passed him, her skirt hiked up so she could run. Jessup was right behind her, waddling like a dirty duck. Sam felt helpless and useless as they left him limping in the leaves. He cursed his own body and picked up as much speed as he could.

"I found him. He's here, Sam!" Angeline's voice guided him through the darkness until he found them near a group of boulders.

She'd taken off her shawl, a threadbare wool one with barely enough warmth to keep a mouse warm, and put it around his father's shoulders. The older man was shaking so hard, his teeth clacked together.

Sam dropped to his knees and took his father into his arms and somehow managed not to cry. He had been selfishly focusing on Angeline, on his love for her, while his father wandered off in the night on his own. He could have died and Sam would have been completely to blame.

"Pa, are you all right?"

"Sam? What are you doing out here in the middle of the night?"

A half-sob, half-laugh jumped up his throat. Sam took off his own coat and handed Angeline's shawl back to her with a grateful smile. Later on, when he didn't feel so overwhelmed, he'd thank her properly for her help.

"I'm cold."

"I know, Pa. Let's get you back to the house."

Between the three of them, they managed to get his father on his feet, but he was nearly dead weight. Likely his legs were too cold to function. It broke Sam's heart to see his father helpless and dependent on strangers to help him back home, dressed only in his union suit and tears.

When they got into the house, every one of them was huffing like a locomotive. He led them to the front parlor, where there was a settee. With less grace and more desperation, they maneuvered themselves like a horse with eight legs until the older Carver was safely lying on the settee.

Jessup coughed and looked between Sam and Angeline. "If'n you folks got this situation in hand, I'm gonna go back to the Blue Plate and get some fresh biscuits."

Sam nodded. "Thank you, Jessup. I'll see to it you have fresh biscuits every day. I don't know what would've happened if you hadn't seen him." He gazed down at his father and his heart pinched hard enough to stop his breath.

"Ain't nothing, but I will hold you to the biscuits promise." Jessup nodded to Angeline, then disappeared out the door, leaving behind a rank odor and an amazing record of good deeds.

She took Sam's hand. "I'm sorry."

"It's okay. I should have been watching him. I should have known something might happen." He could spend all night talking about what he should have done, but it didn't change a damn thing.

His father seemed to fall asleep immediately, his face looking almost childlike. Angeline took an afghan from the back of the settee and covered his father. Sam checked him for injuries. But other than scratches on his feet, he seemed to be fine.

"I smell coffee. Why don't we go warm up?" She tugged at Sam's arm.

Sam didn't want to leave his father yet, but he had to. He needed time to get hold of his emotions, and he also needed to tell Angeline the truth about what was happening.

They walked to the kitchen, her small hand incredibly comforting tucked into his own. He hadn't realized the depth of his love until that moment. Without thinking about it, he kissed her hard and quick.

"I love you, Angel."

Her face flushed pink and she looked down at their joined hands. "Let's go get some coffee."

He wasn't disappointed at her lack of response because he saw the love in her eyes before she averted her gaze. She just obviously wasn't ready to tell him yet. Sam was patient enough to wait.

The coffee was waiting on the stove, hot and strong. At least that small comfort would help him build up his courage enough to talk. Pouring the coffee was an everyday chore, bringing some normalcy to an otherwise abnormal morning.

The sun had started to rise and the predawn light filtered in through the window as they sat at the rickety table. He looked down at the old, splintered top and realized there were many things he'd been ignoring. Their house was full of pitiful furniture and even more pitiful men.

"I have kept something from you. I think because I didn't want anyone to think less of him. My father has been sick for some time. Not sick in his body, but in his mind." Sam sipped at the coffee. "I started seeing it about two years ago. Little things like forgetting where he left something, or someone's name. Before, he never forgot anything."

"It sounds as if it was hard to recognize as anything other than forgetfulness." Angeline watched him with her steady blue gaze.

Sam ran his hand across the tabletop. "I see this table and I realize I've ignored more than my father's memory loss. I've spent so much time thinking about me and my needs that I turned into a selfish bastard."

"You're not a selfish bastard." She put her hand over his. "You're human."

He snorted. "Yeah, I am. After I realized something was wrong with my father, I kept it from everyone. Like it was a dirty secret to hide away."

She pulled her hand away and looked down at her mug. "Sometimes you have to keep secrets."

At another time he'd ask her what she meant by that.

"After I kept one secret, there was another and another. He forgot who I was, who he was. Hell, he was calling my mother's name and she died ten years ago." Sam had never felt so helpless as he did in the woods looking for his father. He'd survived a war, but he'd almost allowed his father to die.

"He needs to have someone take care of him during the day and obviously keep an eye on him at night. I don't know how I can do this." Sam had never imagined he'd be the one taking care of his father instead of the other way around.

"I can help when I'm not working. I could cook, clean up around here. Perhaps if you hired someone to take care of the newspaper, that would give you time to take care of him." Angeline touched his hand again. "You have friends who will help you."

Sam sighed heavily. He couldn't expect anyone to help out indefinitely. No, he had to look to the future and for that he had to have money.

"Angel, you are amazing. I appreciate the offer, but I can't accept it." He smiled at her sadly. "The only way you're cooking in this house is if you marry me."

He didn't mean it, or perhaps he did and needed to get it said. Her reaction, however, made him realize it was far too soon to mention marriage.

Angeline's face drained of all color so quickly, he swore he could actually see the blood travel down her skin. Her eyes grew wide as saucers and her lips pinched together so tightly that they didn't even appear pink anymore.

"I can't marry you, Sam." Each word was torn from her throat, ragged and raw.

He knew he was hearing what she hid deep inside. "Why not?"

She shook her head.

Sam took her hands in his, noting they were cold and trembling. "Trust me, Angel. Please, tell me whatever it is. It won't change how I feel about you. You are firmly inside my heart and nothing is going to dislodge you."

A single tear rolled down her cheek, but still she said nothing.

Sam dropped to his knees beside her and took her face in his hands. The rest of her shook just as hard as her hands. It was fear he saw in her eyes.

"You're scaring me and believe me, I've had enough scaring for one day. Please just tell me."

"You are a wonderful person, Sam. Better than I deserve, but I can't marry y-you because I'm already married."

A roar went through his ears and he could see nothing for a few moments. Then he managed to suck in a breath and his brain recognized what she'd said.

"Oh, Angel." He kissed her forehead. "I still want to marry you, no matter what. Please tell me you don't love him."

She made a sound that sounded something like a laugh but was more a cry of pain. "Love him? I hate him more than I ever thought I could hate anyone. He destroyed my life and my future."

It explained so much, everything really. She had run from a husband she hated, who must have hurt her. Then she came to Forestville and into Sam's heart.

He pulled her into his arms and held her. It was a day of heavy emotions and confessions. Sam didn't know what it meant for the two of them, what the future held for them, but he did know he meant what he'd said.

Sam wanted to marry Angeline, no matter what.

Angeline walked back to the Blue Plate with her heart in tatters. It had been such a strange morning and it was barely past dawn. She had been so worried about the older Mr. Carver when Jessup had come to the kitchen to get her.

This situation was even more stressful than three days earlier when Alice had needed her help to get rid of an unwanted suitor. Then she'd been worried, but not truly afraid. This time she'd been more fearful, knowing that Mr. Carver's life was in danger.

However, fortune had smiled on them when they'd found him hale and hearty if very cold. He needed help, and no matter what Sam said, she would do all she could. Even if it meant reducing the hours she worked at the restaurant.

One of the things she'd been taught as a girl was to take care of family, that parents and grandparents were to be revered and respected, taken care of until they passed. Even if she'd abandoned much of what had been beaten into her, she firmly believed in taking care of older relatives.

After Sam's confession about keeping secrets, guilt immediately settled on her heart. She needed to tell him the truth, not just a small nugget of it. After all Sam had done for her, his devotion to courting her, she owed him the same respect he'd given her.

She would tell him the whole truth that night.

The corners of her bedroom were deep in shadow, with only the moonlight streaming through the small window. Angeline crept in with Sam behind her, his hand firmly tucked into hers. She knew Marta would not approve, much less Pieter, but she needed to be with Sam. With Karen's help in watching Mr. Carver, Angeline had an hour alone with Sam.

"I don't like sneaking around," he whispered harshly.

She didn't answer him, instead closing the door and leaning against it. "I needed to talk to you in private."

"What about my father? I can't leave him alone." His voice sounded pained to admit that particular fact.

"Don't worry. Karen is keeping an eye on him. Daniel was even playing checkers with him when I came to get you."

Angeline sat on the edge of the bed and clasped her hands

together. She couldn't look him in the eye as she prepared to tell him everything she had kept hidden inside. He glanced at the windowsill and smiled when he saw the collection of his gifts perched on it.

"I told you I was married."

Sam sat down beside her. "Yep, I remember that. It's something I'm not likely to forget."

She felt her cheeks heat, grateful for the semidarkness, since all she appeared to do was blush around him.

"I wasn't entirely honest with you about that."

"Do you mean you aren't married?"

Oh, how she wished that was true. "No, I married Josiah. In fact, I was his third wife."

The silence was loud enough she could hear the blood rushing past her ears.

"Excuse me?"

"I grew up in Utah, in a small town called Tolson. My mother died when I was five and my father raised my sister, Eliza, and I, with the help of the church. Our church, you see, is a faith called the Church of Jesus Christ of Latter-day Saints. Have you heard of Brigham Young?"

Sam was quiet enough to make her fidget. "No."

"He founded our church and our faith. I won't go into the details of everything I was brought up to believe, but one of the main practices of our church is allowing a man to have multiple wives." She swallowed the huge lump in her throat. "I was chosen by a well-respected church elder to become his wife. My father told me to do it and although I thought I loved another, I obeyed him as I had always done."

Sam's body tensed at the use of the word "loved." He was sitting next to her like a block of wood.

"My sister, Eliza, tried to stop the wedding, but my father would not be swayed. Although I didn't want to marry Josiah, I did. It was not a joyful day for me, but it was the last day I felt anything but fear."

Sam's gaze snapped to hers in the semidarkness. "What do you mean 'fear'?"

"Josiah had already buried his first wife, his current wife was a shell of a woman who simply took care of his ten children, the second was Let—a friend of mine who did not want to marry him either, and then there was me. All of us lived in one house together." She closed her eyes, remembering the noise, the heat from fourteen bodies, and the shed out back.

"Sounds cozy."

Angeline clenched her hands into fists. "Sam, I know you're angry and hurt, but if you keep being snide, I won't continue. This is hard enough."

He was quiet for a few moments. "I'm sorry, Angel. I don't mean to be snide. It's just, well, I wanted to marry you."

She took his hand in hers and felt the warmth of his skin, the beat of his life force against hers. Angeline brought it to her cheek and let him feel her tears.

"I would like that too, Sam, more than you can ever imagine." She managed to get a deep breath in and tucked his hand onto her lap between hers. "The one thing no one had warned me about was Josiah's strange proclivities. You see, he enjoyed inflicting pain. It gave him pleasure to do so. He was not a young man and he needed all the help he could get to, um, perform as a husband should."

Angeline let that information settle in Sam and his sharp intake of breath let her know he understood what she meant.

"Are you saying he beat you so he could get hard enough to fuck you?"

She would have said something about his cussing, but she didn't. It was understandable, given the mental image she'd just put in his mind.

Her chin trembled as she continued. It was so hard, so very hard to not only relive Josiah's brutality, but to know she would likely never have Sam as her husband to erase those memories.

"Yes, although it wasn't always a beating. Sometimes he used things other than his fists. I'm damaged inside and out, Sam. I can never be whole and I can never marry you."

He gathered her in his arms and held her as they both came to terms with Angeline's statement. It was a bitter truth that would not taste good, no matter who was delivering it.

She burrowed into his warmth, breathing in the scent that had become a part of her. He hadn't run from the room, and he offered her comfort when she needed it. Perhaps telling him was the right thing to do.

"Never say never. I'm going to fight for you, Angel."

Angeline sat back and stared at him. "What do you mean, fight for me?"

His dark eyes were intense in the lamplight. "I won't simply give up on being with you. We are meant to be together, two sides of the same coin. This isn't something that happens every day. People can go their entire lives without meeting their other half. You and me, we got lucky."

She stared at him openmouthed, completely flummoxed. "I don't understand."

"You said you were his third wife. In the eyes of the law, no man can have more than one wife at a time. That means you aren't really married."

Angeline hadn't considered the legality of her marriage, just the church's position on marriage. She was bound to Josiah for life and after death according to her church. Yet, as she stared at Sam, she realized he was right. Completely right.

"I'm not married?"

He cupped her cheek. "You're not married."

Her heart began to beat like a jackrabbit at the possibility Josiah had no legal right to follow her, to make her return to Tolson or ever to lay his hands on her again. She allowed a tiny flare of hope to ignite within her. Yet she hadn't told Sam everything yet. It was time to tell him the rest.

"He sent a man after us. Someone who tracked us from—"

"Did you say 'us'? Who is us?" Sam frowned.

Angeline realized she'd slipped up and said more than she should have. Lettie's secrets were her own to tell, but it was too late to take back the words that had popped out.

"Me and, uh, Lettie. You can't tell anyone though because it's her business, not mine. I didn't mean to tell you about her."

She watched his face carefully for a reaction. Instead of looking shocked, he nodded as if he'd known what she'd say.

"She's his second wife now, and unfortunately barren, so he never had children with her. That was the reason he decided to marry me."

"I hate to tell you this, honey, but that's not the only reason." Sam raised one brow. "You're simply stunning, smart, and have such an amazingly good heart, it humbles me."

Angeline shook her head. "I'm not that good. I've done things in the last year I'm not proud of, including running from my husband."

Sam squeezed her hands. "He's not your husband. Just keep saying it over and over."

"I'll try. Now let me tell you the rest." She opened up the memory of what had happened in the dark forest outside Bowson. The fear, the outright terror of having a gun pressed to her head.

"Lettie and I were on our own for a few months, scared to death and surviving on willpower alone. We thought we had been so clever, but this bounty hunter found us. And my sister was with him. She was using him to find me and, since we look nothing alike, he didn't suspect who she was." Angeline looked away from Sam, unwilling to let him see just how hard it was to talk about the terrifying experience. "We were working in a restaurant in a town called Bowson. Eliza tried to help me escape, but the bounty hunter got to me first. H-he was going to shoot me in the h-head. My sister saved my life by hitting him and tying him up."

"Jesus. You have a helluva sister." Sam kept her at his side, his body touching hers from shoulder to toes.

"She's amazing and I owe her so much. I've never been so scared. The last year has been nothing but sleepless nights and so much worrying my stomach hurts nearly every day." Angeline felt the familiar knot of tension inside her. It was a constant companion she would do anything to cast aside.

"Ah, Angel, I'm so sorry." Sam leaned his head against hers. "If I could take away all the bad, I would."

Angeline's eyes stung with tears at the love she heard in his voice, at the love that was in her heart. "I know."

He kissed her forehead. "Will you marry me, Angeline Hunter?"

This time, the impossible was possible. She could marry him and be his wife, no longer indentured to Josiah, no longer needing to be afraid he would find her and hurt her. It was tempting, so tempting.

She wanted to say yes so badly, she actually tasted it. Something held her back though. If she married Sam, then he would be a target for whatever vicious bounty hunter Josiah sent after her. Josiah could make her a widow before she had a chance to truly be happy with her new husband.

Instead of telling him no, she wrapped her arms around his neck. "Kiss me, Sam."

His breath gusted out on a sigh. "You know I can't resist you, Angel."

She watched his mouth descend and closed her eyes just before it met hers. At first it was a simple brushing of the lips, the lightest touch like a butterfly. Then he pressed himself against her from top to bottom and she gasped.

It was all he needed.

His mouth opened over hers and consumed her. His

tongue coaxed hers out of hiding, caressing, rasping against it. She felt his cock hard and insistent against her hip. His entire body shuddered as he pressed himself closer, then closer still, as if they could occupy the same space.

Her bed wasn't very big, but it was large enough for them to find their pleasure together. She leaned back and pulled him along until they were side by side on the narrow bed. He thrust against her rhythmically, reminding her of just what they could be doing if all their clothes weren't in the way.

"You know we shouldn't do this here," he whispered as he rained kisses down her neck, his hot mouth leaving a trail of tingles.

"I know but it feels so good." Angeline reached down and grasped his cock through his trousers. He was hard as iron and pulsed against her palm.

"Obviously my dick agrees with you." He pushed against her hand. "You've got a magic touch."

Sam started unbuttoning her dress until it was open to the waist. Through the opening, her breasts were only covered by a chemise. She never had much money for undergarments, so this was all she had, along with one thin petticoat. Sam, however, didn't seem to mind at all.

He pulled the chemise down until her breasts were thrust above the neckline, like an offering to him.

"Your breasts are beautiful, alabaster topped by the lightest shade of pink." He bent down and licked one, then the other, sending bolts of pleasure straight to her center. "Delicious."

Angeline simply watched as his mouth closed around her nipple and he sucked on her, pulling her deep into his mouth. She had never realized breasts and nipples were so sensitive and could bring so much joy when touched by the right man.

His hand landed on the other breast and he pinched the nipple between his fingers. She gasped as his teeth closed around her, nibbling gently. The combination of his mouth and hand were astonishing.

Her pussy thrummed with arousal the more he toyed with her breasts. He licked, nipped, sucked, and pinched her nipples. Angeline wanted him to do that while he was inside her. The possibility of what it would feel like made her moan.

"Feel good?"

"I want more. I want you inside me."

He stopped and stared at her in the lamplight, his dark eyes probing. "Are you sure? I mean, Pieter would likely shoot me if he catches me up here."

"Please, Sam, I can't wait. Please." She pulled at his shirt, yanking it from his trousers, then reached for his buttons.

"I guess you're sure." He put his hand over hers. "Let's take this slow."

"No, I can't." She throbbed with need, so wet, moisture trickled down her thigh. "I need you now." Angeline pulled up her skirt until the slit in her pantalettes was easily accessible.

His gaze darkened as he realized her intent. A quick, fierce mating was what she craved. He finished unbuttoning his trousers and released his cock. It sprang free, hard and seemingly as eager as she was.

She inched closer until she could flip on her back. He rose up on his elbows and landed above her. Angeline had never felt such a burning desire, such an unstoppable need to mate with him.

"Now, Sam, now."

Angeline wrapped her legs around his hips and pulled. His cock landed right between her legs and he thrust inside her, filling her until he was embedded within her. Sam wasted no time. He started thrusting inside her, faster and faster.

"My breasts, kiss them, bite them," she whispered.

Sam was like a machine. Never losing his rhythm, he

leaned down and pulled the right breast into his mouth. His sucking mimicked the motion of his cock. Her fingers dug into his back as she felt the now familiar coil tightening inside her.

She closed around him, making him thrust harder, heightening her pleasure until she exploded from the inside out. Sam bit her nipple and her heart stuttered as she found her peak. She scratched at his back, her mouth open in a silent howl of ecstasy. Angeline bucked against him, pulling him deeper inside her.

He buried himself with a powerful thrust, the veins on his neck standing out. Angeline watched him find his own release, his face reflecting the greatest joy. She rode the wave of her bliss as he rode his.

It was over in minutes, but Angeline felt as if she'd been making love for an hour. Her breath came in short gasps and her body virtually vibrated with the force of what had just happened.

He propped himself on his elbow and kissed her. "Amazing."

She smiled and kissed him. "Definitely."

They spent a few minutes catching their breath before they rose and washed up quickly, then straightened their clothes. Angeline had told him as much as she could about herself and he'd accepted her for who she was. She loved him desperately. But could she say yes to marry him?

Chapter Seven

Karen poked her head into the kitchen. "There's a man here to see you."

Angeline's head snapped up. "What man?"

"I don't know. He looks kind of scruffy, whiskers and all. Oh, and he looks like he's been wearing the same clothes awhile. Kinda nervous too." Karen disappeared from view.

Angeline's heart simply stopped beating and she started to see spots in her vision. She managed to suck in a breath as her entire body trembled. Her worst fear was coming true too soon.

"Miss Angeline, what's wrong?" Daniel looked up from his perch on the stool where he was currently shucking peas for dinner.

"I don't feel well, Daniel. I'm going to get some air." Angeline's hand shook so much, it took her three tries to get the backdoor open. She stumbled outside and walked carefully down the steps.

Angeline had to find out who was in the restaurant, but she had to get ahold of her runaway fear first. Josiah was not her legal husband, there was no reason to be afraid. If this man tried anything, she would do what she had to to protect herself.

She took several deep breaths and straightened up. The first thing she would do was go find the sheriff. He had already proved he would stick up by her. He was a fair man—it was time to start standing up for herself.

With more fortitude than she knew she had, Angeline went back up the steps and looked inside to find Marta at the counter, frowning.

Angeline threw her apron inside. "I have an emergency, Marta. I'll be back as soon as I can."

Before the older woman could respond, Angeline closed the door. She marched down the street toward the jail and this time she felt more anger than fear. It was high time she stopped feeling as if she were a rabbit being chased by a wolf.

Angeline was about to become the hunter instead of the prey.

By the time she got to the jail, she felt even stronger, more able to defend herself. She opened the door and stepped in to find Sheriff Henry Booth at his desk with a mug of coffee. He smiled when he saw her. Then his expression changed when she stepped inside.

He rose to his feet, a tall, lanky man with silver hair and wide shoulders. His blue chambray shirt was covered by a black leather vest with a shiny silver star on it. A dark brown hat was perpetually perched on his head.

"Miss Angeline. What's wrong?"

"There's a dangerous man in the restaurant."

"At least you decided not to use a rolling pin on this one." His brows rose and she managed not to blush.

"What happened to that particular, ah, suitor?" She had meant to ask him before now. She'd thought about the sound of the rolling pin on the man's head many times.

"He woke up with a hell of a headache, pardon my language. Said something about an angel kicking his ass, pardon my language again. We found his horse over by the saloon and that cowboy rode on outta here." Booth watched her carefully. "Told me he'd never come back this way again."

"I'm glad he was well enough to leave, but I don't regret protecting Alice." Angeline kept her shoulders back and her spine straight. That night in the darkness of the restaurant, she'd found true courage and she wouldn't be ashamed of it.

"I'm glad you did protect her. She's a good girl, even if she has a sharp tongue. Now what makes you think this man in the restaurant is dangerous?" The sheriff didn't appear to disbelieve her, but he wasn't exactly running out the door to arrest anyone either.

"He's unkempt and suspicious and, unfortunately, I've had some troubles with men, um, following me." Angeline didn't quite want to admit her not-really husband had sent a bounty hunter after her. "He's already asked for me and I think he means to do me harm."

"He'll do no such thing while I'm the law in Forestville." The sheriff picked up the gun belt hanging on a nail behind his desk. "Let's go see what this fella thinks he can do."

They left the jail side by side and hurried down the sidewalk toward the restaurant.

Angeline was grateful Sheriff Booth didn't ask for any additional details. She should tell him everything, but that would have to wait until later. For now she needed to get back to the restaurant before the bounty hunter found her first.

Sam walked out of the general store with a box of penny nails. He needed to finish the table he was making for his father before another job came his way. Fortunately, his father was taking an afternoon nap so he could make a quick trip to the store.

He was turning toward home when a flash of blue caught his eye. His mouth dropped open when he realized it was

Sheriff Booth sprinting down the sidewalk with Angeline. Sam knew immediately something was wrong and she could be in danger. Her loco husband might have sent another hired gun after her.

Sam dropped the nails and ran. He kept her in his sights, following the shiny gold of her hair, which sparkled in the sunlight each time she went between buildings. They had a good head start so they arrived at the restaurant before he did.

When the sheriff pulled his gun and walked in with Angeline at his back, Sam ran harder, his heart lodged somewhere near his throat.

Sam arrived a minute later, his breathing as labored as his heart rate. The sheriff was walking toward the door.

"Henry, what's going on?"

The older man glanced up at Sam and tucked his gun back in its holster. "Darned if I know. Miss Angeline said someone was going to hurt her so I came over here, but turns out she knows the fella."

"She knows the fella?" Sam repeated as if the sheriff were speaking a foreign language. "What do you mean?"

"Said something to him about he wasn't supposed to be here and scolded him a bit for scaring her." The sheriff shrugged. "She said she was okay and now I'm leaving."

Sam was completely confused. He rounded the corner into the restaurant to find Angeline staring at a stranger. Instead of being afraid, she looked sad.

"Jonathan, I told you to leave. You can't stay here."

Sam took stock of the stranger. He was young, likely no more than twenty, with short dark hair, at least three days' worth of whiskers, unkempt but serviceable clothes. It was his eyes, however, that drew Sam's attention. The man looked completely, hopelessly in love with Angeline. Sam's stomach clenched.

"I can't just leave, Angeline. Everything I expected, wished and hoped for just got taken away from me. I'm lost without you, without our future." The man, obviously named Jonathan, was pleading with her.

Sam felt like punching him.

"You've got to find your own path. I can't tell you where to go or what to do, but I know you *can't stay here.*" Angeline sounded firm and unshakable, very different from the sweet, soft-spoken woman.

He wanted to clap for her.

He also wanted to drop to his knees and ask her to marry him again, to mark his territory so this stranger would leave her alone.

Sam stepped into the room and the stranger noticed him. The man's lips curled back into a sneer. He pointed at Sam.

"I see your Indian is still here, sniffing around your skirts."

Sam couldn't have been more surprised if the man had slapped him. How the hell did he even know who Sam was or that he and Angeline were linked?

She snapped her gaze to his and her expression changed to guilt. Sam's heart dropped to somewhere near his feet. What hadn't she told him? He thought they'd been completely honest with each other about everything, including the man she'd run from. This was obviously not her husband because the kid was barely shaving.

"Angeline, what's going on?" Sam was disappointed to hear his voice was husky, full of the dark emotions swirling around inside him.

"I, uh, ran into an old friend a while ago." She sounded shaky and nervous. "I asked him to keep quiet about seeing me and he left Forestville." She turned back to Jonathan and narrowed her gaze. "He was supposed to leave and not come back."

The younger man had the balls to kneel in front of her like a penitent in front of a preacher. "Angeline, darling, I love you. I have since you were five years old. I can't just leave."

Obviously there were things Angeline had not shared with Sam, not the least of which was that she already had a beau who was obsessed with her. Not that he blamed the man—Sam was a little obsessed himself—but the fact remained she had hidden that tidbit of information. As well as the small detail that this Jonathan had been here in town to see her a few days earlier.

Sam's temper began bubbling up from the slow simmer it had been at. "You heard her, now get out."

"I'm not talking to you, Indian." The stranger looked up at Angeline, pleading with his entire body. "Please, please, tell me you still love me."

She looked at Sam and he could see the pleading was wearing at her. That was all it took for Sam's temper to boil over. He grabbed hold of the kid by the collar and dragged him out of the restaurant. Fury drove him to ignore the other man's protests and feeble attempts to stop him.

Sam made it outside and dragged Jonathan out into the street. The dirt wasn't mud, but it was wet enough to leave dark smears on the man's already dirty clothes. He let the kid loose and stepped back, fists up. His anger at Angeline mixed with his love for her, coming together to make him into a man ready to defend his future.

The kid glared at him and rose to his feet. He wasn't small by any means, at least as tall as Sam. Not overly muscular but solid. It was apparent, however, that Jonathan had never been in a fight before in his life.

Sam's grin was positively feral.

"You ready to fight me for her, kid?"

Out of the corner of his eye, he saw the sheriff leaning against the side of the restaurant, watching them. Henry would make sure nothing got too out of hand, but had the common sense to stay out of the way when two bucks were battling over a doe.

The younger man brushed off his clothes and stared warily

at Sam's fists. "I'm not going to fight you, Indian. She will choose me because she's always chosen me."

"Ha! You think so? Then where the hell were you when she married the bastard who beat her?" Sam's anger turned to fury.

Jonathan had the decency to look guilty. "I didn't know about it. She didn't tell me."

Sam clipped the kid on the jaw, sending the younger man staggering back with wide eyes.

"Then she doesn't love you. She ran because there was no man to help her, to save her from that fucking monster."

"Sam, please stop." Angeline stood on the steps, hugging herself while the two men who loved her fought in the dirt for her. "I don't want anyone to get hurt."

"Too late. *You* already got hurt. I'm not going to let this puppy threaten you." Sam turned his attention back to the kid just as the younger man charged him. He caught Sam in the stomach with an exceptionally hard shoulder and they both went down into the dirt. Jonathan had no idea what he was doing, but he could definitely make a fist. Sam's head rang from the blows to his head while he tried to suck in a breath. The shoulder had knocked it all from his body and the kid straddling his stomach kept him breathless.

Sam put all his strength into an uppercut that knocked Jonathan clear off his stomach. He managed to get air back in his lungs and rolled to his feet as quickly as he could. The kid's face was a mask of rage and hate, much different from the pleading, pitiful fool who'd been on his knees five minutes earlier.

The fight was turning dangerous. Sam recognized the kid had been on the edge of losing control, and this altercation was the event that shoved him past it.

With a scream worthy of any battle cry, Jonathan lunged at him, fists flying. Sam deflected most of the blows, but they ended up in the dirt again, wrestling and beating each other.

The younger man was like a caged animal let loose for the first time. Sam kept punching him, but he kept coming back for more. Soon the boy's face started to turn violently red.

"Booth!" Sam grunted as he tried to capture the kid's flailing fists. "Get this kid before I kill him."

Sam heard Angeline's gasp over the sheriff's pounding footsteps. Soon the younger man was trying to wiggle out of the big sheriff's grasp. He was howling like a wolf, snarling and crying. Sam understood what the kid was going through, knew the dark emotions that spread deep inside like poison. Jonathan had lost all sense, lost himself in the black tides within.

The sheriff managed to get the kid on his stomach and put handcuffs on him. Still, Jonathan bucked and grunted, growling and snapping his teeth.

Sam was breathing like a bellows, trying to clear the ringing in his head while his entire face throbbed. "You need help getting him back to the jail?"

"Nah, I don't need any help, but you're coming too, Sam. You started this." The sheriff's blue gaze was stern.

"Fine. I'll come too." Sam met Angeline's horrified gaze. She shook her head in denial over the state of her childhood sweetheart.

"I don't understand, Sam."

He shook his head. "I'll explain later. I've got to be arrested first. Can you please go check on my father? He was napping."

Later on he'd sort out his own dark emotions, the fury that egged him on to starting a fight with a kid half his size. Sam loved Angeline to distraction, and obviously so did Jonathan. She inspired men to great heights and, now he knew, to the lowest depths.

"Yes, I will." She glanced at his face and stepped toward him with her apron raised. "You're hurt."

Sam shrugged off her touch. "Not now, Angel. We can talk about this later, but not now."

He couldn't begin to explain to her how much he wanted to howl like Jonathan did. That he was only a hair's-breadth from losing his control too. Elemental rage still coursed through him, and he wanted to beat the younger man until the breath was knocked from his body for good.

Sam had never felt the killing lust like this. Even when he was at war, he'd reacted with more horror than rage. Yet when his relationship, his future with Angeline, was threatened, he wanted to kill.

She must have seen it in his gaze because she stopped and stepped back away from him. "I'll go check on your father now."

Sam took the kid's other arm and together, he and the sheriff half-dragged Jonathan to the jail. The entire way there, the younger man tried to bite them.

Angeline turned to find Marta and Lettie standing in the door, their faces awash in sympathy. Alice poked her head out beside them.

"Never thought I'd see two men fight over her."

"Shut up, Alice," Lettie snapped. "Get your skinny ass inside and mind your own business."

Normally, Marta would have scolded Lettie and Alice, but instead she met Angeline's worried gaze.

"Go take care of Mr. Carver for Sam. We'll mind your duties until you get the mess sorted out."

Angeline nodded her thanks to Marta, then looked at Lettie. Her friend was more than angry, she was also scared. Angeline could see it in her brown gaze.

"I'm sorry."

"Ain't your fault. Men are always making a mess of things." Lettie's lips were pinched together so tightly they turned white.

Angeline felt terrible about everything, but she knew Lettie was right. It wasn't her fault. She had to keep remembering that or she'd get caught up in the men's feud. They were the ones acting like idiots. She had considered throwing a bucket of water on them as they wrestled around in the street, as if she had to break up a fight between two animals.

That's what they'd been—two animals fighting over her. She walked to Sam's house in a daze, shaken to her core by the fight she'd just witnessed. There wasn't much fistfighting in Utah, and she'd been shielded from life for so long, every time she saw violence, it shocked her.

Then to see Jonathan act like an animal, echoed by Sam . . . she could hardly fathom what had happened to both of them. They were gentle men, soft-spoken, and sweet. What she'd just witnessed told her they had a side to them she had never even imagined existed.

It was as if they became animals fighting in the dirt for her. She didn't understand and certainly didn't like it. When she remembered the look in Sam's eyes, she began shaking so hard, her teeth rattled. He'd been out of control, not quite as much as Jonathan, but definitely not himself.

It scared her as much as it intrigued and angered her. She knew there were so many things she didn't understand about men, about life, even about human nature. Her flight into the world had taught her quite a bit, but she obviously still had much to learn.

She went over to the Carvers' house and found Michael just waking up. He frowned at her as he rubbed his right eye.

"I know you."

"Yes, my name is Angeline. I'm a friend of Sam's." She walked over and handed him an obviously well-loved sweater. "He couldn't be here so he asked me to make you dinner."

"I am a might hungry." Michael got to his feet and slipped on the sweater. "You wore the same dress the last time you were here."

Although Angeline was embarrassed he'd noticed, she smiled at the fact he had recognized it. "I don't have many clothes, unfortunately, so I wash them often, as much as I wear them."

They stepped out into the hallway and walked side by side to the stairs.

"You are the same size as my wife was. She was thin like you, but her hair was like midnight, silky black midnight." As he spoke of his wife, Mr. Carver seemed to come to life.

She smiled as they walked downstairs together, ready to hear every story he wanted to tell about the woman who still held his heart. It reminded her that love was more important than anything.

Sam's jaw throbbed in time with his heartbeat.

Thump-thump-thump.

The young scrapper had a lot of power behind his skinny arms, that was for sure. Sam knew he had crusted blood on his lips, nose, and forehead. His stomach also hurt from the sharp shoulder of his opponent.

Both of them were in cells, facing each other across the tiny space between them. Henry knew better than to keep them together, or they just might hurt each other even worse. The kid had fought all the way to the jail. He'd even bitten the sheriff on the arm and earned a sharp cuff to the head, rendering him unconscious.

Jonathan lay on his bunk like a rag doll, snoring softly. Sam wanted to throw something over there to wake him up. Little shit had come in there like a cock of the walk, stirring up trouble and trying to take Angeline.

Ain't no way that was going to happen, not while Sam lived and breathed.

"You calmed down yet?" Henry Booth leaned against the wall, his arms crossed.

"Yeah, I'm calm." Sam glanced outside, startled to realize

it was nearly sundown. He'd been locked up most of the afternoon, which meant his father might be alone. "You hear from Angeline about my pa?"

"No, I didn't." The sheriff frowned at him, his silver brows creating a vee. "What's wrong with your pa?"

Sam gingerly touched his lip, avoiding the other man's gaze. "He's not feeling well. I, um, asked Angeline to look after him while I was here."

"I heard you ask her and wondered why. Something you ain't telling me, Sam?" Henry always had an uncanny ability to see through a lie, even if the liar was a twenty-nine-year old man.

"Nothing I can talk about just yet. Leave it be for now, okay, Henry?" Sam didn't want to let the town know yet about his father's loss of faculties.

"Fair enough." Booth stepped closer and unlocked Sam's cell. He gestured to the cell to his right. "What do we do about this one?"

Sam got to his feet, his entire body aching from head to toe. He wished like hell he could have a hot bath, but more than likely he didn't even have the strength to heat the water, much less empty the tub.

"Let him sleep for now. After he wakes up, we need to talk to him about getting out of Forestville and leaving Angeline alone." Sam would rather drag the kid back to wherever he belonged, by force if necessary. No doubt when he woke up, Jonathan would have a hell of a headache and a smart mouth.

Booth nodded. "I'll let you know when he does. You should head on home now and tell your pa I said hello."

Sam couldn't quite manage a smile—whether because his mouth hurt or because he felt like shit, he wasn't sure. "I'll do that. Thanks, Henry."

When he stepped outside the jail, he blinked against the brightness of the setting sun. He walked as quickly as he could manage with the soreness of his body. It took longer than he wanted, but he walked through his door in less than fifteen minutes.

"Angeline?"

Silence met his question and he was immediately awash in new worry. Where was she? And for that matter, where was his father? He closed the door behind him and walked into the house, peering into each room, all of which were cloaked in the shadows of sunset.

He looked up the stairs and took two at a time, out of breath with more than just the exertion of the climb. When he finally got to his father's bedroom, he heard what he couldn't discern from downstairs.

Singing.

No doubt it was Angeline and it was no surprise to realize she had the voice of an angel. She sang softly, sweetly, a melody he didn't recognize. Sam pressed his head against the door and let her voice wash over him. The notes were like soothing swipes against his aches and pains.

Her voice trailed off and then she was murmuring softly. Sam stepped back just as the door opened. She didn't appear to be startled, as if she'd known he was out there listening. After closing the door behind her, she gazed at him, apparently cataloging his injuries.

"Let's go downstairs and get you cleaned up." Just like that, she'd taken control of the situation.

Sam followed her, too tired and wrung out to do anything but as she bade. By the time he got to the kitchen, he realized she had buckets already heating on the stove, and she'd dragged in the tub from the back porch.

He was astonished and so grateful tears pricked his eyes. "Angel, did you do all this?"

She stuck her finger into each of the three buckets on the stove. "Did you think I grew up with servants? I know how to work and I'm strong. There's not much I can't do in a kitchen, or in a house for that matter." She pointed to one of the kitchen chairs. "Now sit."

Sam sat and watched her as she gathered a few things, then pulled the chair up and sat down, facing him.

"Let's get those cuts clean first." She dipped a rag into a bowl of hot water and reached for him.

Sam closed his eyes and let her wash away the blood and dirt. Her touch was gentle, soothing, a balm to his battered body and soul. It had been a day filled with too much to take in all at once. He needed time to heal and Angeline seemed to sense that—part of their connection which grew even stronger with each passing moment.

"How is Jonathan?" she asked as she wrung out the rag in the water.

"Sleeping, but fine as far as I can tell. Henry is going to keep an eye on him, let me know when he wakes up so we can sort all of this business out." Sam opened his eyes and met her worried blue gaze. "I didn't want to fight him, Angel."

She nodded. "I know you didn't. He's not the boy I knew. I'm not sure what happened, what made him act the way he did."

Sam looked at her. "Honey, he's in love with you, desperately, hopelessly in love with you. A man who loses the woman he loves so deeply will do anything he can to get her back."

The idea seemed to shock her. "This whole thing is my fault?"

"No, no, that's not what I meant." Sam reached out and cupped her chin. "You inspire men to love you just by being you. Their stupidity is their own, not yours. That kid knew what he was doing, what he was up against when he came back to Forestville. He knew who I was, knew what you meant to me."

Instead of denying it, she nodded again. "He was here earlier this week and saw us together. I explained to him that I was never going back to Tolson, to the church, and especially to Josiah. He seemed to accept that and left. I never expected him to come back." She squeezed the rag so hard, water began dripping on her dress. "I never wanted either one of you to be hurt."

Sam took the rag from her and set it back in the bowl, then kissed her forehead, nose, and lips. "I know you didn't, so stop blaming yourself for our fight. There is no good explanation as to why men fight each other. I guess deep inside we're animals in the forest fighting for what we want."

"You are not an animal."

He couldn't possibly explain to her the things he'd done as a soldier, as a man. Some of them she would never believe, even if he told her. Men did what they had to in order to survive, no matter how horrific or unnatural it might seem. Angeline had obviously accepted the fact there was nothing she could have done to stop the fight between him and Jonathan.

Sam smiled at her, his face aching from one end to the other. "I love you, Angel."

The world seemed to stop, a moment suspended in time as she opened her mouth to speak. Sam's entire life was there in front of him, caught in a single second as he waited for her.

"I love you too, Sam."

Disregarding his soreness, his exhaustion, and his bruises, Sam hauled her close to him and captured her mouth in a kiss. His heart beat so damn hard, he thought it might just jump out of his chest.

She loved him.

This was a defining moment in his life, when the rest of his future was decided. Angeline had made her choice and he could have danced on the roof, he was so excited to be the one she chose.

He forced himself to ease back, releasing her mouth. She stared at him, her gaze full of wonder. Sam felt the same wonder coursing through him.

"Let's get that bath ready for you." Angeline broke their connection, getting to her feet and heading for the stove.

"I'll help you."

"No." Her voice was firm enough to stop him from rising from the chair. "I'll do it. Just sit there and let me do what I need to do."

Sam didn't know what Angeline was thinking, but he respected her enough to do as she told him. He was tired enough to appreciate it too, even if he felt as if he could run to Texas and back after her declaration of love.

She moved efficiently, dumping each hot water bucket into the tub. Then she used the pump in the sink to fill each one with cool water from the well. By the time the third bucket of cold water was in the tub, he was more than impressed with her strength. Angeline was much stronger than she appeared.

"Now let's get you undressed." Angeline turned her attention to him. She removed his boots and socks, then set them aside.

Sam got to his feet and simply watched as she undressed him. It was a sensual experience, although there was nothing sexual about it. She took off his shirt, her breath catching when she saw him in the full lamplight. Her fingers traced the saber wound in his side, then the bullet scar on his shoulder, and the bruises on his ribs.

Her gaze went to his. "You've survived a lot of pain."

He took her hand and kissed the back. "I survived so I could find you."

Tears filled her eyes as she leaned forward and kissed each of the marks on his body. Sam felt his own tears building and blinked them back. Angeline flattened her palm against his chest and his heart reacted by thumping against her small hand.

She reached for his trousers and unbuttoned them, sliding down the rest of his clothes until he was nude. Angeline stepped back and gazed at him, stopping at his leg where the other, larger saber scar shone against his skin.

Without asking questions, or showing him pity, thank God, she held out her hand and led him to the tub. Wisps of steam rose from the water as he stepped into the water. She kept a firm grip on his hand, steadying him so he could sink into the heavenly bath. Sam groaned as the hot water surrounded his tired muscles.

"You have no idea how good this feels."

She smiled and reached for a clean rag and soap on the table. "I think I have an idea."

Angeline washed him from head to foot, without any sexual overtone to her actions. It was a task born of love. With each stroke of the cloth, she told him how much she cared for him. He heard her loud and clear, although she never said a word.

Her nails scrubbed his scalp, washing the mud from his hair until it was squeaky clean. By the time he was done, the water was more gray than clear. She picked up a clean towel from the back of the chair and held it out for him. Sam rose from the water, feeling relaxed and content, something he hadn't experienced in many years.

As he dried off and dressed, she dipped the buckets into the tub and one by one, emptied it until there was only a small amount of water left. Then she filled another bucket and put it on the stove to heat, more than likely to wash herself. When she started to drag the tub toward the back door, he stopped her.

"Let me do that."

"I can empty the tub by myself, Sam. Don't think I'm incapable." She kept dragging it, grunting with each yank.

He put his hand over hers. "Honey, there's nothing I don't

think you're capable of, but I want to do this. For you. Please."

Her face was covered in a sheen of perspiration, her hair a mess of strands sticking to her cheeks. Sam thought her the most beautiful woman he'd ever seen.

"Okay, thank you." She wiped her forehead on her sleeve and stepped back.

Sam kissed her, tasting her sweat, her sweetness, and her love. "Thank you, Angel."

He was rewarded by her eyes twinkling with the same love he felt in his heart. Sam made quick work of the tub, leaving it standing upright on the back porch to dry. By the time he made it back inside, she was filling another basin with water.

"Is that for my father?"

She shook her head. "No, he washed up earlier. I fed him dinner and supper too. He told me lots of stories about you and your mother."

"Really?" Sam's father hadn't told him stories about his mother except when he was not very lucid. After she died, he could hardly bear to hear a story much less tell one.

"Oh, yes. He even said I was the same size as she was." She smiled at him. "He's really very charming."

"I'm glad you got to know each other. And thank you for taking care of him while I was, um, unable to." Sam had relied on himself for so long, he felt odd asking for help. Yet with Angeline, it was different.

She tested the water on the stove again, and apparently decided it wasn't quite ready yet.

Sam's body began to heat, and not from the warmth of the bath. "This water is for you?"

She blushed and glanced down at her feet. That was a habit she had when she didn't want to talk about something. Sam wasn't going to let her get away with it. He chucked her under the chin until she looked up at him, meeting his gaze.

"I need to wash up."

Sam's heart thumped so hard, his cock hardened almost instantly. "Let me wash you."

Angeline's mouth turned cotton dry as she stared at Sam. His eyes were dark and wide in the lamplight, his half-dressed body tempting her to touch him. This time it would be as something other than as a nurse. She'd told him she loved him and she knew he loved her.

She knew he wanted to marry her, and Angeline wanted that too, so much so she could almost taste it. However, before she could experience pleasure with him again, she had to show him her scars. He'd allowed her to see all of his; he'd been vulnerable and open. Now it was her turn.

The warm kitchen encouraged her to be brave, to use that inner well of strength she'd been building over the last year. She stepped back and reached for the buttons on her blouse. His body jerked and she could clearly see the outline of his engorged cock in his trousers.

Angeline knew it was up to her—she controlled the situation rather than being the victim of someone else's power. This time her hands were not shaking. This time she was not afraid to be the woman she'd become.

"Sit."

He obeyed immediately, dropping to the chair, his gaze never leaving her body. She smiled as power surged through her. Angeline had never felt more alive.

First she removed the fossil from her pocket and set it on the table. It was one of her most precious possessions and she was never without it. Then she took off her shirt and skirt, laying them on the back of a chair. Her chemise hid much, but she wasn't about to keep it on. It was time to show Sam everything. Before she pledged her life to his, she needed him to see exactly who she was.

Angeline turned her back to him and pulled the chemise and pantalettes off, exposing every inch of her skin. Each scar from the lash must have shone in the light. Her stomach danced as she waited a full minute until she turned around. His smile had faded and instead she saw sympathy and fury.

"Did your supposed husband do that to you?"

"He could not perform as a man without inflicting pain. I could not refuse him or deny him. We all experienced the lash, each of us caring for the other afterward." Angeline remembered Lettie sobbing softly as her wounds were cleaned and salve applied. Those were the only times she had ever seen her friend cry.

Angeline refused to cry, earning her more lashes from Josiah. She nearly died the last time he'd beaten her. It was the very reason she and Lettie had escaped, the impetus for her flight into the world. Into Sam's life.

"Jesus, Angel, what did he do to you?" Sam reached out with a shaking hand and turned her. His hand ran down her back and buttocks with a gentle touch.

"It doesn't matter anymore. I'm no longer the same girl who accepted lashes for what she'd done or hadn't done." Angeline turned around, inches from his warm skin.

This was the moment when she would decide the rest of her life. She took his hand and put it on her breast. The nipple peaked against his skin.

"Marry me, Angel."

It wasn't the first time he'd asked, but it was the first time she was ready to say yes.

"Only if we can spend the rest of our lives making love." She smiled through her tears.

"I think I can do that." He pulled her closer until her body was pressed against his.

His lips lightly grazed hers. Angeline closed her eyes and took a deep breath as she shook with her awakening passion. Sam claimed her mouth with his and they were lost in a lovers' kiss.

She hadn't expected his lips to be so soft, yet so demanding. He kissed her hungrily, devouring her lips with his. Then she felt his tongue. A delicious shiver ran straight down to her toes. He slowly licked her lips and then tickled his way inside her mouth. Her tongue answered his with bold strokes. He growled in his throat, deepening the kiss. Suddenly his arms were around her, crushing her breasts against his hard wall of a chest. Angeline stopped thinking about what she was doing and let her hands roam over him.

Her body was throbbing painfully as she moaned softly in his embrace. His right hand reached up for her breast and caressed the underside. Angeline caught her breath as his thumb felt the hardened nipple. Her mind reeling, she could think of nothing but the desire that was raging through her body.

This time was different, special, because they had pledged their lives to each other. Sam kissed each inch of exposed skin until she was breathing heavily. He lapped at her nipples, then bit each one gently.

Angeline moaned and swayed on her feet. "Please, Sam, please." She didn't know what she was asking for, but she knew she needed it and soon. Her body was familiar with his and craved his touch.

Sam scooped her into his arms and carried her to his bedroom, laying her down gently on the bed. He climbed up beside her and kissed her softly.

"My wife."

It was as if they'd pledged their hearts and now their bodies. One soul, one heart. She felt tears prick her eyes as he slid into her.

"Oh, God, Sam." She felt out of control, anxious to be his, to join with him and find that perfect moment.

He kissed her again as he began to thrust in and out, slowly at first, then faster and faster. She pulled her knees up, exposing herself to him completely.

"Oh, Angel." Sam held her knees as he plunged in deeper and deeper, touching her very soul.

Angeline cried out as a powerful release hit her so suddenly, she couldn't form a coherent thought. Her mind scattered to the winds, like dandelion puffs. She scratched at his arms, pulling him down to her.

His mouth captured hers in a soul-searing kiss as he found his own release. She felt the tears as they fell, tears of joy, tears of a love found.

Angeline woke suddenly as if someone had clapped right in her face. She sat up, realizing she was in a strange bedroom. It took her a few moments to remember she was in Sam's house, in his bed. She let out a sigh of relief and glanced around the dark room. It would be the first of many nights she would be with him, and she'd need to get used to where everything was.

A sharp smack from her left made her tumble out of the bed. Her hip slammed onto the hard wooden floor, stealing her breath. What had just happened? She shook off the impact of the fall and tried to figure out what was going on.

She heard a rustling on the bed and a moan. Angeline got up on her knees and peered over the top. Sam was tangled in the sheets, which had twisted around his leg while he thrashed.

He was having a nightmare.

Angeline got up and rubbed her hip, then walked around to the other side of the bed. On the small table, he'd left a glass of water next to the pitcher, along with a clean rag around the rim. She guessed it wasn't the first nightmare he'd had, judging by the fact he had everything next to the bed rather than on the washstand at the other side of the room.

She didn't want to wake him too abruptly, but she also didn't want him to suffer any longer than necessary. Angeline leaned down and took his hand.

"Sam, wake up."

He squeezed her hand so hard, she heard her bones rubbing together. She gasped at the pain and decided the quiet method wasn't going to work.

"Sam! Wake up!" she shouted near his ear. "You're hurting me, Sam. You need to wake up."

He moaned and mumbled something that sounded like "Angel," but he didn't release her hand. She didn't want to do anything to hurt him, but she couldn't take the pain much longer.

Angeline pinched the skin between his shoulder and chest. Sam let go of her hand and sat up so fast, he knocked his head into hers. Angeline fell to the floor again, this time on her knees.

"Angel?" He sounded confused and uncertain, scared even.

"I'm here, Sam." She leaned down and pressed her forehead against his.

His breath came in hot gusts as if he'd been running. Both his face and his body were covered in sweat; the acrid odor made her nose wrinkle.

"What happened?"

"I think you were having a bad dream, and I, um, had to wake you up so I pinched you." Her hand still throbbed from the crushing grip he'd used.

"Did I hurt you?" He grabbed her sore hand and a cry of pain popped out of her mouth. "Oh, God, Angel, I hurt you. I'm so sorry."

He sat up and ran his hands through his sweat-soaked hair. Angeline realized he was shaking so hard, his teeth were clacking together. She poured water from the pitcher into the basin and wrung out the rag. He closed his eyes as she wiped the sweat from his face and neck.

"Let's get you out of those sweaty sheets." Angeline helped him to his feet and patiently walked him to the chair in the corner. He leaned on her the entire way.

"My leg stiffens up when I sleep. It takes some time to get the kinks out." He sat down with a heavy sigh and leaned back. Dressed in nothing but the bottom half of a union suit, he was attractive even at his lowest point. She kissed him softly.

"Don't worry, Sam. We'll get you cleaned up."

He stared up at her in the dim light, his black eyes completely unreadable. "I love you, Angel."

"And I love you, but right now I don't love your smell, so let me get busy."

Angeline put a quilt over him to keep him warm and stop the shivers. He looked like a little boy, lost and lonely. Her heart ached at the thought of whatever he'd been fighting in his dreams.

She stripped the sheets and found another set in the trunk at the foot of the bed. Doing something made her calm down enough to be of use to Sam. Her hand still hurt, but she didn't think there was any permanent damage.

By the time she had the bed made, he'd stopped shaking and was just watching her work. She helped him to his feet and this time his gait was a bit smoother.

"Take off that union suit so you can wash up."

"Are you trying to get me naked?" His words were teasing, but the tone was anything but.

"I don't think I'd have to try too hard, now would I?" She stripped his body as she'd stripped his bed.

While she washed him from head to foot, she started humming. It was a lullaby her mother had sung so very long ago. Angeline had been five when her mother died and she barely remembered anything about her. The song, however, had stuck in her head.

It seemed to soothe Sam too. He allowed her to wash him without a peep. When she tucked him under the cool, clean sheets, he sighed.

"Now you climb in here with me and this will be just perfect."

She shook her head. "I need to wash up quickly too." After dumping the basin of water out the window, she used fresh water to wipe herself down. All of the work had made her sweaty and uncomfortable. She didn't have another chemise to wear, so she slipped under the sheets as naked as he was.

"I could definitely get used to this." He pulled her close and they spooned together.

Angeline never remembered feeling so safe, so secure before. Sam's body fit perfectly against hers. Though they were nude, the contact between them was not sexual just now. She was exhausted and, obviously, so was he, but she couldn't help asking the question that had been spinning around in her mind.

"What were you dreaming about?"

"You don't want to know," he murmured against her neck.

"Yes, I do. It was enough to knock me out of the bed, make you into a man I didn't recognize, and give you the sweats. I think if you talk about it, it might help." She always felt better after telling her sister, Eliza, of her troubles. Sharing burdens was what family did—and Sam was now her family.

"I dream about the war mostly. I was there for two years, fighting for the Union in Maryland. It was horrible, men killing their brothers, acting like the animals we pretend not to be." He shivered against her. "I nearly lost myself in that war, Angel. And unfortunately, I relive it in my dreams."

She pulled his arms tighter around her as if she could take on whatever demons haunted his nightmares, get rid of them once and for all. However, she knew it took time for pain to go away, especially pain in the heart and soul.

"Do you dream about something in particular? A battle maybe?"

He sighed again, his breath gusting past her ear. "It was a battle. In Sharpsburg in September, eighteen-sixty-two. I'd only been there a month when the battle began. It lasted three days in the middle of a cornfield and even in a church.

I've never seen so much blood before. I was almost up to my knees in bodies." He made a noise that sounded like a sob.

Angeline wrapped her leg around his from behind and pulled him even tighter against her. "Oh, Sam, I'm so sorry."

"I survived, of course, but most of my battalion was wounded or killed. General Lee just kept pushing, but McClellan ended up standing his ground. So many people died in those three days." He pressed his forehead against her neck. "I killed my first man that day. He was barely old enough to shave and I took his life."

Angeline rolled onto her other side so she could face him. She took his face in her hands and kissed him softly. His pain was palpable, coming off him in waves. He still suffered so much from the war.

"Have you ever talked to anyone about this before?"

"No. I can't."

Although her eyes felt like they had a cup of dirt in them, she propped herself up on her elbow. "Yes, you can and you will. You've got a festering sore inside you, Sam, and it's eating you up in your dreams. If you never told anyone before, no wonder it's still bothering you ten years after."

"Angel, I don't want to talk about it."

"Too bad, you're going to anyway. I refuse to marry a man that can knock me clean off the bed and nearly break my hand while he's having nightmares that he refuses to talk about."

Sam was completely silent for a few moments. "I broke your hand?"

"No, you didn't, but it still hurts. That's not how we need to live. If we're going to start over, you have to show me your scars and I don't mean the ones on your body. I mean the ones inside your heart." Angeline knew she was right; she just had to make him see reason.

"I'm tired. I really don't want to talk anymore." He sounded almost a bit whiny. That was the final straw for Angeline.

She got up out of bed and reached for her clothes.

"What are you doing?"

"Leaving. I won't be in the same bed with you until you talk about this. Obviously, it won't be tonight." She had her chemise on and was pulling on her petticoat when he fumbled out of bed.

"Angel, please don't go. I'm sorry, it's just so hard to put it into words."

He sat down on the edge of bed and leaned his elbows on his knees. "We were part of the left flank of the battalion," he began.

Angeline sat and listened to his story, ached with him, cried with him, and sympathized with him. His tale was one of blood, honor, and sheer fortitude. She was proud of him, of the fact he'd survived to tell her about it.

By the time he finished talking, they were back in the bed, naked and under the covers. She held him as he wept, as he'd done for her. When he finally drifted off to sleep with his arms wrapped around her, Angeline knew she'd chosen the right man as her husband.

She'd never loved him more.

Chapter Eight

Sam and Angeline walked to the restaurant in the sunlight, side by side, hands and fingers interlocked. He'd been craving peace for so long, he was surprised to find it in the guise of a young woman with more scars than he had. He hadn't wanted to tell her anything about the battle at Sharpsburg. Hell, he hadn't even wanted to think about it.

She'd bullied him into confessing every single detail until he nearly vomited. Damn sure cried about it too. Yet Angeline didn't make him feel stupid about having emotions. She listened to him, made him purge every bit of the past from inside him.

For the first time in ten years, he'd slept soundly and he'd never felt better. Angeline had taken a chance in the darkness of his bedroom and he couldn't be more glad she had. Sam felt as if their relationship had reached another level the night before, grown even deeper than when he'd asked her to marry him.

They had bared their souls and in doing so, become one. Sam gently held her hand, knowing he'd hurt her in his dream state. He never wanted to be responsible for causing her pain again.

His father walked ahead of them, somewhat lucid and

chipper that morning. It was as if the world had woken up in a good mood. Sam certainly had. It was the first of many mornings he would wake up with her beside him. He intended on having as many as he possibly could for the next fifty or sixty years.

They were about to tell everyone at the Blue Plate that Angeline was leaving permanently. Sam fingered the ring in his pocket, the worn gold band a gift from his mother. She had put it in his palm and told him he would know the woman to wear it when he met her. He would put that ring on Angeline's finger when they got married. Although he had no idea if it would fit her finger, something told Sam it was the perfect size.

When they walked into the restaurant, Pieter rose from a table by the kitchen door, his gaze locked on their entwined hands. Anger was evident in his expression.

"I hope you have a good reason for keeping Angeline from her bed all night." Pieter's frown could have turned iron into a molten mess. "You have ruined her."

"No need to worry, Pieter. She helped me with my father and with my, ah, wounds from yesterday." Sam smiled at Angeline. "And she's agreed to marry me."

The three waitresses were all serving various customers in the restaurant. At Sam's pronouncement, Karen gasped and ran forward to hug Angeline. Alice simply stared at them with something that almost looked like wistfulness. Lettie shook her head and in her gaze Sam saw disapproval. He squeezed Angeline's shoulder because he knew she held Lettie's opinion in high regard. He hoped the older woman would support Angeline's decision and not cause problems in their wedding or their marriage.

When Angeline wrapped her arm around his waist, he knew everything would be all right.

"Marta!" Pieter called toward the kitchen door. "Come quickly."

Within seconds Marta had come out of the kitchen, wiping her hands on a cloth. "What is it? There's no need to bellow." She caught sight of Angeline. "Ah, girl, we were worried for you. What were you thinking staying out all night? We almost went to find Sheriff Booth."

"He says they're going to be married." Pieter's frown had not lightened even a smidge. "Although he hasn't asked my permission."

Sam realized the two of them had adopted Angeline as family, like a daughter to take care of and keep safe. He watched her face as she walked toward them, her back straight and her spine stiff.

"I love him and he loves me. That's all that's important. I love you both, but if you don't approve, I'm still going to marry him." Angeline was a different girl, one he was proud to call his own.

"Ah, this is good. I am so glad to hear this!" Marta walked forward with her arms outstretched. "*Liebchen*, all we want is for you to be happy and you have found a good man for that." She pulled Angeline into a hug and everyone in the room felt the genuine affection between them.

Pieter grunted and eyed Sam with a father's intensity. "You will do right by her or you answer to me."

Sam smiled and nodded, knowing the older man simply wanted to make sure Angeline was in good hands. He could only hope that with time the Gundersons would come to love him too. Most folks didn't get close enough to him to even care what he needed.

"What's happening, Sam?" Sam's father walked up beside them. "Why is our angel crying?"

Sam put his arm around his father's shoulder. "Because she's happy, Pa. We're going to be married tomorrow."

"Tomorrow?" Marta exclaimed. "That cannot be. I must have more time to prepare. And we'll have to close the restaurant for the afternoon, have a party to celebrate." She let go of Angeline and beamed at her. "We cannot let her be married without a celebration. I will make strudel and a pie, oh, and some of that lovely pot roast with the rosemary."

"You don't have to have a party or even cook for us, Marta. We just want to be married in a quiet ceremony with the preacher." Angeline glanced back at Sam. "Or maybe at the lake."

Although they hadn't discussed it, he agreed with her decision completely. The lake was a special place for both of them, and it was only fitting they join together forever on its shore. His mother would have approved and he had no doubt her spirit would be with them.

"At the lake? That sounds lovely," Karen piped in. "It's a perfect time of year too."

"Too many bugs and it'll likely rain." Alice obviously didn't approve of the location. "Maybe even muddy. Your dress will get dirty. Besides you met here at the Blue Plate."

Angeline smiled at the young woman. "That's very romantic, Alice."

"Muddy? You are a breath of sunshine." Lettie had no qualms about being nice to the pretty young woman. "If you don't want to be nice, then keep your mouth closed." She walked over to Angeline. "Can I talk to you alone?"

Angeline looked at Sam and he told her with his gaze he understood. "Of course. Let's go into the kitchen."

Marta came toward him and Sam prepared himself for a round of hugs and affection from the effusive German woman. She was nothing if not full of love for the people she cared about.

"Are you sure you know what you're doing?" Lettie speared her with a probing look Angeline had been subject to more than once. "You are committing yourself to a man you've known less than two months. A man who beat your former beau in the street yesterday. A man who by all accounts is a half-breed Indian with a hitch in his step. It's a hard road you're choosing here."

They stood in the back outside the restaurant, the shadows keeping the area chilly in the morning air. Angeline shivered a bit without the warmth of the sun on her. Everything her friend said was true, of course. They had made some hard decisions over the last year, but this one wasn't a hard decision to make at all.

She knew Lettie was being harsh because she cared about her. "I know it's a hard road, but it's *my* choice, my decision." She took her friend's hands. "I love him and I can't imagine not spending my life with him. It's as if my soul was made to be with his. It sounds silly but I believe it's true."

"Don't forget you already have a husband and he's not going to like sharing you." Lettie pulled away from Angeline, her brown gaze full of worry.

"Josiah has no legal claim to me. The law only recognizes one wife to one husband." Angeline's voice grew stronger with each word. "He has no right to hurt me, hit me, or hunt me like an animal. I refuse to give up this chance of happiness because he might not like it."

Lettie's eyes widened. "I don't think I've ever heard you talk like that before."

"Good, because I want to change. I want to be able to make my own choices and live the way I want to live." Angeline didn't even realize she was crying until Lettie handed her a handkerchief.

"You deserve to." Lettie's voice was low and thick. "I envy your courage."

Angeline shook her head. "Don't envy me. You are stronger than any person I've ever known, man or woman. I hope one day to be as strong as you."

"I can't believe you think I'm strong," Lettie scoffed. "I stayed with Josiah for five years. *Five years!* You showed me what it means to be strong."

The two women stared at each other, humbled by the qualities each saw in the other, knowing no other person would ever understand. Angeline's throat grew tight as she stared at her friend, her comrade, her confidante. The woman who'd picked her up from the ground and dragged her to her feet, who'd taught her how to survive. Lettie was so much more than she let everyone see. Angeline loved her for that and more.

"No matter what happens, I will always be there for you. You will always have a place in my life." Angeline was surprised to find herself in Lettie's embrace, to feel wetness on her cheeks. Lettie was crying.

Lettie pulled back as quickly as she had pulled Angeline into a hug. She wiped her eyes and cleared her throat, seemingly embarrassed by the show of emotion. Lettie had grown such a hard shell around her heart, she rarely let anyone close to her, much less see her vulnerable.

"I don't agree with what you're doing, but I do agree it's your choice. You have the right to do what your heart tells you to." Lettie hugged herself and stepped back.

"Thank you. Now will you be my maid of honor and stand beside me?" Angeline couldn't imagine anyone but Lettie at her side when she made Sam her husband.

"Are you sure? You know I don't want you to marry him."

Angeline smiled. "I'm sure. You're closer to me than anyone else. I'd be honored if you would be my maid of honor."

Lettie sighed heavily. "I'm going to say yes, but only because I agree with what you said. There isn't anyone closer to me, and likely never will be."

Angeline's heart pinched with the realization that her friend would remain lonely until she allowed herself to be free. She was still trapped in the horror of Josiah's control, hiding from the woman she could be. There was nothing Angeline could do except continue to be her friend and never lose hope that something or someone could change her mind.

"Thank you. You mean a lot to me. I hope you know that."

Lettie murmured her thanks and walked back up the steps into the kitchen. Angeline stood outside a few minutes longer until she no longer felt the urge to cry. Her life was about to change drastically and her excitement was mixed with fear.

She was strong and she would be okay. There was nothing she couldn't do with love in her heart. Sam was her mate; she felt it deep down into her bones. Now she just had to get through the wedding and truly take him as her husband.

Angeline went back into the restaurant and was pulled into the heated discussion of where to hold the wedding. Pieter apparently agreed with Alice, while Karen and Marta thought the lake was the perfect place.

Angeline finally got a word in while they were all sucking in breaths. "Everyone, I appreciate you all being enthusiastic about the wedding. I don't want anyone's feelings to be hurt. What if we wait a few days and have the wedding and the party in the restaurant? Alice is right—this is where we met and it's special to all of us."

She looked at Sam and he nodded. It honestly didn't matter to him where they married, just that they did. The lake did hold special meaning for them and that wouldn't change, but it would make peace among them all if they stayed at the Blue Plate. After all, it's where her new family was.

"That would be wonderful," Marta exclaimed. "We will make you a dress and oh, such lovely food for the party."

With that, the Gundersons and the rest of their group started planning the wedding in earnest. Sam kissed her and led his father out, leaving her to be a part of the madness.

Angeline sat back and listened to them all chatter and exclaim. She felt a wave of sweet love for all of them; even Alice seemed to warm up to the idea of a wedding. She sat down next to Angeline.

"I think it's right nice."

"What is?"

Alice looked down at her hands. "The way he looks at you. He loves you for truth and it ain't the fake kind neither."

"I love him too." Angeline put her arm around the other woman. "I think there's someone out there for you too."

"I haven't seen hide nor hair of him yet." Alice snorted. "You know the kind of fella that's attracted to me."

Angeline remembered all too well exactly what kind of man liked Alice. She hoped the girl had learned her lesson about how to pick a beau.

"Well, all you have to do is stop picking them and like I told you, he'll find you." Angeline smiled and was rewarded with a genuine smile from the petite brunette.

"What's this? The wedding has made everyone into happy little critters," Lettie teased.

Alice stuck out her tongue and everyone laughed, including Alice. Pieter kissed Angeline's forehead.

"You have a good man, little angel."

Yes, she had found a good man and he had given her the power to heal. It would be a marriage of equals, a partnership born of love and trust.

Sam left Angeline with the ladies at the restaurant and went down to the jail with his father by his side. He had to explain to at least six different people that the paper wouldn't be published for a while. He had had no idea so many people actually read it.

It just made his father's confusion worse and Sam's guilt sharper. If only he could find some way to keep publishing the paper and keep his father safe.

First, though, he had to find out how young Jonathan was and make sure the sheriff took care of the kid. They stepped into the jail and his father peppered him with questions.

"Why are we here? Did you get arrested? What did you do

wrong?" His father looked around, like a young child visiting an intimidating place for the first time.

Sheriff Booth was drinking coffee at his desk. He smiled and rose to his feet.

"Well, good morning, Carvers. I'm glad you came by."

"Samuel, who is this person?" Sam's father reared back, obviously frightened by the tall and boisterous lawman.

Booth held up his hands, apparently understanding something was wrong with the elder Mr. Carver. "I'm Sheriff Booth, Henry Booth. It's good to see you again, Michael."

His father turned to Sam. "Do I know him?"

"Yes, Pa, he's your friend," Sam reassured him. "Now why don't you look at the wanted posters while I talk to him?"

"Do I know them?"

"Maybe. If you recognize them, it would help the sheriff catch them and put them behind bars where they belong." Sam felt a bit of hopelessness wash through him seeing his father, once a healthy, strapping man full of life, reduced to a confused old man.

"How long has this been going on?" Sheriff Booth came up beside him and they both watched Sam's father peer at the wanted posters hung on the wall behind the desk.

"A while. It's only been bad about three months." Sam sighed. "I've got to find someone to watch him all the time. He's already wandered off in the middle of the night."

Henry whistled through his teeth. "Hard to believe. Something hit him in the head maybe?"

"I wish it were that simple. He's just simply . . . fading away, Henry." Sam's voice started to break so he took a breath and swallowed a few times. "I'll work it out, but I came down here to check on Jonathan."

"Ah, the kid. He's a scrapper, that's for sure. I had the doc in here earlier. Had a look at the kid and he tried to run out of the jail." Booth shook his head. "Not sure what to do with him. I'm afraid he'll go after you or Miss Angeline and I can't let that happen."

Sam was afraid of that. "Can you keep him in custody for a few days? Maybe he'll calm down and see reason. I don't want him to hurt Angeline or do anything to jeopardize our wedding."

"Wedding? You're getting hitched?" Booth's blue eyes twinkled as he clapped Sam on the shoulder. "She's quite a find. Congratulations, Sam."

Sam's smile was genuine. "Thanks, Henry. We're going to work out the details today and hope to get married in a couple of days."

Henry winked. "I don't blame you for wanting to get it done quickly. She's, ah, quite a beauty."

Sam didn't bother to tell the sheriff that particular party had already happened three times. Instead, he simply smiled and nodded.

"My father seems fascinated by your wanted posters. Do you mind if he stays awhile? I'll be back in an hour or so."

"Don't worry, Sam. I'll keep an eye on him."

Angeline walked to the jail with a determined stride. She needed to speak to Jonathan, to find out what had happened and why. He had seemed to accept her decision when he'd left a week earlier. Now he was back and acting like someone she didn't even know.

While everyone at the restaurant was busy making plans for her wedding, she left quietly. Jonathan's behavior made no sense to her. It was as if he'd become a different person.

The morning coolness had given way to a gentle warmth. She breathed in deeply, pulling in courage from the fierceness of the glowing sun. By the time she arrived, she was ready to face him.

At first, when she stepped into the gloomy exterior, she was momentarily blinded by the change from bright to dark.

"I know you. You're the angel from my house." Michael Carver's voice came from her left.

She blinked until she could see him sitting at the desk, a stack of papers in front of him. He smiled at her and she returned the smile.

"Hello, Mr. Carver."

"I'm looking for crooks, helping my friend Henry." He went back to the stack of papers, peering at them as if they held great secrets.

She was glad to see him interested in something. He'd seemed so lost before. Perhaps spending time at the jail would be a good thing for the older Mr. Carver.

"Is the sheriff here?"

"Went to use the necessary. But since it's after coffee, he might be there a while pooping."

Angeline smiled, despite the fact she shouldn't find it amusing to talk about the sheriff using the outhouse. Mr. Carver's illness had made the clock turn back so he sometimes had the brutal honesty of a child.

"Angeline?"

Jonathan's voice came from the cells. Her smile forgotten, she walked toward him, knowing she should wait for Sheriff Booth, but realizing she didn't want to.

As she stepped around the corner, the smell hit her first. It was a combination of urine, feces, and blood. When she saw him in the cell, her discomfort at the stench gave way to shock.

Jonathan was a different man, someone she didn't know at all. His clothes were covered in dirt and dried blood, his face a mask of bruises and cuts. His normally neat brown hair was sticking up every which way. He'd obviously thrown the chamber pot against the wall, judging by the stains currently oozing down to the floor.

It was his eyes, however, that told her the true story. He

looked like a caged animal, with a wild, feral gleam in his gaze.

"Angeline," he breathed, reaching through the bars toward her. "I knew you'd come for me."

"I haven't come for you, Jonathan. I came to speak to you."

Her hard-won courage didn't desert her, although it was a near thing. She faced the man who would have been her husband if things hadn't gone so horribly wrong and Josiah hadn't turned his leering gaze her way. Jonathan was a good man, she firmly believed that, but he had definitely lost himself.

"What happened to you? Why are you here acting this way?"

His smile faded and turned into a baring of teeth. "You forced me to."

She shook her head. "I forced you to do nothing. This was all your choice. I asked you to leave, to understand that I could never be your wife or return to Utah." Her throat grew tight with sadness as she gazed at her childhood friend. She pulled a handkerchief from her pocket and he yanked at it, hauling her within reach.

Angeline dropped the handkerchief, but it was too late. He took hold of her braid and pulled her tight against the bars. She had never been afraid of Jonathan until that very moment. His brown eyes were full of anger and hate.

"Let me go."

"Not yet, Angel. I want to find out what I've been missing." He reached for her breast and she slapped at his hand.

His eyes widened. "Did you just hit me?"

"Let me go," she repeated, her voice growing stronger. "You're hurting me."

"Hurting you? Hurting you? Now that's funny. You have completely destroyed me and you complain I'm hurting you." He tightened his grip on her hair. "I could kill you right now, choke you until you turn blue."

She stared into his eyes and finally saw the fear and sadness hidden inside the crazed man who held her captive. "Jonathan, please let me go."

"I saw you with him. Don't think I don't know what you've been doing with that Indian. Fucking him like a common whore in his bed. You're a married woman. How dare you throw away the vows of marriage so quickly, and for what? A fucking Indian." Spittle flew from his mouth, landing on her cheek and lips.

She wanted to wipe it off, but dared not move just yet. Shock kept her immobile—he'd been spying on them? How could he do such a thing?

"I love him, Jonathan. Do you understand that? What you and I had was friendship, nothing more. I could never be with you."

"And I could make it so you could never be with him." His hand closed around her throat and too late Angeline realized she should have called for help already.

As he began to squeeze her throat, she knew she had only moments to stop him, to save herself from the madness that seemed to have taken over a normally sane man. Angeline leaned forward as far as she could and kissed him.

Astonishment lit Jonathan's face long enough for her to twist from his hold on her hair and bite his hand. He howled and tried to slap her, but she fell to the floor and scuttled out of his reach.

"You bitch."

She trembled so hard she could barely stand, but she got to her feet anyway. Angeline dusted off the dirt on her clothes, but realized the rest of her would require soap and water. She forced herself to look at Jonathan, at the man she really didn't know.

Instead of being the furious animal she'd found in the cell, he sat on the edge of the bed, staring at his hands.

"I tried to kill you."

"You didn't succeed." Her voice was hoarse with a hundred different emotions, not the least of which was profound sadness. She'd lost the boy she grew up with, her best friend.

He glanced up at her. "Your neck is red from my hand. I don't understand what's happening." Finally the real Jonathan had come through the haze of fury surrounding him. "Angeline, what have I done?"

"You've made a choice, same as me. I'll forgive you this time, Jonathan, but there's nothing more between us. I'm going to leave this jail and I don't want to ever see you again." She straightened her spine and put some force behind her words. "Do you understand me?"

"Yes," he whispered and curled up on the bed in a fetal position. "Just go then. Get out."

"Good-bye, Jonathan." She picked up her handkerchief from the floor and walked out of the cell area.

Mr. Carver still sat at the desk with his stack of posters. He waved happily at her as she left the jail. She waited until she was outside to cry.

The next two days were a flurry of activity for the ladies. Angeline seemed to be swept along with the tide of happenings, while Sam stepped back out of the way. She spent each day at the house with his father and her nights with Sam in his bed. Pieter disapproved, but Angeline refused to change her mind about where she slept.

Sam had never loved her more.

He was watching her cook breakfast the day before the wedding, her lovely behind swishing this way and that as she made eggs in the skillet. His father walked into the kitchen with an armful of clothes.

"I heard you're getting married."

Sam smiled at him. "Yes, sir, we sure are."

"Good, then I'd be right pleased to give these to your

angel as a wedding gift." Michael laid out clothes on the chair and turned to Angeline. "These are for you. She'd want you to have them."

Her hand flew to her mouth as she walked over to the table. Sam took the wooden utensil from her and took over minding the eggs. He took great pleasure in watching her pick up each article of clothing.

He'd actually had no idea his father had kept his mother's clothes. The very notion he was ready to give them to Angeline made Sam's throat tighten. He knew he'd found the right woman.

Angeline held up a wool coat and whipped around to look at Sam. "It's lovely."

"I bought that for her in Denver. She looked right pretty in it." His father sat at the table and picked up Sam's mug of coffee, sipping happily.

"Thank you, Michael. You're so kind to give these to me." Angeline knelt beside him. "Are you sure?"

"Of course, I'm sure. You'll need to keep fixing me good suppers and singing to me though." Michael shook his finger at her. "I like that a lot."

Angeline nodded and kissed his cheek. "Thank you."

Sam had never felt more content, more at ease than with the two people he loved the most in the house with him. Everything was proceeding without a hitch for the wedding. The one thorn in his side was the disappearance of Jonathan. The young man had been in the jail one day and the next morning, he was gone. Angeline didn't seem to want to pursue him or even find out where he'd run off to.

Sam, on the other hand, kept one eye out for any man he didn't recognize, or even those he did. He didn't want to tell Angeline how much it worried him, so he only spoke to Jessup.

The older man had proved to be a good friend, who had

taken to living in the barn behind Sam's house. The barn was cold, but Jessup refused to live in the house with them. He just barely accepted the offer to live in the old barn.

Sam didn't even own a horse anymore. The only thing the barn was good for was catching dust. Might as well have someone living there who would appreciate the shelter.

Each morning Sam went to the Blue Plate before dawn and brought back biscuits to Jessup. He had promised the old man and he intended to keep that promise. It was late morning and Sam was headed off to find Lettie. He needed to talk with her.

"Hey Sam, wait up there." Jessup appeared from the side of the house, a hustle in his step. "I done what you asked."

Sam stopped in his tracks, his interest piqued. "And what did you find out?"

"That man had been here a week ago. Folks seen him talking to Lettie and the angel. He left the next day, but he come back." Jessup whistled. "And, boy, he didn't look the same. In fact, he looked more like me." He apparently thought that funny because he chuckled.

"Yeah, he was dirty and could have used a bath." Sam pointed to the tub on the back porch. "You have no excuse anymore."

"Baths make ya sick. I don't want no bath but once a year. Anyway, ain't nobody seen the boy since day before yesterday." Jessup poked at the dirt with one muddy boot. "And that was after, ah, someone else went to see him in the jail."

Before the older man told him, Sam knew who the visitor had been. His stomach flipped, then flopped. "It was Angeline, wasn't it?"

"Ayup, it sure was. She was in there for a bit. Your pa was there too. Word has it Booth was in the shithouse the whole time." Jessup scratched his dirty nose. "When she come out, her neck was red and her hair was all messy."

Sam refused to accept what the evidence seemed to suggest. Angeline had not gone to the jail and given herself to Jonathan. It wasn't possible.

"What do you think happened?" His voice was tight and strained. The dumb kid was causing him stress, even after he'd disappeared from Forestville.

"I think the boy tried something with your angel and she put him in his place."

Sam let out a breath at Jessup's theory. It was exactly what he needed to hear.

"So what happened to him night before last? Where did he go?" Sam was still worried Jonathan would reappear.

"Dunno. Somebody must've let him out. That jail can't be broken out of. I know 'cause I tried more than once." Jessup stared at Sam. "I can keep nosing around to see if folks know anything."

Sam put his hand on the shorter man's shoulder. He had trouble remembering what he used to think of Jessup, because the man now had his utmost respect and friendship.

"Thanks, Jessup. I appreciate you doing that. I just don't want my wedding to go haywire because of Angeline's old beau." Sam stared down the street and spotted Lettie walking on the sidewalk. "I'll talk to you later today."

"You betcha." Jessup disappeared into the shadows as he usually did.

It was Friday afternoon and the wedding was scheduled for Saturday morning at ten. He didn't have much time to get Lettie alone, so Sam raced to catch up with her.

He'd been surprised to learn Lettie was making a dress for Angeline. Given the history of where they'd come from, he'd expected her to disapprove of the entire marriage.

Yet he knew she was making the dress despite her own misgivings. Sam respected her feelings, although the woman had barely said two words to him in the entire time she'd been in Forestville. Though she probably wouldn't like it, he had to speak to her.

"Lettie, I need to talk to you."

She didn't slow her stride. In fact, he swore she actually sped up. "Got nothing to say to you."

Sam was a tall man and she only came up to his chin but, damn, the woman had the speed of a thoroughbred. He practically tripped over his feet to keep pace with her.

"Please, Lettie, you're the only one she truly trusts."

She halted so abruptly, Sam continued past her a few feet, then stopped to turn around. Lettie's eyes were narrowed to near slits and her hands were on her hips.

"If I'm the one she truly trusts, then why has she been sneaking around with you? Why did she agree to marry you without talking to me first?" Lettie snorted. "Trust me? Ha, she barely could see past your handsome face."

Handsome? She thought he was handsome? Before Sam could react to that, Lettie started to walk away. He put his bulk in her path and crossed his arms.

"You and me need to talk honest like."

She pinched her lips together and held his gaze for what seemed like ten minutes. "Fine. but make it quick. I've got to get something at the store."

Sam hadn't expected her to give in so quickly. He glanced around and realized he was only a block from home. "Why don't we go get some coffee then?" He gestured toward the yellow building. "My father is at the jail with Henry, looking at wanted posters."

It had become a habit with Michael Carver. Each morning he insisted on helping the sheriff review the posters. It kept him busy and Henry didn't mind the company. It also allowed Sam to prepare for his wedding and get some work done, preparing the house for its new mistress.

Lettie walked toward the house, leaving Sam to catch up again. Truthfully, he was a bit nervous about talking to her. She held a big place in Angeline's life. He had a feeling if he didn't work out a truce with Lettie, then his marriage would always have a shadow over it.

Sam got to the door first and opened it for Lettie. She stepped inside and glanced at the newspaper equipment, then her head swiveled back again. He was surprised to see keen interest in her gaze. She didn't say anything though, so he didn't offer any information. Perhaps after the wedding, he might find out if she wanted to know more about publishing a newspaper.

"Let's go into the kitchen. I can make coffee right quick."

Again, Lettie said nothing but allowed him to lead her into the kitchen. The brand-new table he just finished shone brightly against the rest of the roughness in the room.

"Nice table."

Sam was pleased by the compliment. "Thanks. I hope Angeline likes it too. I'm still working on chairs to go with it." He held out one of the rickety old chairs for Lettie. "Sorry these are so pitiful."

"I've certainly sat in worse." Lettie was an odd duck, that was for certain.

Sam busied himself getting water on the stove for coffee, then sat down across from her. He laced his fingers together and thought about what he wanted to say. It had to be said just right because he'd only get one chance with this woman.

"I wanted to talk to you about Angeline. She thinks the world of you, and your opinion is very important to her. I think this marriage is going to be a thorn in your friendship if you and me don't find a way to get along." Sam knew it was silly to talk to a woman about her friendship with his intended, but he damn well wanted to do this right.

Lettie sighed. "You're right to be concerned. I don't approve of you two getting hitched and that isn't going to change." She met his gaze with a completely unwavering one. "She's told you about Josiah?"

At the mention of the bastard who had hurt Angeline, Sam's hands tightened until his nails were cutting into his skin. "She did."

"All of it?"

"Enough of it. I've also seen her back. Believe me, if that bastard comes within a mile of her, I'll shoot his head clean off." Sam had already made sure his rifle and shotgun were cleaned and ready. He wasn't about to take a chance with his new wife's safety. Aside from that fact, he wanted to kill the man who'd dared to treat Angeline as if she were a thing put on earth for his pleasure. The man didn't deserve even a shred of pity or mercy.

Lettie nodded. "I'm glad to hear it, but he'll send hired killers after us. He won't bother to do it himself. She escaped one already, but only because of her sister." She leaned forward. "To be honest with you, I don't think an ex-soldier with a crippled leg can defend her against a hired gun."

Sam didn't take offense. Lettie was only telling the truth. "Fair enough. I can also alert the sheriff to be on the lookout for strangers. Besides, once Angeline changes her name to Carver, it'll be that much harder for anyone to find her."

"That's clever thinking, but you don't know Josiah. I'm sure Angeline didn't tell you everything."

The water was bubbling on the stove so Sam rose to put the grounds in. He wasn't sure he'd like what Lettie was going to tell him.

"Then why don't you tell me what she hasn't? I would never judge her for things she's done." He knew Angeline would feel the same way. Both of them knew the other was flawed, with more mistakes than they could carry, but none of it seemed to matter. They were deeply connected and nothing could break that bond.

"He beat his wives so he could get his staff hard." The words were yanked from her, spat out as if they tasted bad.

"I knew that." He put cool water in the coffee to settle it and kept his gaze on the brunette at the table.

"The more pain he inflicted, the harder he got."

"He's a lousy bastard."

Lettie's voice began to rise. "He also liked to watch. Did she tell you that? He would make us pleasure each other so he could then beat both of us and make us pleasure him."

Sam couldn't help being shocked. He had trouble imagining sweet Angeline touching another woman. "He did what?"

Lettie's eyes began to burn like coals. "Oh, yes, he did every filthy thing imaginable to give himself pleasure. There wasn't anything Josiah didn't enjoy if it involved pain and humiliation. Angeline was lucky she only had to live with him for two months. There's *nothing* in this world, no love or understanding, that could possibly erase my hideous memories of that black-hearted son of a bitch."

Sam poured the coffee, glad to see his hands weren't shaking. There was so much rage in Lettie and she obviously kept it bottled up if this small exhibit was any indication of what bubbled beneath the surface.

"I'm sorry, Lettie. I'm sorry he took so much from you." He set the mug down in front of her, pleased to see she didn't smack it away.

She stared at the coffee, swallowing repeatedly. Sam realized she was swallowing tears. The unflappable, unmovable Lettie had been reduced to tears at the memory of what her supposed husband had done to her.

"You have no idea how much he took." Her voice had sunk to a whisper.

"I'd be pleased if you would consider moving in with us after the wedding." The words had jumped out of Sam's mouth before he realized he was even thinking of them.

Her head snapped up and surprise danced across her face. "What did you say?"

"You and Angeline are closer than sisters. I know she loves you and would want you to be safe." Sam began warming to the idea the longer he spoke. "I desperately need help with my father and the newspaper. We could all live here together as a family."

Lettie sipped the coffee and that's when Sam realized *her* hands were shaking. He was truly surprised by how much she hid beneath the gruff, hard exterior she showed the world.

"A family?"

He nodded. "A family ain't just bound by blood. Look at you and Angeline. You two are family with no shared blood. I'd be right pleased if you would consider yourself my new sister and this as your home."

She glanced around the kitchen. "If I'm to live here, we're going to have to fix this place. It's in terrible condition."

Sam grinned. "Does that mean yes?"

Lettie took another sip of coffee. "It means yes, but I'm going to warn you, Carver. If you hurt either one of us, nobody will ever find your body."

He would have laughed, but he knew she was serious. Instead, he held out his hand to shake hers. "Agreed."

Her handshake was firm, with the calluses born of a woman who worked too hard. Sam thought he even saw a hint of a smile hidden somewhere in her fierce expression.

"I can't wait to tell Angeline." Sam gazed around the room. "Then I'm going to need to buy some more wood and nails."

This time Lettie actually chuckled, and Sam joined her. They would definitely have a unique family, but the one thing it wouldn't lack was loyalty and love.

Chapter Nine

Angeline's wedding day dawned bright and sunny, a perfect spring morning in May. She laid the dress on her bed and stared at the ivory material. It was softer than anything she'd ever felt and would be her only wedding gown. In only a few hours, she'd be Mrs. Samuel Carver, a wife in truth to the man she loved.

She hugged herself and twirled in a circle, too happy for words. If she could find her voice, she might have even started singing.

Her first wedding was only a dim memory. On that day she'd worn a raggedy dress and tears. This wedding was as different as day from night. She was filled with hope and love, a far cry from fear and loathing.

"I guess you're excited to get hitched." Marta chuckled as she came into Angeline's small room. She'd never felt closer to Marta and Pieter than when she realized she was more important to them than their restaurant. In fact, the ceremony was taking place downstairs; they'd closed the restaurant and set it up for the guests. It was a gesture that humbled Angeline.

"Yes, this time is, I mean, today is perfect." Angeline pushed away the dark memories and focused on Sam.

"Good, now let's get you in that gown and downstairs. The preacher is here and so is your anxious bridegroom." Marta touched Angeline's hair. "Never was blessed with children, so I hope you don't mind me filling in as your ma."

Angeline's eyes pricked with tears. "My mother died a very long time ago. I never really knew her, but I do know I'd be blessed if she was anything like you." She hugged Marta, immediately enfolded in the older woman's embrace.

"Ah, *Liebchen*, you will make me cry now." Marta laughed and held her at arm's length. "Let's make you a missus."

Angeline smiled, unable to speak since her throat was tight with emotion. Marta helped her put on the dress, then brushed her hair and twisted it into a lovely bun at the back of her head.

"Come look at yourself in the looking glass in my room." Marta took her hand and led her to the larger bedroom at the end of the hallway.

When Angeline stepped in front of the mirror, she gasped at the image. The woman standing there was a stranger, a vision in ivory and lace, shining in the sunlight like an angel. For the first time in her life, she saw what others did. She had never considered herself pretty until that moment, until she was ready to marry the man who had claimed her heart.

"You are a sight, Angeline. Sam will likely fall on the floor when he sees how beautiful you are."

"Oh, he certainly will." Pieter stood in the doorway, a wide smile on his face. "She is beautiful."

Angeline turned and curtseyed to the older man. "Thank you, kind sir."

Lettie appeared behind him. Her gaze sought Angeline's.

"Can you give me a few minutes with Lettie?" Angeline looked at the Gundersons. "I know we're close to the time to go downstairs, but I need to speak to her."

"Of course, of course." Marta herded Pieter out into the hallway and closed the door behind her.

Lettie looked Angeline up and down. "You look stunning."

"Thank you. The dress is, well, it's amazing. You are a gifted seamstress." Angeline fingered the lace on the sleeve, never having owned anything even half as lovely.

Lettie waved her hand in the air. "It was my pleasure. I know I don't always show it, but you mean a lot to me."

Angeline sat on the chest and patted the spot next to her. Her friend lowered herself slowly beside her.

"I came to confess something to you. I hope you won't be angry with me."

Angeline frowned, wondering what Lettie could have done to make her angry. "Confess what?"

"I helped Jonathan escape from jail."

At first Angeline could only gape at her friend. It was more than shocking news, it was simply unbelievable.

"Lettie, why would you do that without asking the sheriff first? Or me? Did you know he tried to choke me?" Angeline's voice rose and she had to take a deep breath to calm herself down. She had no doubt Lettie had a good reason for what she'd done.

"I went down there at first to talk to him. He was a shadow of the young man he used to be, before he left on his mission. I've never seen a man so low before. We started talking and he told me what he'd done." Lettie took Angeline's hands. "When he was here a few weeks ago, he sent a telegram to Tolson."

Angeline's mouth dropped open. "What?"

"He sent a telegram to Tolson and told them he'd found us here in Forestville."

This time Angeline's heart stopped beating. She couldn't find enough air to even form a sentence or get a breath in.

"He was truly sorry he'd done it, but the deed was already

done. Jonathan begged me to let him go so he could put the wrong to rights. He was going to find a way to tell them he was mistaken, starting with a telegram from another town." Lettie rubbed Angeline's back. "I know this isn't what you wanted to hear today, but I had to tell you. You need to know what you and Sam are up against."

Angeline finally was able to breathe again. "Jonathan did what he thought was right, just as I am about to do. I know you were trying to help and I appreciate your telling me."

"You're still going to marry Sam?"

"Yes, I'm still going to marry him. I love him, Lettie. That doesn't change because I think Josiah will come after me again. He no longer has power over me. I refuse to let him." Angeline got to her feet and smoothed out the front of her dress. "I am living my own life now."

Lettie stood and hugged Angeline tightly. "Someday I want to be as strong as you."

The door opened and the Gundersons peered inside at them.

"Are you ready?" Pieter held out his arm.

Lettie kissed Angeline's cheek and left the room. Angeline wiped her eyes and stepped forward to take Pieter's arm, Marta right behind her.

Angeline was about to change her future.

Sam was nervous. He didn't need to be, but that didn't seem to matter. There were only about a dozen folks there for the wedding, including his father and Jessup, who were currently conversing quite avidly in the corner.

He glanced at the pocket watch he'd borrowed from his father. It was two minutes after ten. Angeline would be downstairs any moment. He could hardly wait to see her.

Lettie came down the stairs and walked over to one corner of the room, watching him with her steady gaze. It was a bit disconcerting. She didn't appear angry or disapproving, yet she unnerved him with her unblinking stare. He knew he'd get used to her in time since she was important to Angeline. That definitely made his embarrassing discomfort worthwhile.

"Here she comes!" Jessup announced like a proud uncle.

Sam stepped beside the preacher, Will Baker, a young man currently living as a boarder with an older couple in town. He had no permanent church, but with his friendly open face, light brown curly hair, and warm brown eyes, the young minister was already a favorite in town.

Will smiled at him. "Are you ready, Mr. Carver?"

"More than you know." Sam watched the stairs as Marta came down, grinning widely.

He saw a flash of ivory and his stomach jumped. Suddenly there Angeline was, his angel with the sun shining on her, surrounding her with a halo of goodness.

She got to the bottom of the stairs on Pieter's arm and turned into the room. In her hands she carried a bunch of wildflowers, their colors bright against the creaminess of her gown. She smiled at him, a radiant expression of pure joy.

It went straight through Sam's heart, reminding him of just how much he loved her. He'd never felt such overwhelming happiness. Tears actually pricked his lids and he had to blink rapidly to clear them. He didn't want to miss a second of his wedding.

Angeline seemed to float on air until she arrived beside him. Pieter kissed her cheek and put her hand on Sam's arm.

"Take good care of her."

Sam nodded, simply unable to speak as he turned to face Will with Angeline on his arm.

"Dearly beloved, we are gathered here today to join together Samuel Carver and Angeline Hunter in holy matrimony. Marriage is a holy union, blessed by God and sanctioned by man." Will looked at both of them in turn. "Are you both prepared to pledge yourselves to each other for the rest of your lives as husband and wife?"

They both nodded as Sam squeezed her hand on his arm.

"Do you, Samuel, take this woman to be your lawfully wedded wife, for better, for worse, in sickness and in health, 'til death do you part?"

"I do." Sam's voice was hoarse with emotion.

"Do you, Angeline, take this man to be your lawfully wedded husband, for better, for worse, in sickness and in health, 'til death do you part?"

"I do." She laced her fingers with Sam's.

"Do you have a ring?" Will asked Sam.

He nodded and pulled the ring from his pocket. The gold winked in the morning sunshine.

"Repeat after me. With this ring, I thee wed."

Sam repeated the words and slipped the ring on her finger. She stared down at it, rubbing it with her thumb, then met his gaze. He saw his future in the depths of her blue eyes.

"I now pronounce you man and wife." Will smiled widely. "You may kiss your bride."

A chorus of whoops filled the air as Sam leaned down and kissed Angeline. It was the absolutely perfect moment. One he would remember, pull out, and review again throughout the rest of his life. He pulled her close and breathed in her scent.

"Happy?"

"More than happy. I just married the man I love."

The celebration continued throughout the day with drink and food. Sam had never realized he could find such joy. He was anxious to get his wife alone and start their marriage, though. After an hour of eating strudel and other delicious delights, he went up behind his new wife and pulled her back against him.

As he felt her soft bottom, his entire body came to life. He was sure she felt the movement in his trousers because he saw her smile widely.

"Are you ready to leave, Mrs. Carver?"

"Yes, I believe I am, Mr. Carver." She giggled and leaned against him.

Sam looked around and saw a few knowing glances, a couple of winks, and a dozen smiles. The one face he didn't see was his father's.

"Where's my father?"

Angeline stiffened and pulled away from him, her brow furrowed in concern. "When was the last time you saw him?"

"He went out back a while ago. Said the coffee was making him fart." Jessup forked more strudel into his mouth.

"How long is 'a while ago'?" Sam's voice took on an edge that made everyone stop and stare.

"I dunno. Mebbe twenty minutes." Jessup seemed to understand that Sam was worried. He set down the plate, although he looked at the strudel with longing. "I'll go look for him."

"We'll go too." Angeline took Sam's hand.

"I'll head toward the north end of town." Booth put on his hat and went out the door, followed by Jessup.

Everyone else stared at Sam with questions in their gazes. It was time he confessed to them what was happening.

"My father gets confused. He's, ah, well, he doesn't remember things like he used to, even what year it is or who I am. I've been watching him with Angeline's help just about every hour of the day." Sam squeezed his new wife's hand. "He already disappeared one night into the woods by the lake—"

Angeline gasped, her eyes wide. "The lake."

They ran out of the restaurant as fast as they could, heading south toward the lakeshore. Sam prayed to every god who was listening to save his father. There was no need to take a doddering old man yet. He still had grandchildren to spoil.

Sam had felt fear before, but this kind made his mouth go completely dry and his heart thump so hard he could hardly catch his breath. Somehow he knew they would find him, he just knew. Perhaps his mother was guiding him, or maybe he was imagining it.

Either way, they arrived at the lake breathless and started calling Michael's name. The leaves had grown in fully so it was harder to see through the trees. With each passing minute, Sam's stomach grew tighter and tighter.

Angeline stopped and yanked his arm. "In the water, Sam. In the water!"

Sam howled, "No!" as he ran toward the shore, toward the body floating facedown in the sun-warmed water. Tears streamed down his cheeks as he fought his way through the water. By the time he reached the body, he tasted the salty tears of grief.

It was his father. Sam sobbed openly as he turned him over and searched for signs of life. It was too late. Too late.

Michael Carver was dead.

Angeline was numb as they walked back to the restaurant. She felt like a warrior returning alive from a battle. Her body, mind, and soul were bruised and battered. Sam was silent by her side, his sadness and grief as real as the tears on her face.

She was so exhausted, she wanted to sleep for hours, but she had duties to attend to first. That began with Lettie.

The group of them had set the restaurant back to rights. Karen and Marta were cleaning up the dishes, while Alice stood by the kitchen door with her arms crossed. Rather than a mulish expression on her face, she looked a little lost. Lettie wasn't even in the room.

Marta met Angeline's gaze. "Did you find him?"

"He's dead. Jessup and Pieter have brought him over to the house." Sam's voice sounded so raw, Angeline's heart hurt just to hear the pain in it.

Marta pulled Sam into an embrace. "I'm so sorry, Samuel."

He closed his eyes briefly as he accepted the hug, but to Angeline's surprise, he stepped away within moments. "Thank you. I'm going to see about a coffin and find Will to get the burial done today."

Sam kissed Angeline's forehead, then took her hands in his. She was distressed to realize hers were shaking.

"If you can prepare my father for the burial, I will get everything else done."

"Of course. I'd be honored to take care of Michael." Angeline didn't recognize her own voice either. They truly were different people than they had been an hour earlier.

"Thank you, Angel." With that, Sam left her at the restaurant.

Marta met Angeline's gaze with a worried one. "What happened?"

Angeline shook her head. "He drowned in the lake. Perhaps he was trying to swim, or maybe he was just ready to join his wife in heaven. I don't know."

Marta pulled her into a hug. "I'm sorry, Angeline."

"Sam wants to bury him today, so I'm going over to the house to get the body ready. I won't be able to work tonight." She was simply doing what she had to, not really thinking about the fact she'd already told Marta she wouldn't work anymore.

"I wouldn't expect you to. Now go take care of your new family. I'll be at the funeral."

Angeline nodded and left the restaurant. It was time to say good-bye to the father-in-law she had just found.

Chapter Ten

Jessup readily volunteered to dig the grave for Michael Carver. They'd apparently become friends over the last few weeks and he told everyone what a good man had been lost. The entire town wept over Michael's senseless death.

The wedding night would wait. They would hold the burial before dinner, with Will Baker there to speak over the grave. Sam hadn't wept since his father had died. He appeared to be shutting himself off from emotion, taking care of business and working with Jessup at the cemetery to dig.

That left Angeline to prepare the body, which she'd done before at home. Yet this time it was someone she'd come to know and love. It was the man who would have been the only grandfather her children knew. Now they would have none.

Angeline scrubbed her hands clean, then changed out of her wedding dress and into her old, but serviceable, navy blue one. She carried her bags over to her new home with grief rather than joy. She put a sheet on the new kitchen table, then prepared the rags and a bucket. Sheriff Booth and Pieter laid out the body on the table. The tall lawman stayed in the kitchen with her, hat in hand.

"Well, Miz Carver, I don't know rightly what to say. Never

had a wedding go so wrong before." He watched as she brought the bucket to the table.

Angeline undressed her father-in-law with care, then covered his lower half for modesty. She tried not to cry, she really did, but she couldn't help feeling responsible for what had happened.

"It ain't your fault." The sheriff seemed to want company as much as she did. "I know'd it was hard to keep track of Michael. He was a wanderer. More than once I caught him leaving the jail with wanted posters in his hand."

Angeline ran the rag down Michael's body, wiping away the dirt that clung to his damp skin. As she worked, tears rolled down her cheeks. She wiped them away on her shoulder, knowing Booth was right, but not wanting to let go of her guilt just yet.

"Would you please go up to Michael's room and check what he has to dress him in? I'm sure there has to be something."

"Oh, of course, of course. I know just the clothes. I'll be back in a jiffy." The big lanky man left the room, leaving Angeline alone.

She needed a few moments to grieve and find the strength to carry on with what was to have been a joyous occasion. Angeline took Michael's hand in hers.

"I'm so sorry this happened. I never meant for you to leave us so soon. You were such a good man, a wonderful father to Sam." Angeline got to her knees beside the table. "Dear God, please take good care of this man. He deserves every accolade you have, happiness and peace."

A whisper near her ear made Angeline shiver. It sounded as if it said "Angel" and it was a woman's voice. She smelled something sweet, almost like vanilla. Angeline got to her feet and looked around the kitchen, but no one else was around.

When she looked back at Michael, a single feather lay on his chest. Angeline jumped back in surprise, crashing into the chair and landing on Booth's hat. Her heart thumped against her ribs as she tried to reason why and how that feather came to be there.

Booth walked back in the kitchen with a black suit and a blue shirt. He frowned at Angeline, who was still perched on his hat.

"Ah, Miz Angeline, can you get off my hat?"

She rose to her feet, her gaze never leaving the body. Booth handed her the clothes and started reshaping his hat.

"Good thing you ain't a heavy girl or this'd be squashed flat for good." He glanced at Michael's body. "Oh, good, you found a sparrow's feather. He must've had some in the box on the mantel."

Angeline gaped at the sheriff. "A sparrow's feather?"

"Ayup. He used to say it was the way he paid tribute to his wife. Every year on her birthday, he would carry one next to his heart all day."

"Why?" Angeline's voice was hoarse, barely controlled emotions bubbled through her.

"Didn't you know? Sam's mother's name was Sparrow."

Booth's voice echoed through Angeline's head and then a buzzing began; it turned into a wave and then suddenly she was on her knees with her head on the floor. The cool wood felt good on her forehead. The sheriff fluttered above her, shouting something about women and the vapors.

She wasn't having a fit of the vapors though—it was much deeper than that. Sam's mother had just shown Angeline she was watching over them. Not only had she whispered to her, but she had put her mark upon her husband. Angeline's tears leaked from the corners of her eyes as she held them tightly closed. It was so much, too much.

"Henry, what's going on?" Sam's voice cut through the cloud of grief.

"I don't know. I went up to get your father's suit and when I come back, she was sitting on my hat. Then she fell on the floor crying and sobbing." Booth sounded exasperated. "This is why I ain't never gonna get married."

Angeline felt Sam's hand on her back.

"Angel?"

She sat up and fell into his arms, holding on to her new husband as she let the grief run its course. A shuffle of boots let her know the sheriff had stepped out of the room. Sam simply held her while she cried, never murmuring silly things or telling her to calm down. Angeline loved him even more for that.

She felt the tears begin to subside and finally let Sam loose. A handkerchief appeared in his hand and she gratefully took it. He helped her onto a chair and squatted beside her as she cleaned her face.

He watched her with his dark eyes, patient and steady.

She took a deep breath. "I was talking to the sheriff and getting your father's body cleaned up when something happened."

Sam frowned. "What happened?"

"I thought I heard someone whisper in my ear."

Instead of looking dubious, he nodded. "Go on."

"Then when I looked, there was a feather on his chest." She pointed a shaky finger at the body.

Sam rose and looked at his father, reaching out to touch the feather. He looked back at her expectantly.

"Booth told me it was a sparrow feather and about how your mother's name was Sparrow. A-and I realized she must be here in spirit, looking out for you, and for him." Angeline smiled sadly. "It was a bad time to cry, but at that moment, I felt the purest love imaginable. It was overwhelming. You probably think I'm hearing things."

Sam took her hands and brought her to her feet. "No, actually I think you just met my mother's spirit. And I think she is telling you everything is going to be okay."

Angeline had feared he would think her silly or discount

her story. Yet he believed her; not only that, he reaffirmed her feelings. She knew she'd fallen in love with the right man, and it was a love blessed by the two people who loved him best.

The wind picked up on the hill as the wagon rolled up to the cemetery with Michael's coffin in back. Angeline walked beside the wagon with Sam. A trail of mourners followed them.

Jessup stood at the top of the hill, waiting for them. When the wagon rolled up, six men were there to carry the coffin, including Sam, Booth, Pieter, and Jessup. Angeline was pleased to note the old man had bathed for his friend's funeral.

The day had started with so much excitement and happiness, and was ending with death and sadness. Angeline barely heard the words Will spoke as the wind whipped around them. Sam closed his eyes and looked toward the sky, his lips murmuring. She squeezed his hand and tried to give him all her strength.

Too soon Sam was taking a handful of dirt and throwing it into the grave. Then others did the same, each one saying good-bye to the man who had graced them all with his skill as a schoolmaster, then as a newspaper publisher. He'd been well loved and respected, and he would be sorely missed.

Sam helped Jessup fill in the grave while Angeline said good-bye to each person who had come to the funeral. She felt a bit odd doing so since she had only been his daughter-in-law for thirty minutes before Michael's death. Yet no one made her feel awkward or out of place. In fact, their grief was as real as hers and it made her feel better to know how they mourned him.

After the grave was filled in, Jessup pulled out a wooden cross he'd made.

"I know Michael didn't want nothing fancy, but I carved

him something." Jessup put the cross in place and pounded it into the ground, each hammer swing echoing around them as if the world were grieving with them.

"Thank you, Jessup." Sam shook his hand after the older man finished. "I know he would have appreciated it."

Everyone left the cemetery but Sam and Angeline. She wasn't sure if he needed her there or not, but she wasn't about to leave just yet. The wind blew his dark hair as he stood beside his father's grave. Sam was murmuring again and she stood there patiently waiting for her husband.

He pulled out a knife from a scabbard in his boot that she didn't know he had. Before she could ask him what he was doing, he pried a large chunk of the cross open and slipped the sparrow feather in the opening. He glanced up at her with his dark gaze unreadable.

"I want to make you a part of this. Will you trust me?"

She nodded, unsure of what he was doing, but what she did know was that he was saying good-bye to his father. He rose to his feet and walked toward her with the knife. Angeline knew no fear—she loved Sam and he loved her. He reached for her hair and cut off a lock near her hairline. Then he did the same on his own head.

Angeline watched as he braided the two together, blond and black woven into one. He'd obviously braided hair before, judging by the speed with which he completed it. With a knot she didn't recognize, he looped the two ends together until they were a perfect circle.

Sam went back to the grave and slid the circle onto the cross until it fit perfectly right over the spot where the sparrow feather was. He'd made both of them a part of the family, together with his parents, a talisman of sorts.

She didn't know much about what he did, but it touched her heart deeply. This man believed in family, in loving and respecting those within his circle, even after death. She had always known loyalty to God and church first, the ward second, and family a distant third. It wasn't wrong, it was just different. Angeline understood that now.

Being born into the Church of Latter Day Saints was simply fate, but neither she nor her sister, Eliza, were meant to be a part of that church. Angeline believed God would show her the right path in His own time and He had.

Sam pulled her into an embrace and they stood together on the hill. The wind whistled through the trees, a mournful sound, as if the earth were grieving along with them.

Sam and Angeline made their way home slowly. He told her stories of his father, giving her a piece of what was a good man. She laughed and gasped, cried and listened as her husband dealt with his father's death in his own way.

As they stepped inside, Angeline heard noises from the kitchen. She looked up at Sam, but he didn't seem to be worried. They walked in to find Lettie cooking and Jessup at the table with clean hands and a scowl.

"Lettie, what are you doing here?" Angeline hugged her quickly. "I'm so glad to see you." She'd been worried about her friend.

"He didn't tell you, did he?" Lettie leaned against the sink and folded her arms, her gaze locked with Sam's.

"Tell me what?"

Sam glanced at Jessup and Lettie. "I invited Lettie to live here with us. She's family."

Angeline smiled as she realized she would have a part of her old family here with her new family. She leapt into Sam's arms and kissed him hard.

"Thank you."

His arms closed around her and he stuck his nose in her neck, tickling her as he breathed in her scent. "You're welcome."

"Ahem, there are other people in the room and this stubborn old man is one of them." Lettie waved a wooden spoon at Jessup. "He washed the dirt off his hands, fortunately, but he won't change out of those dirty clothes. I don't serve supper to folks in dirty clothes."

Lettie's brown gaze narrowed as did Jessup's. Angeline held back a chuckle as they faced each other like a hen and rooster determining who ruled the roost.

"I told you, I ain't got no clothes but these. I ain't running around buck nekkid in front of everyone." Jessup slurped the coffee noisily. "That there stew smells good and this hag's been torturing me with it."

Before Angeline could tell him not to call Lettie a hag, her friend surprised her completely by laughing. In the entire time she'd known Lettie, Angeline had never heard her laugh once. She stared at the older woman in astonishment.

"Hag, hmm? I'll accept that nickname if I can call you old fart." Lettie smiled at Jessup and her entire face lit up. "But you still have to have clean clothes to sit at my table."

Angeline turned to Sam and saw the same shock on his face. Whatever had happened to Lettie had allowed her to shed the cloak of darkness she'd carried for so long. Lettie looked years younger than before. She looked free.

"Jessup, you were about the same size as Pa. I think he'd be pleased if you put his clothes to good use." Sam pointed upstairs. "Let's go on up and sort things out while the ladies take care of supper."

"I don't take no charity, but seeing as how they was Michael's things, I think you're right. He was a good man and gave me stuff all the time." Jessup rose from the table and, after one more glare in Lettie's direction, left the room with Sam.

Angeline had never had such a unique family before, but she knew it would never be dull and she'd never stop loving all of them. She shook her head at Lettie.

"Old fart?"

Lettie laughed again and Angeline joined in. The healing process had begun.

Sam felt as if there was a big hole in his heart, one that pulsed and ached with every breath he took. He missed his father so much. Only by staying busy could he keep the most intense pain away.

Angeline was his anchor whether or not she knew it. As they ate stew together with their two new family members, it was her smile that kept him from howling to the heavens. He'd never expected to lose his father so quickly and at the same time gain the woman he loved. It was a bittersweet day.

"I need to go outside." Sam rose to his feet abruptly, startling everyone. "I'm sorry, Angel."

He left the house quickly, barely pausing to grab his coat as he stepped out into the evening air. Sam took a deep breath and then another. He wasn't surprised to feel a small hand at his back. Somehow he knew Angeline would follow him.

"What are you doing?" His voice was low and hard.

"You were there by my side when I needed you. Do you think for one moment I won't be here when you need me?" She slipped her hand into his. "Let's go to the lake."

Just like that, he realized Angeline had given him the exact destination he'd been searching for. They walked silently down the street. Angeline managed to nod or wave at folks who spoke to them, giving Sam the opportunity to simply ignore everything around him.

He had been a young man when his mother died and her death had devastated him. With his father's help, they had recovered from her loss. Now he had lost his father and he knew the spirits had seen fit to give him Angeline by his side.

Before he could start his life with her, however, he had to be able to say good-bye to his father, to grieve for him. Sam should know what to do, but he was lost and it was a difficult thing to admit to himself.

When they arrived at the lake, Sam felt the tightness in his chest easing a bit. The setting sun left an orange glow on the water, turning it into a pool of cool fire. Sam closed his eyes and listened to the world around him.

A cool breeze brushed past his face. Beside him, Angeline shivered and he knew she felt the wind as well. Sam opened his eyes and walked toward the lakeshore and sat down with his legs crossed. Angeline did the same, although in a skirt it was a bit more difficult.

The grass was a bit damp beneath him, but Sam ignored the discomfort and focused on the water. The orange and red rippled across the small waves, almost dancing in front of him. Sam opened his mind and his heart to the world around him.

At first, he wondered if his journey to the lake would help, if sitting in the cold grass would bring him the peace he needed. Then to his surprise, he started to hear something other than the wind.

It was a low chant, a steady murmuring all around him, echoing in his ears and heart. He breathed slowly in and out, and with each breath the knot deep within him unraveled bit by bit.

Sam was awash in memories of his father, the good, the bad, the difficult, and the joyful. He didn't even realize he was crying until Angeline wiped away his tears. She didn't push him to speak or question him on what he was doing—she sat beside him and simply gave him her love.

He didn't know how long he sat there, but it was full dark before Sam finally felt peace. Perhaps it was the spirits comforting him along with his mother, or perhaps it was just allowing himself to grieve. He wanted to believe he'd been guided to the lake. The spirits there helped him find the peace he'd been seeking.

Sam got to his feet and held out his hand to help Angeline up. She stared at him with her wide blue gaze, waiting for him to speak. His heart hiccupped at the love he felt for her, the pure connection they shared.

"I love you, Angel."

She smiled widely, her beauty shining brightly in the deepening twilight. "I love you too, Sam."

He held her tightly on the shore of the lake, with the breeze gently caressing them and the spirits around them at peace.

They walked back to the house quietly, although this time their silence was easier. Angeline didn't know exactly what had happened, but whatever it was, Sam had allowed himself to grieve for his father. She thought she'd heard someone singing, a low chant that made her feel comfortable, at ease. Most men would not have grieved so openly, but Sam wasn't most men.

He was her husband.

When they walked in, they found Lettie examining the newspaper equipment. She looked just a little guilty to be doing it, but Angeline was pleased to see Sam smile.

"Tomorrow we can talk about how this all works. It's been weeks since we published a paper. I'm sure everyone in town would appreciate it if we started up again." He ran his hands down the side of the printing press. "My father would want someone like you to take over."

Lettie's gaze snapped to Angeline, then back to Sam. "What does that mean?"

"It means I see passion in you, Lettie. You will put your heart and soul into this paper. You're not the type of person to give half of yourself. I think my father will be pleased to see what you can do with it." Sam kissed Lettie's cheek. "I'm glad you agreed to be part of our new family."

Lettie looked at Angeline with her brows raised, speechless

for the first time since they'd known each other. Angeline chuckled.

"I think you've actually done what no one else has been able to do, Sam. You've shut her up."

Lettie threw a wadded-up paper at Angeline and they both laughed. Sam raised his brows and Angeline smiled at him.

"I think it's time to turn in for the night." Lettie made her exit gracefully, leaving the two of them alone.

Angeline's heart sped up and her body suddenly came alive. She walked toward Sam and cupped his cheek, his whiskers rough against her skin as her fingers explored his sharply planed face. Yes, he was beautiful. Her fingers found his lips, so full and sensual.

"Mr. Carver."

"Mrs. Carver."

This time when they kissed, the darkness of the day slid away, leaving only the light that glowed between them. It made every small hair on her body rise, along with her temperature.

He was holding back. She could sense it. She ran her hands through his raven-black hair. Her fingers continued their exploration to his neck, his quickened pulse visible beneath his smooth, golden skin. Slowly, she leaned over and placed her lips on that pulsing spot. Life.

Sam groaned. She knew she was playing with fire, and she wanted to be burned.

"Angel." His voice was strained.

"Hmmm?" she answered as she kissed his neck, making her way back to his lips. His jaw was set tightly as she tasted his salty skin.

"Want to go to our new bedroom?"

She didn't answer. Looking into his deep black eyes, she lowered her lips to his. It was a delicate woman's kiss, but he responded. Her tongue ran the length of his lips. Sam growled deep in his throat.

She deepened her kiss, letting her tongue invade his mouth. She unbuttoned his shirt and ran her hands over his smooth chest. Unable to quell his own passions, Sam anchored his hand in her thick hair and kissed her back. The force of his passion enveloped Angeline. It was an endless kiss as their tongues darted and teased. His hard chest felt like fire against her breasts. Unable to catch her breath, she grabbed his shoulders, feeling the muscles bunch as she touched him.

"Upstairs." His voice was husky with need.

She smiled at him and pulled him toward the stairs and up to what was now their bedroom. With a wicked grin, he closed the door and began to undress.

Angeline felt her mouth go dry as she watched her husband reveal his nude body. He was well muscled and tan from the waist up. His chest was broad and sleek. From the waist down, he was pale as milk, but still so beautiful. She couldn't help staring at his cock, her body readily responding to the sight of his.

He took her into his arms and lowered his mouth to hers. Angeline moaned as Sam's tongue entered her mouth. He pulled his lips away from hers and looked down into her face. His eyes held no secrets as they shone with passion and love.

Sam lay down on the bed and waited for her, his expression full of hope. "How about you ride me tonight?"

She stared at him, not really understanding what he was asking. "Ride you?"

"Yes, honey, you climb on and ride me." He took his cock in hand and held it up straight. "Like a horse."

She blushed, unaware women and men did that kind of thing. It was always the male on top in her experience, even with horses. However the sight of his hard cock made her even wetter. She was prepared to try anything with this man. He was her soul mate and much more.

Angeline undressed slowly, giving Sam a show he wouldn't

forget. His cock twitched on more than one occasion as he watched her strip. As she cupped her breasts for him, she felt the power of his arousal and of her own surging through her. It was heady, and it was wonderful.

She approached the bed, eager for him to teach her what to do. "What do I do?"

"Climb on, honey. Spread your legs and guide me in." He licked his lips as she straddled him.

A shiver of longing raced through her as she felt the head of his cock nudging her entrance.

"Now it's up to you how much and how long." He held her hips and pulled down slightly, letting her feel the motion.

Angeline braced herself on his chest and slowly lowered herself onto his erection. It was the most titillating experience of her life. She was in control—she had the ability to pleasure herself and him at the same time.

With a saucy grin, she raised herself up, then back down only an inch, then up, then back down an inch. He groaned and gripped her hips tighter.

"You're torturing me, Angel." He didn't pressure her to go faster or deeper—he simply thrust his hips up a bit with each downward stroke.

Soon Angeline had the rhythm and started riding him in earnest. He reached up and tweaked her nipples, sending tingles through her. She decided it was a must to have him do the same each time she rode him.

"God, you feel good." He blew out a breath of choppy air. "I don't think I will last much longer."

Angeline closed her eyes and focused on the intensity of their joining, on the pleasure coursing through her. When his hand settled between her legs and flicked her nubbin, she jerked and let loose a groan of pure ecstasy.

"Yesss," she gasped. "Yes, Sam, yes."

He flicked her faster and she fucked him faster. Harder and harder, she rode him as the sensations built to a crescendo.

He shouted her name, coming nearly off the bed as he found his peak. She was seconds behind him, clutching his shoulders and slamming her mouth into his.

Their tongues danced as her orgasm took over her body, wave after wave. His hand never left her nubbin, drawing out her pleasure until she begged him to stop.

Angeline slid off him, a boneless heap of woman. She didn't resist when he tucked her under his arm and pulled up the quilt. It was a mating, a joining of man and woman, heart and soul, mind and body.

She loved him and now he was her husband.

Chapter Eleven

Within a few weeks of the wedding, life returned to normal in Forestville. Angeline, Sam, and Lettie lived in the house together, although Jessup insisted on living in the barn until it got too cold. They were a happy family, if an unusual one.

Lettie learned the newspaper business quickly, taking over the paper and making it a monthly publication to give her time to gather stories. She was now a devoted newspaper person.

Sam was working on new chairs to go with the kitchen table. He was out behind the house with a planer finishing the seats of the chairs when Angeline stepped outside with a stranger.

He stopped working and waited for them. Sam didn't know who the man was, but he was wearing a fancy suit and even carried a case. The man looked like a lawyer.

"Hey there, Angel, did you make a new friend?"

She shook her head and frowned. "He's not here to see me. He's asked for you. Mr. Bennington, this is my husband, Sam Carver."

The nattily dressed man held out his hand. Sam tried to

wipe off some of the sawdust, but his hands were filthy. Mr. Bennington shook his hand anyway.

"Ty Bennington. It's a pleasure to meet you, Mr. Carver. I hope you don't mind mc saying so, but you favor your mother quite a bit. You have her look about you." Mr. Bennington seemed to be in his late thirties, with light brown hair and brown eyes.

Mention of Sam's mother made him start. "How the hell did you know my mother?"

"Sam, be nice," Angeline scolded. "Just listen to what he has to say."

"I met your mother about thirty-two years ago, right after she married your father. I was just a boy, but I remember how beautiful she was. Her hair was fascinating to a six-year-old." He grinned.

"She did have beautiful hair. Now tell me what you're doing here and why." Sam was done trying to figure out what the stranger wanted.

"I work for Bennington and Hargrove, a law firm in Denver started by my grandfather and his partner. My family has always handled legal matters for your father's family." The wind blew a cloud of sawdust on the attorney but, to his credit, he simply ignored it.

"My father doesn't have a family." Sam had asked many times as a child if he had a grandpa like his friends.

"Yes, actually, he does. Why don't we go inside and sit down? I have some papers for you to sign."

"Papers?" Sam had no idea what Bennington wanted, but the mention of papers made him suspicious.

"I will explain everything, I promise. Your wife offered me some coffee. If you don't mind, I'd appreciate a cup. I'm parched from the ride over." Bennington watched him with a gaze that could have been honest or deceptive. Sam couldn't tell which.

"Fine, let's go inside and I'll wash up." He met Angeline's

gaze and she shrugged her shoulders. Whatever Bennington wanted, it would be a mystery until the man got a cup of coffee.

The three of them walked back inside to find Lettie at the kitchen table. She glanced up at them, her gaze turning distrustful when she spotted the stranger.

"Who the hell is that?"

Bennington stared at her with surprise clearly written on his face. "I'm Ty Bennington."

"I don't know who you are, Ty Bennington, but I don't take kindly to strangers staring at me." She got up and left the room.

"You'll have to forgive Lettie; she doesn't like strangers much." Angeline headed for the coffeepot on the stove.

"I could tell." Bennington sat down and opened his case.

Sam washed up in the sink quickly. He was curious to figure out what the man was talking about, whether he was loco, and most of all, whether he had information about his father's family. All his life, his pa insisted he had no family—no uncles, grandpas, or cousins. His mother's family had moved around so much, she'd lost contact with them when Sam was a small boy. He had had no one but his parents until he met Angeline. Now he only had her.

Angeline poured three cups of coffee just as Sam finished drying his hands. They sat down with Mr. Bennington, who had placed several documents on the table.

"I don't know what your father told you about his family. I'll tell you what I know. He was born Michael Andrew Carver on February first, eighteen-twenty to Benson and Mary Carver in Denver, Colorado. He was the only son in a family of four children. His three sisters stayed in Denver while your father, well, he had a wandering spirit." Bennington smiled. "After he turned eighteen, he spent a few years exploring and returned with your mother in eighteen-forty-two. She was already pregnant with you."

"That sounds about right. I was born in January eighteen-forty-three." Sam sipped the coffee while his insides were jumping like frogs. He had no knowledge about his father's life or where he'd come from. The fact that his father had *three* sisters was simply astonishing.

"Your mother was gracious, beautiful, and soft-spoken, but she was also half-Indian, the daughter of a white man and an Indian woman. The elder Mr. Carver, he didn't appreciate his only son and heir marrying what he termed a 'savage.' After what I hear were epic battles over the marriage, Benson Carver disowned his son and kicked him out of the house." Bennington looked apologetic, but the information was devastating nonetheless.

"This is why he told me he had no family? Because his father was an ass?" Sam was angry and disappointed. To think his own family had shunned him before he was even born left a bitter taste in his mouth.

"Benson Carver was somewhat overbearing. He used to scare me when I was a child. Mary Carver was just as sweet and soft-spoken as Sparrow. In fact, they got along well. So well, in fact, I discovered your mother corresponded with your grandmother for years after they left Denver." Bennington set down a stack of yellowed envelopes tied with a pink ribbon. "When Mary passed away two years ago, she left these in trust for you."

Sam felt as if he'd been punched in the gut. He stared at the stack of letters, knowing his mother had learned to write after insisting his father teach her. Now he knew she'd done it to keep in contact with Sam's grandmother. Yet she'd never said a word about any of it to Sam. His grandmother had been alive until only two years ago. He'd missed the opportunity to know her. The realization left a bitter taste in his mouth.

"The firm knew where you and your family lived in

Wyoming. We've kept track of you under the provisions of Mary's will. She had taken over the business ten years ago when your grandfather died. The business belonged to your father, although we've held it in trust for him. We tried to contact him, but he never responded to any correspondence." Bennington handed Sam a thick document. "This is Mary's will, naming your father, Michael, as the heir to Carver Industries. In the event of his death, you are the named heir."

Angeline moved her chair closer to his while Sam tried his best not to run from the house. He didn't understand any of it and he was too overwhelmed to form a coherent thought. His angel, however, saved him yet again.

"Mr. Bennington, this is a lot of information. Are you saying that Sam has a family in Denver, that he owns something called Carver Industries, and you've come here to give him the legal paperwork for all of it?" She held on to Sam's hand with a firm grip.

"Yes, that's a good summary of everything." Ty looked apologetic. "I know it's a lot of information, but if you'll travel to Denver, I can show you all of it."

"What do you mean, all of it? What is Carver Industries?" Angeline sounded much calmer than Sam was. In fact, she was beginning to sound angry.

"Carver Industries is a company begun by Sam's grandfather. It has become the leading transportation provider in Colorado and beyond. He began with stagecoaches and wagons, and expanded into trains. Denver is a major shipping hub providing goods to people all over the west. Your company alone is worth approximately fifteen million dollars."

A blackness roared through Sam's head as he gaped at the lawyer. He could not handle any more information. Not one shred of it. Sam left the house at a dead run, leaving Angeline to deal with the lawyer. He didn't want the man to see him cry.

* * *

Angeline stared at the lawyer, who stared at Sam's retreating back. She was shaking, wondering if this man was a shyster or if everything he'd said was true. If it was, then Michael had given up a fortune for his Sparrow. Love had sustained him all his adult life, and it had helped him raise Sam and thrive without much to live on.

It was amazing, astonishing, and somewhat humbling. She had liked Michael. He'd been a good man and a good father. There were so many questions she had for him, ones that would never be answered now.

"You've come now because Michael is dead," Angeline stated flatly. "Where were you two years ago?"

"I told you, we tried to contact him, but without success." Bennington gestured to the papers. "We've sent copies of Mary's will and the business information on numerous occasions."

"Michael was suffering from a loss of faculties the last two years. He was forgetful, confused and, oftentimes, living in the past rather than the present." She touched the edge of the will with one finger. "He probably didn't understand what you sent him, or perhaps the mere mention of his family made him so upset he burned the papers without reading them."

Ty looked stricken. "I had no idea."

"Of course, you didn't. Sam hid it from everyone. Sparrow died ten years ago, so there was no one to watch over Michael but his son." Angeline stacked everything neatly on the table. "It's going to take some time for Sam to accept all this. If you can leave these here, I will make sure he reads through them."

"Yes, of course, these are copies for him. I was planning on staying here in town until everything was signed. We've had an offer to purchase Carver Industries and I have to present it to your husband, in addition to the rest of the legal paperwork giving him possession of the house and assets in

Denver." Ty rose to his feet. "I'll be over at the hotel. I was also told they serve good meals at the Blue Plate."

Angeline smiled. "The food is wonderful there. You'll not leave hungry."

"Okay then, I'll wait to hear from you or Sam." Ty took her hand and shook it gently. "It was a pleasure to meet you, Mrs. Carver."

Angeline walked the lawyer out the front door, then leaned her forehead against the jamb. She was shaken and confused, but not nearly as confused as Sam was. He was hurt and she knew there was only one place he would go—the lake.

Sam contemplated going swimming, but the water was still very cold. It might do him good to jump into the cool water, help numb the confusion and pain he felt. His parents had kept secrets from him, and not just little white lies told to children. These were huge, life-changing secrets.

He felt betrayed.

Soft footsteps behind him didn't make him move an inch. He knew by her scent that it was his angel. She sat down beside him, as she'd done before, and looked out on the lake with him. Without a word, she simply took his hand and sat beside him, giving him her quiet strength.

"Is he gone?"

"Yes, but not far. He's got papers for you to sign so he's staying at the hotel until everything's done."

Sam nodded. The lawyer wasn't to blame. He was a messenger sent to bring information, not to wreak havoc, yet that was exactly what he'd done.

"I'm not very good company right now."

"I know. That's why I'm protecting everyone else in town from you." Angeline sounded completely matter-of-fact.

Sam managed to squeeze her hand lightly. "I'm angry with them."

"I would be too."

"They kept information from me, kept my family from me. Dammit, they lied to me." Sam's chest hurt just contemplating how much lying his parents had done.

"They loved you and they loved each other. Your father gave up his family because he loved Sparrow so much. It wasn't his fault his father could not see how wonderful she was. Many people are taught to hate, taught to never see beyond the outer shell of a person." Angeline smiled sadly.

Sam thought about the fact he owned a business worth a staggering sum of money when yesterday he was counting pennies to buy nails. Then his mind returned to what Angeline had said about his parents' love. His father had been devoted to his mother, blindly in love until the day she died, and then part of him died as well. He could have returned to Denver then, but he didn't. Sam would never know why.

"People make choices, decisions they can never reverse. It doesn't mean they're bad people. It just means they're human and they shape their lives by those decisions." She kissed the back of his hand. "I would give up my life for you, Sam. I know your parents had the same kind of love."

Sam's anger began to dissipate. She was right, of course. He would give up everything for Angeline, no matter what the consequences. The fact was, there wasn't anything he wouldn't do for her. When his mother had gotten sick, his father spent every waking moment taking care of her until she wasted away to nothing. The pain he suffered must have been unbearable. No wonder he didn't return to Denver. He'd built his life in Forestville and he would have wanted to stay where Sparrow was buried, never straying too far from her grave.

They sat side by side for a bit longer. Sam felt more in control of himself, calmer and ready to learn more about the Carvers in Denver.

"Did Bennington leave the papers for me?"

"Yes, I asked him to. They're on the table whenever you're ready to look at them." She got to her feet and held out her hand.

"The letters too?" He accepted her help and stood.

"Yes, the letters too."

Sam pulled Angeline into an embrace and held her tight, their hearts beating against each other. He felt a breeze on his neck again and closed his eyes. Sam wasn't quite ready to forgive his mother, but he was done being angry with her. It was time to get more information and then decide what he needed to do.

He kissed Angeline, a sweet, hot kiss that made his body ache. She sucked in a lungful of air when he finally let her loose.

"Well, that was nice." She raised one blond brow. "More later?"

Sam laughed and turned to walk back home with his wife, his love, tucked under his arm. He'd need her strength to get through the next few days and even beyond. His life had changed last fall when Angeline arrived in Forestville, and again when she became his wife. Now it seemed his life was taking another sharp right turn and he had no doubt it was going to be a rocky path.

The wind was at their back as they walked home. The spirits were already guiding him to where he needed to be.

Angeline watched him as he read through the letters. She didn't ask to see them or even what he found in their yellowed depths. It seemed better to simply be there if he needed her.

She spent her time making the kitchen into something that functioned as a kitchen rather than a dirty dish storage area. Somehow the two men had forgotten how to clean up after themselves. The chore of cleaning gave her the opportunity to watch him without actually watching him.

After he stacked the letters and tied them with the pink ribbon again, he started on the rest of the papers. By then Angeline had cleaned the pantry closet, which had nothing in it but dust and a can of old peaches, and scrubbed every inch of the kitchen until it sparkled.

He sat back and pinched his nose between his fingers. When he sighed, she hung up the rags on the side of the sink and sat down across from him. Angeline had learned how to be patient, although she wanted to shake him so he'd start talking.

"Everything he told us appears to be true. I still have trouble believing all of it, but those letters are in my mother's writing." He met her gaze. "I have a friend who works in the government in Colorado. I'm going to send him a wire to make sure this is all on the up and up."

"That's a good idea. No matter what papers Bennington has in hand, it doesn't mean he's not a shyster." Angeline agreed with Sam's methodical review of everything, but she still wanted to find out more. That curiosity of hers wouldn't let her rest. "How long will it take your friend to find out the information?"

"Not long. A few days probably." Sam gestured to the letters. "If you want to read them, go ahead. They are daily diaries of what I did growing up—when I lost my front teeth or broke my arm, even when I climbed a tree and got stuck."

"She was allowing your grandmother to watch you grow up even if she wasn't able to see you." Angeline knew Sam's mother had been a good woman, and this was a prime example of why. She had no connection to Mary Carver, no compelling reason to do what she'd done. Sparrow was a busy mother with a boy to raise and a house to take care of. Yet she'd spent her time painting pictures of young Sam's life for his grandmother to read.

"Yep, I guess that's what she was doing." Sam's gaze connected with hers, their depths still full of dark emotion. "It would have been better to let me actually see my grandmother."

"I don't think your father or your grandfather would have allowed it. This was the best she could do under the circumstances." Angeline wanted to reach inside and absorb all his pain. He'd gone through so much with his father's death. This news, all of the history behind it, was like kicking him when he was down.

"What do you think I should do?" His question surprised her, but she'd been thinking about the answer since Mr. Bennington had left the house.

"I think we should find out what is true and what isn't. If you want to get to know your family, we should visit Denver, but not live there." She took his hand and kissed it this time. "Family is more important than any money. You only have one life to live, and living it with regrets will make it that much less."

Angeline tried not to think about Eliza, but all the talk of family brought memories of her older sister to the surface. If only she knew where her sister was, she would find a way to see her.

"I can't even begin to imagine how much fifteen million dollars is."

Angeline shook her head. "Neither can I, but I guess it means I don't have to darn your socks for winter."

Sam chuckled. "Seems like that's true. Would you want it? The money, I mean?"

Angeline wasn't going to lie to him. "All my life I've lived without much except the bare necessities, and sometimes even those were a bit thin. I can't say that the idea of having everything I've ever wanted doesn't sound delightful, but it sounds scary too."

He nodded. "Yep, that's how I feel too. Let me go send that wire and then we'll find out if we're dreaming or not."

Angeline kissed him hard. "I love you, Sam Carver."

He smiled. "I love you too, Angel. Here, this is for you." Sam opened her hand and put a shiny black stone in her palm. "I found it down by the lake when I was kicking dirt around."

Angeline treasured each one of the gifts he gave her because they were from the heart, and no store-bought trinket could ever mean as much. Her hand closed around the pebble and she had an idea of what they could do if Sam truly did have enough money for anything.

Over the next two days, Sam went back to work on the chairs, making six of them to match the table so they could have folks over for dinner. Then, because he didn't have work and the waiting to hear from his friend Philip was killing him slowly, he started on a rocking chair for Angeline.

After his mother died, one of the things his father had burned was her rocking chair. For some reason, he needed to destroy something and it was an easy target. Their house had not had a need for a rocking chair in the last ten years. Sam didn't tell his wife, but he was hoping within a year, they'd need one.

Having a child with Angeline would be the greatest gift he could ever receive. Knowing a life grew within her would be more than wonderful. He could make a crib or a cradle later on, but a rocking chair, well, that was something he could make now. She could always sit in front of the fire in it, reading. Angeline had already started going through his meager collection of books.

"Sam?"

He looked up to see Angeline at the back door waving a yellow piece of paper. A telegram.

Sam dropped the sanding tool and ran for the house as fast as his bum leg could carry him. She looked as nervous as he felt, her blue eyes shining in the afternoon sun.

"I didn't open it."

"You could've. I don't have any secrets from you." He took the paper with sawdust-covered, shaking hands and opened it.

SAM

INVESTIGATED CARVER INDUSTRIES STOP WELL KNOWN BUSINESS WITH MULTI MILLION DOLLAR VALUE STOP MATRIARCH MARY CARVER DIED TWO YEARS AGO STOP MICHAEL ANDREW CARVER THE HEIR OF RECORD HELD IN TRUST BY ATTORNEYS STOP THREE SISTERS JANE ANN, GERTRUDE ELLEN, AND ALISON MARIE LIVE IN DENVER WITH FAMILIES STOP ALL SEEMS LEGITIMATE STOP STILL LOOKING INTO OTHER REQUEST STOP

PHILIP

At first, Sam could hardly believe what he was reading. Bennington had been telling the truth about all of it. "Looks like I have a family and a wagonful of money in Denver."

"A family?" She smiled and clapped her hands together. "Sam, that's wonderful!"

"Yep, three aunts and their families are in Denver." He kissed her hard. He had thought he'd lost every bit of his family when his father died. Although he had his Angel, Jessup, and Lettie, there had been no blood relations to speak of. He'd been an orphan and now, he had a large family just waiting for him. "Do you want to take a trip?"

She nodded. "Yes, let's plan on going to Denver. First you need to speak to Mr. Bennington though. He's been waiting for four days now."

"Don't like lawyers," Sam grumbled. "They make me itch."

"Now, he hasn't bothered you since you asked him to wait. In fact, he's been at the Blue Plate for every meal. Alice tells me he sits at the same table each time."

"Is he sweet on Alice?" Sam pulled her against him. "I'll warn him off."

Angeline chuckled. "No need. He seems to be sweet on Lettie."

Sam gaped at her. "Lettie? Well, she's as nice as a porcupine. What in the world would he see in her?"

"Everything. She's smart, sweet, funny when she wants to be, and fiercely loyal. Not to mention the fact that beneath the scowls, Lettie is quite pretty. And she runs a newspaper as her second job." Angeline nibbled on his earlobe. "I think perhaps before we head over to speak to Mr. Bennington, we need to celebrate your good fortune."

Sam growled as his cock rose to attention, pressing against her skirt. "I'm up for celebrating."

She waggled her eyebrows. "You're very funny, Mr. Carver."

Sam tossed her over his shoulder and headed into the house, eager to be naked with his wife.

"I'm pleased to hear you're going to Denver. I know your aunts were apprised of my journey here and Miss Jane in particular wanted to be sure to extend an invitation to you." Ty Bennington sat at their kitchen table, the first guest they'd had for supper.

Jessup eyeballed him with his usual table manners. The old man had told Sam to refuse the money. After all, he lived every day without a cent and he was just fine.

"I'm more interested in my children, or our future children." He squeezed Angeline's hand. "I want to be sure they're taken care of. For us, well, we're going to live here, but we'll visit Denver whenever we can."

"Perfect. I'm sure we can decide on someone to run Carver Industries in your stead. There are some good candidates we can speak to while you're in Denver if you prefer." Bennington sipped at his coffee with impeccable grace. The man really was a gentleman.

"I don't know about interviewing folks for a job. I wouldn't know the first thing about what to ask them." Sam looked nervous about the possibility.

"We can provide you with questions, or even sit in on the interviews, but the most important thing for you to determine is whether you like the candidate. The man will be responsible for your entire family fortune. You must trust your instincts here."

"I like that plan," Sam said. "Who's heading it up now?"

"Your Aunt Jane's husband, Dominic Archer, is the acting president. He worked for your grandfather and then your grandmother. He's got quite a bit of experience." It was what the lawyer didn't say that niggled at Angeline.

"You don't think he's the right person for the job."

Ty's gaze swung to her, his brown eyes full of surprise. "What makes you say that, Mrs. Carver?"

"We might be the poor relations, but I can tell when someone is telling a half-truth, or not giving all the information they have." She raised her brows, waiting for him to contradict her.

He grinned sheepishly. "Your wife is very intelligent, Mr. Carver."

"She is that, and more." Sam winked at her. "I want to meet this Dominic Archer, then decide if he's the right man for the job."

"Mr. Archer is a good man, a smart man, but he's a lot older than you. I'm afraid he might not be around long." Mr. Bennington shrugged. "I'm only thinking of the company and its leadership. However, your plan is a sound one. We can definitely decide while you're in Denver."

Angeline was proud of Sam and glad to know that Mr. Bennington would be traveling with them in two days' time back to Denver. She was hoping to have someone to assist them since her own travel experience was limited to horses, carriages, and wagons. She'd never been on a train or in a fancy coach. The very idea was intimidating.

After everything was cleaned up and the lawyer left, Angeline tugged on Sam's hand and pulled him outside to take a walk. The sun had already set, and the twilight was bright enough so they could see where they were going. She held his hand as they strolled toward the lake.

Sam was quiet, but he was thinking about a million different things, as Angeline likely was too. Their lives had already changed so much in the last year, now things were about to change even more.

As they arrived at the lakeshore, Sam breathed in deeply. The lake had a calming effect on him, one he was certain came from his mother and her people.

Angeline turned to Sam and opened his hand, placing the black rock in his palm this time. "I want to build a house here for us, our family, our children. I want to wake up to the sun on one side of the lake, then see its mirror image on the other side at the end of the day. I want you to teach our children to swim in it. I want to make love in it and be here for the rest of our lives."

Sam stared at her, realizing she was absolutely right. Coming to the lake had suddenly made it all clear in his mind. He knew it was the right thing to do. It was already their home. Now all they needed was a house.

Sam's smile was as wide as a country mile. He whooped and held her up in the air, spinning her around until she protested. "My angel, you are a genius! We'll design a perfect house, then we'll build it when we get back from Denver." He kissed her, then spun her around again, laughing.

The air had turned summery, and the warmth of the lake beckoned. She sucked in a breath when he set her down and she looked at the water, then back at Sam.

"Can I have my first swimming lesson now?"

He grinned. "Oh, I think we can arrange that."

They shucked their clothes quickly, eager to find out just how warm the water was. Sam hadn't been swimming in years, but he'd never forgotten how. He led her out past the "squishy mud" between her toes and into the deeper water.

"Now you can float. Don't fight the water, be at peace with it. It can't drown you if you don't let it." He held her arms. "Now kick your legs slowly."

She struggled a bit, but soon had the rhythm of treading water. He smiled at her and pulled her against him, water splashing up between them and into his nose.

Angeline laughed and swatted his shoulder. "Sam!"

"I can't help myself. I love you so much, I need to be near you always. My body just takes over."

And take over it did. His cock rose to attention, pressing against her wet thigh in the water. She raised her eyebrows at him.

"See?"

"You don't need an invitation Sam. Make love to me." Her simple statement summed up their relationship.

They loved, and were loved. No apologies, no need to stand on ceremony. Sam would never hurt her and she would never hurt him.

"Wrap your legs around me."

Her long legs wrapped around his waist, nestling her opening nicely against his waiting cock. He jerked against the wiry curls caressing him. She smiled and leaned forward to kiss him.

Since Sam could still stand with his head above water, he braced himself on the bottom and slid her down until he was fully sheathed inside her.

The lake, the woman, the perfection of the moment was not lost on him. This was where they were meant to be, where they would make babies and raise a family. He thrust slowly in and out, feeling each movement in the water around him. It was the most sensual experience of his life.

Her hard nipples rubbed up and down his chest as they moved. Their tips teased him, making him hotter and hungrier for her. He took her hips and started pushing her down as he thrust up.

Water splashed between them, but he didn't care. All that mattered was mating with her, being part of Angeline in this special place. His balls tightened as he drew closer to his release.

Sam reached between them and flicked her clit. She moaned and threw her head back, which put her breasts at nearly eye level. Her hair fanned out in the water behind her like a blond curtain.

His mouth closed around her nipple, tugging and lapping at her while he held on as long as he could. She tightened around him, and he knew she was coming. Sam bit her nipple and she shouted his name.

The walls of her passage clenched so tight, he came immediately, spilling his seed into her. Black spots danced behind his eyes as he roared her name.

His Angel, his wife, his love.

Chapter Twelve

The trip out to Denver from Wyoming opened Angeline's eyes to a great deal of experiences. While Sam had traveled on trains back East ten years earlier, she'd never set foot on a train before. The sounds, the smells, the rumble of the locomotive as it rolled out of the station, all seemed like a different world to her.

Sam smiled at her wide-eyed innocence, but he never made fun of her, which she appreciated. She truly felt like a small-town girl suddenly thrown into a big city, and she hadn't even gotten to Denver yet.

Unfortunately, the first hour on the train, Angeline discovered exactly what Alice was talking about when she'd called Sam a half-breed. A woman passing by with her daughter stared at him with a horrified expression. She pulled the little girl against her skirts.

"Oh, sweet Lord, it's a savage. Don't look, Laura Sue." She hurried past, pale as milk, while everyone in the compartment turned to look at them.

"Why are they staring at us?" Angeline whispered to Sam. "It's not as if we haven't paid for our tickets."

In fact, Mr. Bennington had paid for them, saying he would

be reimbursed from the company accounts when they arrived in Denver.

"I'm used to it, Angel. People are going to think whatever they want." He looked out the window at the passing scenery.

It wasn't the last time people treated them badly. By the time they pulled into Denver late that night, Angeline was so upset, she wanted to punch somebody. He'd been called a savage, an injun, a heathen, and a scalper. She'd never heard most of those words used before.

No matter what Sam said, he wasn't used to being called names. People sneered, shouted, and even spit at them. She was also called names, but only because she sat with Sam. It was simply infuriating.

Angeline decided right then she would never live in Denver if that was the way people in Colorado behaved. No wonder Sam's parents had left.

"Miss Jane is waiting for us at the house, along with some others," Bennington said as he gave Angeline his hand to disembark the train. "They're most anxious to meet you."

"The house?"

"The Carver house. It's housed each generation of Carvers until your father left." The lawyer led them outside the train station while two porters trundled behind them with their bags.

A beautiful black coach sat outside; it had a driver perched on top with a nicer suit than anyone in Forestville. Angeline had a feeling she and Sam were about to embark on a rather uncomfortable day.

"Good evening, Chambers." Mr. Bennington obviously knew the driver personally.

"Good evening, sir." The young man could be no older than she was and his avid curiosity was plain. He stared at both of them, his gaze wide.

They all climbed in and Angeline sat on the softest cushion she'd ever felt. The coach was lined with blue satin and the seats were obviously stuffed with feathers or something equally as soft. Her stomach flipped at the knowledge this was only the coach—what must the house be like?

They drove along smoothly, more smoothly than she thought a coach could. Sam sat beside her, his hand laced with hers. Mr. Bennington glanced at their joined hands and smiled.

"You two are a love match, that's very evident." He leaned forward and spoke softly. "I will warn you that some members of your family won't be happy to have the heir apparent appear. They've grown comfortable assuming the fortune is theirs."

Sam scowled. "That was something you could've shared in Wyoming."

"I thought perhaps you wouldn't come if I told you too much. I was your grandmother's personal attorney and she so hoped your father and you would return. It was her fondest desire to see her grandson at the helm of the company." He had affection in his voice when he spoke of Mary Carver. "She was a great lady, an amazing business leader. Hers are some rather large shoes to fill."

"You're not making me want to stay here, you know. I already feel like a fish out of water and I ain't never sat on anything so soft before." Sam's grip on her hand tightened. "The first person that speaks rudely to Angeline gets tossed out of the house on their ass. I'm not a businessman or a great leader, but I'm smart enough to spot a snake."

Angeline felt as if they were girding themselves for battle. Mr. Bennington made it sound as if there might be a battle waged over Carver Industries and the fortune it represented. Angeline was very afraid she and Sam would be woefully outgunned.

The coach stopped in front of the biggest house on the block, an enormous structure with columns in front and a rolling green yard on either side. A fountain splashed merrily as they circled round the horseshoe-shaped entrance.

"It looks like one of the mansions I saw out in Virginia." Sam gaped just as much as she did.

"Well, truthfully, you could call it a mansion, but everyone in the family simply refers to it as the 'House.' " Bennington looked uncomfortable.

Sam narrowed his gaze. "House, hmm? How many rooms does it have?"

"Forty-seven."

Angeline gasped. She couldn't even imagine the size—it made her mind spin.

"Jesus." Sam turned to look at her. "Say the word and we'll turn around and go back to Forestville. I'll just give it to the greedy bastards waiting for us."

She looked into his dark gaze, reached out and ran her hand through his silky black hair and smiled. "You are stronger than any one of those people in there. You've fought a war. You've survived things they can't even fathom. There's no way we're going to let them run us out of here without a fight."

Although her stomach actually quivered with fear, she kept her smile steady. He took her hand and kissed it.

"I love you, Angel."

"I love you too, Sam. Now let's show them what a real Carver can do."

This time he smiled and she knew he was ready to face his family. She wished she was as ready. Angeline had never felt so intimidated in her life as they stepped out of the carriage and into the warm night air.

The front door was enormous, at least ten feet high, with a huge brass knocker. Mr. Bennington didn't knock, however. He just opened the door and gestured for them to enter. Angeline and Sam stepped through together, hands tightly entwined.

The brightness of the crystal chandelier made everything

glow. Coming from the darkness of the evening, it was almost blinding.

There were at least thirty people in the entrance to the house. More than half were people dressed in black-and-white uniforms, lined up to the left. Angeline assumed they were the servants. In front of them were men, women, and children of various ages, sizes, shapes, and hair colors.

Angeline didn't know whom to speak with first, so she looked to Mr. Bennington for help. He seemed to understand what he was doing because he bowed to the crowd.

"Everyone, may I present Mr. and Mrs. Samuel Carver."

A few titters sounded from the center of the crowd. Someone else gasped, and more than a few murmurs echoed in the enormous entryway. No one, however, came forward to greet them. Sam's hand tightened around hers and she knew he felt as awkward as she did.

"Where is Mrs. Archer?" Bennington apparently had had enough of the silence.

A servant on the left answered. "The Archers have not yet come downstairs."

"Ah, then I will begin introductions." The lawyer seemed to have a knack for names because he rattled off the names of the dozen or so people in front of them from the smallest to the tallest. It seemed there wasn't one Carver in the bunch.

None of them offered to shake hands and none of them said hello. Angeline had a feeling they'd made an enormous mistake coming to Denver. If this was the way they would be treated, she would not be a part of it. It was hard enough to be without her sister every day—she could not endure being shunned and ridiculed again.

"Darlings, there you are." A striking woman with silver hair and a slender build came down the stairs. She wore a dazzling green gown with gold ruching, topped by a glittering necklace and earrings. She made a beeline for Angeline.

Up close, the woman was just as beautiful as any young lady, with the deepest green eyes Angeline had ever seen. "You must be Angeline." The woman kissed both of Angeline's cheeks. "I have heard countless wonderful things about you from dear Mr. Bennington. His description of your ethereal beauty does not do you justice."

The woman turned to Sam. "Oh, my. He is devastatingly handsome, isn't he? That dark hair is like a midnight waterfall, so like his mother's, as are those lovely eyes." She kissed his cheeks too. "I hope you don't think me too forward, darlings, but I must talk to you in private." She leveled a gaze at the various people waiting like a class of schoolchildren. "As for the rest of you, go home. You don't need to gape at the Carvers any longer."

The littlest one, Meredith, if Angeline remembered correctly, tugged at Angeline's coat. "Are you really an angel? And is he a devil?"

"No, sweetheart, neither of us is an angel or a devil. We're just people."

The little girl nodded sagely, then was hauled off by a rather severe woman with a large nose and a face full of freckles.

"Please, come into the study. We can speak in private." The older woman sashayed ahead in her sparkly green dress.

"Meet your Aunt Jane." Ty raised both his brows.

"Who are all those people?" Sam whispered.

"Neighbors, distant cousins, and some of the groundskeeping staff."

"Bennington, be a dear and make sure they come to the study." Jane's voice echoed from down the hallway.

"I think she wants to talk to you." He smiled and ushered them down a very long hallway into another room filled with ornate furniture, amazing rugs, and a collection of beautiful books lining the walls.

Angeline tried not to gape, she did, but she'd never seen so many books before.

"Do you like to read, Angeline dear?" Jane sat on a settee with cream-colored fabric and claw feet.

"I love to read. It's my favorite thing to do." She ran her finger along the spines, noting not a speck of dust. The books were simply gorgeous.

"Sit down please. I'll get a crick in my neck trying to look up at Samuel. He's tall like Michael was." Jane's gaze grew melancholy as she watched the two of them sit across from her on a loveseat of blue damask. "You've journeyed here to speak to me and to Dominic. I thought it prudent if we spoke alone first. Of course, I'd like to hear Samuel speak at least once tonight."

"I didn't have anything to say. Besides, you didn't leave much room for anyone else's words to fit in." Sam's impudent answer made Angeline pinch his hand.

Jane, however, laughed. "You're absolutely right, of course. I plan it that way." Her expression turned serious. "Mr. Bennington has told me there is a great deal of information your parents did not share with you. I'm sorry for that. Michael was a stubborn man, full of pride, but even more full of love for Sparrow. My father could not abide an Indian in his house. He was unmovable on the subject."

Sam gazed at his aunt. "I didn't really know what I missed out on. Maybe my parents did the right thing, keeping us together as a family of three." His voice was low, thoughtful. "It wasn't until my father died that I realized how important family was. Mr. Bennington handed me a treasure at the same time he cast shadows over my entire life."

"Eloquently put. We do make many choices in life that define not only who we are but the paths we take. I think Michael deliberately chose the path that would bring him the most peace and love." Jane smiled sadly. "I respected him for that, but I've missed him. It's difficult knowing he's gone." Her eyes grew suspiciously moist and she jumped off the settee. "Let's have some coffee and get to know each other."

With a twist of her hand, suddenly there were servants in the room with a tray of piping hot coffee in a shiny pot and the most delicate cups Angeline had ever seen. They poured the coffee and left the study as abruptly as they'd entered.

She stared at the cup and felt a bit dizzy. The travel, the stress, and the emotional strain were wearing on her. The room began to spin and all she saw was Jane frowning at her.

"I do believe your wife is about to faint, Samuel."

Everything went black.

Sam carried Angeline up the stairs, right on his aunt's heels. If he was any kind of husband, he would have noticed Angeline wasn't feeling well. Now she was unconscious and he had no idea what was wrong.

Jane led him to a huge bedroom down the right-hand hallway. The carpet was so soft, his shoes practically sank into it. He laid her on the bed, which was as high as his waist, and starting removing her coat and shoes.

"Was she ill during your trip?" Jane watched with a worried gaze.

"Not at all. She was fine all day. I don't know what happened." Sam told himself that she was just tired and hungry, nothing more.

"Is she with child?"

Jane's question knocked him completely sideways. He hadn't considered the possibility yet. Their relationship had only been about them and the idea that they could have conceived a child already was amazing.

"I don't know. It's possible." He looked at Angeline, searching for signs she might be pregnant, but if anything, she looked thinner and less healthy. Weren't pregnant women supposed to glow?

"It would be early on if she is indeed with child. I wouldn't take any chances. Let's get her into bed, bundled up warmly. If she wakes, we should have her eat broth and drink some tea with honey." Jane bustled off to the door. "I'll return momentarily."

Sam took Angeline's cold hand and pressed it to his cheek. "Wake up, Angel. Please wake up."

Her eyelids fluttered and then slowly opened. Her gaze was unfocused. "Sam?"

"Yes, honey, it's me. Thank God." He kissed her forehead, annoyed at himself for shaking like a leaf in a storm. Couldn't he handle one fainting spell? What if she was pregnant? Was he going to start fainting too?

"What happened?" She pressed the back of her hand to her forehead. "I feel woozy."

"You fainted in the study. Jane asked me . . . well, she wondered if maybe you're pregnant." The words came out in a rush, tumbling on top of each other.

Her gaze widened. "She wondered what?"

"Well, you fainted, and we have been married a month." He shrugged, although he felt anything but casual. "It's possible."

Angeline licked her lips and stared at him. "A baby?"

"I wouldn't get my hopes up yet; it might just be exhaustion. I figured I should ask." He managed a small smile.

"Oh, Sam, you are the first person, okay the second person after me who would know." She touched his cheek. "I love you."

"You two are the most amazing couple. Remind me so much of Michael and Sparrow." Jane appeared at the foot of the bed with a hearty-looking mug of steaming liquid. "I'm glad to see you're awake, Angeline. I brought you some tea."

Angeline sat up slowly and then took the mug from Jane. As she sipped, Sam kept sneaking glances at her to see if she was okay. He'd been worried about her before, but nothing like this.

"Carver Industries is run by my husband. I could have taken over the reins when Mother died, but Dominic had been by her side for thirty years. He knew more about everything, and he loves it." Jane leaned against the bedpost. "The lawyers would have him step down because he's nearly sixty. They're afraid he's going to drop dead because of his advanced age."

"You don't think that at all, do you?" Sam watched his aunt carefully.

"He's too full of passion for life and for the company to die. Dominic is the heart of the business right now. He wouldn't know what to do with himself if someone else took over." Jane smiled at them. "We can talk more tomorrow. You need your rest. I can have a bath drawn for you." She pointed in the corner toward another doorway. "The bathing room is in there. All you need to do is ring the bell cord near the door and the maid will come upstairs to assist you."

Sam felt a bit dizzy himself. Aunt Jane talked more than any person he'd ever met. She stepped forward and kissed them both on the cheeks again.

"Good night, darlings."

With that, and a big whiff of her perfume, she left them alone. Sam shook his head.

"She's something."

"She sure is. I like her." Angeline sipped the tea. "She put lots of honey in the tea too, just the way I wanted it."

Sam smiled at his wife. "Finish that tea and we'll get ready for bed." He yawned widely. "I think we both need a good night's sleep."

Angeline nodded and dutifully drank her tea. Sam looked around the room and wondered how he'd gotten there. This place was not his home. He didn't feel at all comfortable there. He was thirty years old, much too old to be starting a completely different life.

Even if Jane welcomed him, he didn't feel comfortable. Bennington had already warned him about the rest of the family, some of whom resented him without even meeting him. No, he didn't want to stay.

In the morning he'd tell Angeline they would meet his family and then go back to Wyoming, leaving Carver Industries the way they'd found it. Sam wanted to go home.

Chapter Thirteen

Breakfast at the Carver mansion involved copious amounts of food. Sam gaped at the heaping piles of eggs, toast, some kind of dark meat, and many kinds of other food he didn't recognize. He and Angeline seemed to arrive downstairs first, just past seven. When the two of them sat down, the servants even opened their napkins and put them on their laps.

Sam knew he'd made the right decision. All of this didn't feel right to him. No wonder his father had left. Sparrow would have suffocated in such a huge place.

"Good morning." A tall man with graying hair, brown eyes, and an impeccable blue suit walked into the dining room. "I'm Dominic Archer. You must be Samuel and Angeline."

After he shook hands with them, Dominic helped himself to food, then sat down with a contented grin. "I love breakfast. Favorite meal of the day, don't you know? Cook makes the eggs extra fluffy."

"I heard there were people in here eating breakfast already." Jane walked in wearing a blue morning gown and her hair in a braid. She looked as if she'd just woken up, but it appeared as though the maid had already coiffed her perfectly. "I'm glad you got to meet my Dom before he went to work. Perhaps Samuel would like to accompany you, darling?"

"Oh, that'd be right fine." Dominic was busy eating toast and eggs, but at least it was a positive response.

"Actually, we wanted to talk to you about that." Sam glanced at Angeline and she nodded. "I've decided to sign the company over to you."

Dominic dropped his fork, and eggs went flying across the table into Angeline's hair.

"What did you say?" Jane gaped at them. "You've only just arrived, darlings. Don't you at least want to stay here a few weeks before you decide? I can't imagine the lawyers will simply let you give it away."

"It's not what we want. Don't misunderstand me. I don't want to give up being a part of the family. It's just, well, I, um—"

"We don't belong here. Both of us grew up with enough money to survive, and not much else for extras. Each day was a gift and I think it made life that much sweeter for us." Angeline gestured to the heaps of food. "I was serving food a month ago to strangers in a restaurant. I can't be served every meal by someone else or have a maid put water in a bathtub for me." She shook her head. "I already love Jane, but we can't stay."

Jane looked genuinely hurt. "Are you sure, darlings?"

"Yep, we're sure. We'll stay a few days, but then we need to go home. I'll tell Mr. Bennington to do what he needs to put the control of the company in your hands, Mr. Archer." Sam felt a hundred pounds lighter just telling them what he felt. "It seems you've been doing a good job up until now. I don't think it's right to make any changes."

"Dom is a genius." Jane kissed the top of his head. "He turns a profit each and every year. Tell me you'll visit though. I can't bear to think I'll not see you again."

"We'll visit each summer," Angeline announced. "I don't

have any family of my own, except for my sister, but I don't know where she is. I'd love to be part of the Carvers."

"Then you shall." Jane met Sam's gaze and he saw his aunt had questions for him. "Now let's eat breakfast."

Sam felt relaxed enough to enjoy the meal, but each minute that passed, the food on the buffet grew colder. No doubt it would be used for the pigs or worse, simply thrown in a heap of trash. No, he couldn't live there, but Angeline was right. He could visit.

Later on, Angeline admitted she was tired and took a nap. Sam went in search of his aunt for a talk. He found her in the parlor, talking with two women. They all got to their feet and he noticed the resemblance immediately. They were all tall with the same silver hair.

Jane smiled and clapped her hands. "How lovely! Samuel, meet your aunts, Gertrude and Alison."

As Sam accepted their effusive hugs and kisses, he wondered if his mother had ever gotten used to their affectionate ways. It was different from what he was used to.

"Now sit with us. Gertie and Allie want to know your plans." Jane's gaze told him it was she who wanted to know.

"We're going to stay on another few days, to get to know you all and Mr. Bennington. Then we're headed back to Wyoming. I have a house to build on a lake there." Sam leaned forward. "I don't need much, so I'll only take a hundred dollars a month."

"For what?" Gertrude asked. "If it's for a clothing allowance, that's not nearly enough."

"Perhaps it's for books. His Angeline loves books."

"No, ladies, I mean for us to live on." He couldn't imagine spending a hundred dollars a month on clothes. What could they possibly need to purchase that cost twelve hundred dollars a year?

"Ridiculous. You should have at least five thousand a month deposited automatically. You can spend it on your wife, on your children, on whatever you want. A hundred dollars won't buy Gertie's handkerchiefs." Jane speared him with a gaze that brooked no argument. "There's no need to scrimp and save for things, Samuel. You can have whatever you want."

"I'll tell you what I want. I want a house by the lake with lots of bedrooms for my future children. I want to wake up each morning with my Angel and go to sleep with her kiss on my lips. I want to visit my family each summer in Denver." He smiled at Jane. "And I want to find my wife's sister so she can visit her family too."

"Ah, I knew there was a story there." Jane leaned forward. "Tell us what we can do."

Angeline woke slowly, stretching on the soft bed until she felt more awake. She sat up and rubbed her eyes until she spotted Sam watching her in a chair by the window.

He smiled. "Have a good nap?"

"Yes, it was wonderful." She swung her legs over the side of the bed and stood. Suddenly she knew exactly why she was so tired.

Angeline made haste to the bathroom, hoping against hope there were rags in there for her to use. She now knew for certain there was no baby to celebrate. It was simply her monthly courses.

She shut the door before Sam could ask her any questions. After a brief search, she found something suitable in the cabinet in the corner of the bathing room. She took care of herself, then went back out to the bedroom. Sam was standing there watching her with his dark gaze questioning.

"Everything all right?"

She smiled sadly. "Yes, everything's fine. I'm definitely not pregnant though."

Sam's shoulders deflated and disappointment flashed across his face. "Oh, ah, I guess that's just the way it is then."

He turned away, but not before she saw a deeper emotion in his gaze.

Angeline took his hand and tugged. "Just because there's no baby today doesn't mean we won't make one in a week or a month."

"I know." He kept his eyes averted until she took hold of his chin and forced him to look at her.

"I love you, Sam. This is simply a bump in the road, nothing more."

"I just wanted, well, I wanted to have a family with you and when I thought you were pregnant, I was overjoyed." He blew out a breath. "It sounds silly, hmm?"

She pulled him into an embrace, holding him tightly. "No, not silly. I want a family with you too, Sam. When it's our time, it will happen."

He kissed her forehead, her nose, then her lips. "My Angel."

Her stomach picked that moment to rumble noisily. He laughed and she blushed.

"Let's go find something to eat."

Downstairs, they made their way to the kitchen and caused a ruckus when they tried to get some food. The cook and somebody with a big ladle chased them out and told them to wait in the dining room. Angeline was embarrassed and Sam was furious.

"I want to go home, Sam. I want to be able to eat when I'm hungry and not wait for someone to make it for me." She fiddled with the lace tablecloth on the table.

"We've only been here two days."

Angeline sighed. "I know."

He sat beside her. "Truthfully, I want to go home too. I have to meet with Mr. Bennington later to sign some papers, but then we can catch the train in the morning."

Angeline felt better just making plans to go back to Wyoming. "Really?"

"Really." She climbed onto his lap and started kissing him. Soon their kisses turned heated, then molten. She felt his hardness pressing into her hip and wished they could go upstairs and spend the afternoon making love. That, however, wasn't going to happen for a few days.

"Ahem."

Angeline looked up to see the aunts all standing in the doorway. She smiled and waved; the three older women laughed.

"I heard we were having tea and cake." Gertrude, the aunt with the blue eyes, glanced around the dining room. "I don't see any though."

"Perhaps they ate it all." Alison was the youngest, with apple cheeks and a ready smile.

"Or perhaps they were too busy to order it." Jane raised her brows.

Angeline extricated herself from Sam's lap and got back into her own chair with a sheepish grin.

"We have something to tell you all." Sam looked at his aunts, no longer smiling. "We're going to go back to Wyoming tomorrow."

Protests immediately ensued and he held up his hands. "We love you all, but we miss home. Angeline and I both agreed we'll come visit regularly and she is already planning to write to you."

"We don't want you to leave so soon, but I guess we can't stop you." Gertrude frowned.

"We could hide the carriage," Alison suggested.

"We could hide the horses," Jane countered.

"Ladies, we'll be back, I promise. But for now, we need to go home and start on that house. I want to get it built by the fall so we can be cozy all winter long." Sam rose and hugged each of his aunts in turn.

Angeline's eyes teared up as she witnessed the genuine affection that had developed between them so quickly. She liked the warmth of the Carver family and felt blessed to be a part of it. When the aunts came to hug her, a few tears slid from her eyes.

They were interrupted when the maid arrived with the coffee, tea, and cakes. Angeline gladly sat at the table with her husband and her new family. She enjoyed every second spent with them, secure in the knowledge she was loved.

Sam stood at the door while Angeline hugged each of his aunts for the third time. She was so well liked and apparently liked them so much, it was a very teary, extended good-bye. Their train left in less than an hour, but he didn't want to rush her. They had the rest of their lives, of course, even if it took her half an hour to bid his family farewell.

"Don't you forget, Angeline, we're your family now too. You come visit us anytime you want." Jane squeezed Angeline's hands. The older woman glowed in a brilliant blue dress as the sun shone on them through the open door.

"And I hope one day you can visit us. Once we get the new house built, that is." Sam glanced at his father's pocket watch, running his thumb over the brass cover.

"That's Michael's, isn't it?" Gertrude noticed Sam's fiddling.

"Yes, it is." He blew out a breath. He was glad to have met his aunts, but he still grieved for his father.

"Our daddy gave that to him on his eighteenth birthday." Alison eyed the watch. "It was Michael's prized possession. I'm so glad he kept it all these years so it could pass to you."

Jane led Angeline to his side. "Don't wait another thirty years to come see us."

Sam smiled. "Don't worry. I plan on visiting you enough that you'll be tired of seeing us."

"Never." Jane hugged both of them. "Now be off with you. I don't like long good-byes."

Well, it was too late for that, but Sam decided it wasn't

prudent to say anything. He and Angeline left the Carver mansion and headed home to Wyoming. Sam took one last glance as they started down the street. The house was bigger than the entire main street in Forestville.

He knew they'd be back in Denver, but for now he needed to go back to where he belonged. "Let's go home."

Angeline smiled and he knew they'd made the right decision.

Chapter Fourteen

October blew in chilly, with the promise of a cold winter. Their new house was nearly done. The roof was two stories above the ground and the interior was simply beautiful. A huge picture window in the bedroom would bring in the morning sun, while a wraparound porch would allow them to watch the sunset.

It was idyllic. It was perfect.

The leaves were almost off the trees and Sam could hardly wait to move into the house. It had been a year since his Angel had come to Forestville, but it seemed like a lifetime ago.

They walked arm in arm to the Blue Plate for dinner. They wanted to celebrate not only the imminent completion of the house, but the anniversary of Angeline's arrival. She told him he was silly, but he insisted.

No matter how many new clothes she could have, she still wore his mother's wool coat. It was sturdy and warm, and she told him, "It's a piece of your mother. Since I never met her, it's the closest thing I have to a part of her."

He didn't ask her again to buy a new one. To be honest, he was touched by her sentimentality. She was just slightly round, only two months pregnant and very healthy. He could hardly wait to meet their child in the spring.

They arrived at the restaurant and said hello to everyone. Lettie still worked there because she said she liked it. The people of Forestville were one great big family.

They sat near the center of the room so they could talk to everyone as they passed. Lettie brought them coffee with one brow raised.

"You gonna tell everyone soon?"

Sam chuckled at Lettie's perceptiveness. Angeline opened her mouth to answer when a shot split the air. Someone screamed and Sam jumped to his feet, putting both women behind him.

He saw three men by the door. Two were older with graying hair and black clothes. The third had the gun in his hand, smoke curling from the barrel. He was dark, hard looking, and had another pistol slung low on his hip. Sam knew he was facing a man who killed for money.

He whipped around to look at Lettie and saw true fear on her face. Angeline gasped and that's when he realized one of the older men must be Josiah. There was no other man in the world who could possibly strike fear into both women's hearts. Sam's protective instincts surged forward and his jaw tightened so hard his teeth almost cracked. It had been months since they'd seen Jonathan Morton. Yet somehow Josiah Brown had found Angeline.

The taller man, whipcord thin with dead eyes, pointed at Angeline. "This slut is my wife in the eyes of God."

"Get out of here." Sam kept his eyes on the hired gun, but he spoke to the old man. "She is not your wife in any way at all. She's my wife."

"She has lain with me, said vows with me, and lived in my house. She is *my wife*." Josiah stepped forward, his hands locked behind his back. He had a commanding presence and blazing eyes; clearly, he was a man who was used to having the attention of a room.

Sheriff Booth rose to his feet from the corner table, hand on his pistol. "Why don't we step outside and sort this out, fellas?"

Josiah ignored him. "There is nothing to sort out. Her name is Angeline Brown and she is *my wife*."

"Well, near as I can figure it, she's Sam's wife." Booth tugged his hat down lower and widened his stance. "I saw the wedding myself back in June."

"How dare you?" Josiah walked toward Sam and Angeline, his face a mask of rage and hate. "You dare defile our holy union?"

Angeline rose to her feet and put herself between Sam and the man who claimed her as his wife.

"How dare *you*? You are not my husband. You're not even a man." She looked like an avenging angel. "Leave now and never come back."

Josiah slapped her so hard, she fell into Sam. Then all hell broke loose. Jessup appeared from somewhere and jumped on the other older man, while Booth dealt with the gunslinger. Sam heard a screech of pure fury and a body flew at Josiah.

Lettie scratched, slapped, and punched him while Sam held Angeline close. The older woman seemed to have the strength of ten men as she beat the man who had abused her so horribly.

Sam started to back away toward the kitchen, but Angeline resisted.

"I won't leave her like this. I can't."

Sam understood her loyalty, but he didn't want things to get more violent than they already were. "Please, Angel, I don't want anything to happen to you. To the baby."

"It won't, not if we stand together."

Although Sam's instincts told him to do all he could to protect his wife and child, he respected her choice. He would stand by her side, and fight her battles with her.

He glanced over and saw the gunfighter punch Booth so hard, the sheriff fell like a sack of potatoes onto the floor. With a feral grin, the gunslinger focused his gaze on Angeline and took aim.

Time seemed to slow to a crawl as Sam ran toward the man with the gun. He shouted at Angeline to run, but the muzzle of the gun flashed in mere seconds. Sam tackled the man and the gun went flying. He felt out of control and possessed by a black rage he'd never experienced before. Punches, blood, and spittle flew as he knelt on the man's chest and pummeled him.

"Sam!" Angeline's voice cut through the red haze surrounding him.

His hands were covered in blood and his knuckles throbbed. "Angel?"

"Sam, Jessup's been shot."

Sam rose to his feet as if in a daze, drawn by Angeline's voice. He saw Jessup lying on the floor in a pool of blood. The world tilted sideways as Sam walked toward him. He heard someone crying and realized it was Lettie. She sat next to Angeline, her face a mass of welts and smears of blood.

"What happened?" Sam dropped to his knees as his heart began to beat so hard, it actually hurt his head.

"He saved me." Angeline had tears running down her face. "He threw himself in front of the b-bullet." Her blue eyes were full of grief.

Sam took his friend's hand in his. "Jessup, what the hell did you do?"

Jessup's eyes fluttered open and he smiled as he focused on Sam. "You know I ain't never had a son or a nephew. I kinda thought you were a good one to pick." He coughed, blood spewing from his mouth.

Sam wiped his eyes and finally looked at the gaping wound

in Jessup's chest. He'd seen too many wounds on the field to have even a shred of hope the older man would survive the bullet. Jessup was already dying.

"You old coot, I don't know what I'll do without you." His voice broke as he allowed himself to face his friend's death.

"Sam, you're a good man, and you have a good woman." Jessup looked at Angeline. "You have an angel at your side."

Before Sam could say anything else, Jessup slipped away, his chest still, his eyes unfocused. Angeline made a soft noise of distress and took Sam's hand.

This time the howl that erupted from within him was the primal sound of a warrior. Angeline jumped back from him as did Lettie.

"Where is he?"

The women shook their heads.

"The bastard you used to call husband. Where is he? And that other man too?" Sam got to his feet, his friend's blood staining his hands.

"He ran like the coward he is." Lettie's gaze was as feral as his own. "After I beat him, he proved himself to be as much of a coward as I thought he was."

"And that other man, who was he?"

Angeline glanced at Lettie before she looked back at Jessup's body. "My father."

Sam could hardly fathom that the man was her father. He'd accompanied a hired killer and the man who'd beaten his daughter to Forestville. Though he'd had no part in the actual shooting, he hadn't done a thing to stop it. He was as bad as Sam had feared. Now was not the time to be discussing Mr. Hunter's obvious flaws though. Now was the time to hunt the sons of bitches down.

Sam pointed at the two women. "Stay here and keep everyone safe. You can protect them."

Both of them rose, their backs straight and their faces set.

They looked like female warriors, ready to do battle for those they loved. He wouldn't have chosen anyone different to keep the rest of the group safe while he dealt with the sons of bitches who dared shoot up his town, his *family*.

Booth was bloodied but alive, waving Sam on. Sam saw Pieter protecting Marta in the corner.

Sam nodded at the hired gun.

"Make sure that son of a bitch gets tied up."

Pieter nodded and walked toward the unconscious stranger. Sam knew the man would be secured and in the jail before long. Now it was time to go on the hunt.

Before he stepped outside, Sam scooped up the gunslinger's weapons. He planned on killing Josiah, not only for Jessup's murder, but for Angeline and Lettie. Sam would protect his own.

He heard footsteps behind him and glanced back to see Angeline running toward him, her dress spattered with blood.

"What are you doing?"

"I'm going with you." Her jaw was tight and her chin set.

"No, you're not." Sam refused to allow his wife to put herself into danger again.

"Yes, I am. That's my father and my, um, former husband. I am tired of running, tired of hiding. I want this done with *now*." She marched down the street, leaving Sam to catch up.

He grabbed her arm, stopping her with more force than he'd meant. "Angel, there's likely to be guns involved. I don't want to be a widower yet."

"Men of the Mormon church do not carry guns."

Sam's anger surged again. "No, they just hire gunslingers to do their killing for them." He held up the pistols for her to see. There was no visible blood on the barrel, but he saw it just the same. He carried the instrument of Jessup's death in his hand. It nearly made him vomit.

"I know. I'm sorry." Her chin trembled, but her back stayed straight as a rod.

He blew out a frustrated sigh. "This gun in my hand killed a member of my family, a man who was my friend. I don't plan on letting the men responsible just walk out of this town. I can't."

"Mormon men don't walk either, especially elders." Her eyes widened as she realized what she said. "They'll probably have a wagon or carriage."

"The livery." Sam started running, somehow hoping Angeline wouldn't keep up. He meant what he told her—he didn't want to be responsible for her death too. This wasn't vengeance as much as it was justice. He didn't believe killing the man who'd killed Jessup would solve anything, but he was damn sure not going to sit idly by and let Josiah Brown escape so he could hire another killer.

He heard footsteps right behind him and realized not only hadn't she gone back to the restaurant, but she was fast enough to keep up with him. Granted he had a leg that didn't work so good, but sheer rage drove him to ignore any pain.

In the distance, he heard Booth calling him, but Sam had no intention of slowing down for anyone. Angeline stayed behind him the entire way to the livery. They were only minutes behind the two older men; no doubt Sam would arrive in time to stop the old bastards. He'd run after a damn carriage if he had to.

The door was wide open, which meant someone was inside. Sam burst in, his heart thumping like a horse and his breath coming in gasps. Splinters lodged in his shoulders as he pushed the inner door open.

The two older men in black were apparently trying to put the traces on the team themselves. Neither one of them seemed to know what he was doing. When Sam burst in, he saw anger in the one man's gaze, and a glimmer of fear in the other's. The thin, angry one was Josiah. His face was covered in welts and scratches—obviously Lettie had gotten some good swipes in before he threw her off.

Behind him, Angeline gulped in air as she stepped up beside him. Her presence actually gave him a boost of strength he didn't expect.

"Where the hell do you think you're going?" Sam snarled.

"We are leaving this Godforsaken town." The man Sam assumed was Angeline's father spoke as if Forestville was beneath his notice.

"Father, why are you here?" Angeline's voice was steady.

"I thought to show you the error of your ways. To bring God back into your soul, but I am too late. From now on, I do not acknowledge you as my daughter. You are dead to me, dead to my church. I am ashamed to even be here."

Sam winced inwardly at Mr. Hunter's harsh words.

"Then why are you here?" she repeated as she walked toward him, an avenging angel in a bloody dress.

"I had to see for myself just what a whore you've become."

Sam growled and surged forward, but Angeline stayed his hand by putting her body between them.

"You are the one who should be ashamed. You made me into a whore—his whore." She pointed at the thin man. "The man who used pain and humiliation and perversion each day to bring himself pleasure."

Josiah's face flushed red and he shook with what Sam assumed was rage. Mr. Hunter glanced at him with a narrowed gaze.

"You lie, Angeline. This man is beyond reproach, a humble man of God who was saddled with wives who disobeyed him." Mr. Hunter turned his back on Angeline.

Sam heard her breath catch, but she didn't move, didn't back away.

"He is a sadistic bastard and I wish he'd been the one to die back there." Her voice was full of pure hate.

Josiah had yet to say a word, but Sam could see he was itching to. Angeline walked toward him.

"I want you to leave here and never come back. Do you hear me? Don't send any more gunslingers or killers either." She pointed a shaking finger at him. "You will burn in hell for what you've done, but I refuse to allow you another moment in my life. I *refuse*."

The man's smile was feral as he witnessed her brave words. Sam was proud of her, but he was terrified something would happen. She was so small, and she had a babe in her belly. Sam would go loco if anything happened to either of them.

"You are my wife and will always be my wife." He grabbed her so quickly Sam had no time to react. Josiah wrapped his hand around her hair and yanked, bringing her to her knees. "Now you're not so brave, are you, little one?"

"Let her go." Sam didn't recognize his own voice as he aimed the pistol at the man who dared threaten his wife. His thumb landed on the hammer and cocked it.

Josiah's grin widened. "Oh, no, I never plan on letting this one go. She's perfect for my needs and she's already my wife in the eyes of God."

"You are an abomination in the eyes of God." Sam pulled the hammer back. "Now let her go or I will put a new hole in your head. You will not hurt my wife."

Angeline, however, had one more surprise up her sleeve. She twisted one way, then the other, and suddenly she was free of the man's grasp. She scuttled away from him, hissing like a cat. When she got to the stall wall, she scrambled to her feet, unbroken and undefeated. She was a warrior at heart.

"You may never touch me again. Do you hear me, Josiah? You have no right. I've taken control of my life and my future and you have no place in it."

Sam didn't lower the gun because he could see Josiah wasn't done yet. The older man had the look of a snake, one who would allow his prey some room to fight, but not escape.

"I have every right. You are my wife and you will obey." Josiah circled around her and she backed away from him. "God has commanded you to be mine."

"God did not command me." Angeline glanced at her father. "My father did." Mr. Hunter did nothing but keep his back turned to her.

"Be that as it may, you cannot change the past. And your handsome young man can't either."

Sam knew something was going to happen. The hairs on the back of his neck stood up. He felt a whisper near his ear that sounded like "gun." In a flash he understood that although the Mormon elders didn't carry guns or walk anywhere, Josiah was armed.

The older man brought the weapon out from beneath his coat, but instead of aiming at Sam, he turned it toward Angeline. A shot split the air and Sam screamed her name. Yet it wasn't she who fell to her knees. Josiah did.

A hole appeared in his forehead and he pitched forward into the hay. Sam looked behind him to see Jonathan Morton with a smoking pistol in his hand. He had gotten cleaned up in the months since he'd been gone and his eyes were focused and clear.

"Jonathan." Angeline stared at her old beau with astonishment. "You killed him."

"You killed him!" Mr. Hunter picked that moment to start ranting. "Jonathan Aloysius Morton! Your soul will burn in hell for the crime of murder. You have committed a cardinal sin."

Jonathan leveled the gun at the older man. "I can always make that two sins."

Mr. Hunter held up his hands and looked at Angeline. As if she would help him because he was outnumbered and in trouble. "Daughter, tell your young man he cannot threaten me."

"He's not my young man and he's obviously not concerned

about the Mormon church any longer." She stepped toward Jonathan. "Thank you for saving my life."

When she kissed his cheek, the young man closed his eyes for only a second, but Sam saw the longing in his gaze. The kid was still in love with Angeline, but he was too late. She was Mrs. Carver now and always.

"You're welcome." Jonathan frowned at Angeline's father. "As for you, Silas, what are you going to tell the folks back in Tolson? That you sold your daughter to Josiah or that you hired a killer to bring back her body?"

Mr. Hunter paled. "You wouldn't tell them that."

"Oh, yes, I would. You will simply tell them Josiah died from a snake bite and you could not find Angeline. But you heard a tale she had died in a carriage accident going to visit a sick relative." Jonathan grinned at Angeline. "She was always such an angel to everyone."

"Thank you." Sam held out his hand and to his surprise, Jonathan shook it.

"I did it for her, not for you. There's no force on earth that could make me save your life." At least the kid was honest. Sam had no doubt he'd like another crack at kicking his ass. "I'll go back to Tolson with Silas, make sure he tells everyone the right tale. I think my mission is finally done and perhaps God has a new path for me to follow."

"Good luck, Jonathan." Angeline turned to look at her father. "Good-bye to you, Mr. Hunter. I wish you good journey."

Like a true lady, she walked to Sam's side and took his arm. Together they left the barn. Beneath her warriorlike exterior, her bloody dress and bruised cheek, she was trembling. Sam felt the same way and couldn't wait to put all of this darkness behind him. First though, he had to bury his friend.

Angeline went back into the restaurant and found Karen and Marta scrubbing the floor. She couldn't bear to look at the bloodstain, so she walked quickly to the kitchen to find Lettie.

She found her beating the dough so hard, it might rise to a foot high. Lettie looked up at her when she walked in the door.

"Josiah's dead."

Lettie cried out softly and sank to the floor, her arms wrapped around herself. Angeline rushed over and crouched beside her.

"He and my father were trying to leave, to run like cowards, and Sam and I tried to stop them. Josiah tried to force me to go with them, but I wouldn't allow it." Angeline tried to tell the story without reliving every intense moment, but it was so hard to detach herself from the tale. "Josiah was about to shoot me when Jonathan killed him."

Lettie's head jerked up at that and she stared at Angeline hard. "Jonathan?"

"Believe it or not. If he hadn't shot Josiah, I'd be dead right now." Angeline began shaking as the reality of what had happened sank in. She had come close to death again. The man who had been her husband had tried to kill her, not only her, but her unborn child.

Lettie put her arm around Angeline's shaking shoulders and pulled her close. They sat beneath the counter, giving each other strength, coming to terms with what was truly an end to the dark times. The man who had hurt them both, had hunted them, was dead.

They were finally free.

Sam walked back toward the lake after visiting the cemetery. He missed Jessup, who was now buried next to Michael Carver. It was a fitting resting place for the two men who had been important to him.

It had been a week since the old man's death and Sam and

Angeline were moving into the new house that day. Sam arrived back at the house just as a wagon pulled up outside covered in a huge tarp. He frowned, wondering who or what was in there.

A driver jumped down and hailed him. "You there, are you Samuel Carver?"

"Yes, I am." Sam walked toward the wagon, filled with curiosity.

"I got a delivery for you." The man was a typical driver with a mouthful of chaw and a layer of dirt from driving a team across dusty ground. He could have been twenty or forty—there was no way to tell.

"What is it?"

"I dunno. I didn't look 'neath the tarp. I just brought the wagon here." The man started untying the ropes.

"Are you saying the entire wagon is the delivery?" Sam gaped at the enormous pile.

"Ayup." He finished one side of the wagon, then yanked the tarp over to the right side.

"What's going on, Sam?" Angeline stepped out on the front porch, a blue shawl wrapped around her shoulders.

"I think Aunt Jane has sent us a gift for our house." No doubt his effusive aunt thought they could use something or a lot of somethings.

"What is it?"

Sam jumped up and started untying the burlap sacks and ropes on the back of the wagon. As he untied everything, he found furniture, including a sofa, a table and chairs, a wingback chair, rugs, and even a kitchen stool.

"I think she's furnishing our entire house." He couldn't believe the number of things on the wagon, but what really made him pause was the fact the furniture was all handmade and it was all exactly what he would have picked.

Jane had gone to a great deal of trouble to give them a gift just right for their new home. He should send the wagon back, but he knew she meant it as a gift of love. He grinned at Angeline as she gaped at the pile.

"Makes your new rocking chair look small, doesn't it?"

Angeline laughed. "What was she thinking? There's so much here."

"I think she wanted to make sure we felt at home." Sam jumped down and pulled her into a hug. "You know, I think we're going to need help with all this."

Angeline grinned. "I think you're right."

She walked into town and asked for help from folks, and soon a small army arrived, including almost everyone from the Blue Plate and the sheriff. Like a team of people who were used to working together, they unloaded the furniture.

Angeline directed the placement of each piece, while the rest kept bringing more in. Soon the house was full of beautiful furniture. Sam looked around with wonder at how the empty house had become a home.

"It's all so beautiful." Angeline smiled at him. "We'll need to send a wire to Jane to say thank you."

"Mr. Carver," the driver called from outside. "I got one more package for you."

"Go on. I'm going to get some cold water and cornbread for our helpers." She went into the kitchen and left Sam to deal with whatever else Jane had sent.

Sam stepped back outside and found the scruffy driver waiting for him at the door. The man handed him a small parcel wrapped in brown paper and twine.

An hour later, he watched as Angeline walked around the house, touching each piece of furniture with amazement. He should have expected something extravagant from Jane, but this went beyond anything he'd imagined. It was so much all at once.

Everyone had gone home and instead of the house feeling

empty, it felt warm and cozy. She picked up her new black-and-brass kindling bucket and headed toward the door.

Sam stopped her from leaving the house. She frowned at him and set down the bucket.

"What is it?"

"Sit down, Angel. There's something I need to tell you."

He led her to the kitchen table and sat down. It wasn't bad news, but he wanted her to be sitting when he told her what he knew.

"Coffee?" She wiped her hands and headed for the stove.

"No, please just sit." He set the papers in the middle of the table. "When we were in Denver in August, I asked Jane for a favor. Since I'd found my family, I wanted to give you the same gift and find your sister."

Angeline's face drained of color as she sank into the chair. "What are you saying?"

"If there is one thing money can do, it can make people talk. I knew that if I asked Jane, she could find Eliza." Sam pointed to the papers. "This came with the wagon from Jane. I think you should read it."

Angeline stared at the papers. "What does it say?"

"You need to read for yourself." Sam knew what the papers contained, but it was her sister, therefore it was her right to know what Jane had found.

With shaking hands, Angeline opened the sheaf of papers and started reading. After she read the note on top from Jane, she gasped and looked at him.

"They found Eliza?"

Sam smiled. "Keep reading."

She read through the rest of the papers, then read them again. Her hand went to her mouth and a sob escaped.

"She's in Idaho?"

"Lives in a cabin in the mountains with her husband, a man named Grady Wolfe." He felt nothing but love for his wife as joy spread across her face.

"Can we go visit them? Please? I need to see her."

"And we will. I promise. I think we should wait until spring—"

"No, I want to go as soon as we can. I want to see them by Christmas." She took his hands and squeezed tightly. "Please, I need to see her."

Sam brought her to her feet and pulled her into a hug. "Yes, we can go visit them. I think we should at least finish moving into the house, then ask Lettie to stay here while we're gone." He looked into her beautiful blue eyes. "Are you sure you want to do this? You are pregnant and I don't want anything to happen to you."

She cupped his face. "Nothing is more important to me than you and this baby. We have months and months until I give birth, so this is a perfect time we'll have to find them. From what I've read, their cabin is hard to find, so we'll need to hire a guide."

"Angel, I'll do whatever you want. You're my whole world." He could still hardly believe she was his wife and that she loved him as much as he loved her.

Angeline ran her hands through his hair. "How did I get so lucky?"

He snorted. "Woman, I'm the lucky one. You are like a shining star, almost too bright and shiny for me. I'm just a half-breed who can swing a hammer."

She pressed her forehead to his. "We are truly blessed, Sam. Truly blessed."

He felt a breeze on the back of his neck and a whisper that sounded like "love." Sam said good-bye to his mother's spirit and hello to his new life with Angeline. Nothing had ever felt so right.

It took two months to track down the exact location of the cabin. On Christmas Eve, they trekked the ten miles from the small town at the base of the Rocky Mountains. Angeline's stomach jumped around like a fish, floppy and jittery. She told herself there was nothing to be frightened of. They had a guide, were wearing sturdy clothes, and had plenty of time to get there before nightfall.

It didn't matter a whit to her stomach. She was still so scared about seeing Eliza. According to the detective's report, Eliza had married the gunslinger, the man who had tried to kill Angeline.

They rode up to the cabin nestled in a valley covered with a foot of snow winking like diamonds in the sunlight. Towering trees hung over a brook that was frozen in the cold of the Idaho winter. A small red barn with a corral lay to the left of the house.

It was more than just a house. It was a beautiful home. Angeline was glad Eliza had settled there, finding a perfect place for herself.

They dismounted and walked toward the door. Their boots echoed as they walked across the porch. Angeline took off her thick mittens and knocked.

She heard a voice from inside. "Who the hell is that?" The deep voice sent a shiver up her spine. It was enough to make her want to hightail it back to Wyoming, but she waited. She was more eager to see Eliza than to run from her new brother-in-law.

Angeline heard laughter; then the door opened. Eliza stood in the doorway, her mouth agape, looking happier and healthier than Angeline had ever seen her.

"Merry Christmas, Eliza."

Eliza turned to look at her husband, who stood there with a gun in his hand. She turned back to Angeline and opened her arms. "Merry Christmas, Angeline."

Mark Chambers closed the door of Marianne's Diner and glanced back through the paned window. The woman he'd passed as he turned into the parking lot was walking toward the building.

Sunshine backlit her so he couldn't make out her features, but he saw a dazzling halo of white-gold curls, a slim silhouette, and a long, loose skirt that was so filmy the sunshine cut straight through it, outlining her long legs. All the way to the apex, where the breeze plastered the fabric against her thighs and the sweet triangle between them.

Lust rippled though him, thickening his blood, shocking him. He didn't make a habit of lusting after strangers—usually he was so caught up in work he barely noticed women—but the picture she made was strikingly erotic. And it was . . . hmm. Months since he'd had sex, now that he came to think about it.

"Good afternoon," a voice behind him said, and he swung away from the door.

Behind the restaurant counter, a middle-aged African-American woman with short, curly hair and round cheeks smiled at him. "Take a seat wherever you like."

The place, a renovated fifties-sixties diner, was maybe half full, all the patrons seated in booths or at tables. He chose a bar stool and dropped his reading material, the latest issue of the *Journal of Experimental Marine Biology and Ecology,* on the blue Formica counter. "Thanks. Could I get a coffee and a menu?"

"You bet." She poured a mug of coffee and handed it to him along with a plastic menu. "The fruit pies are great if you're in the mood for something sweet."

For him, things fell into one of two categories: those to be taken seriously and those that weren't worth paying attention to. Food fell in the latter category.

Coffee, though . . . He lifted the mug to his lips and sniffed. Mmm. Rich, robust, not acidic.

He should have asked if the beans were fair trade, but he doubted the answer would be yes, and he needed coffee. Every man was entitled to one indulgence. Though, to be strictly accurate, as he tried to be, it was more of an addiction. Even if the stuff was poorly made, as was so often the case, he'd still drink it. Now, he savored the scent a moment longer, then lifted the mug to his lips and took a sip.

Well, now. Another sip, to confirm his first impression. "This is excellent," he told the woman approvingly. If you were going to do a job, you should do it well.

Behind his back, the diner door opened and closed. It'd be the blonde. And it would be rude to swing around and look.

"Thanks," the woman behind the counter said. "You should try the fresh strawberry pie."

"Strawberry pie?" The feminine voice from behind him was light, eager, like a kid who'd been offered a present.

A moment later, she slid onto the stool beside him, and this time he did look.

She was stunning in a totally natural way. Her face was heart-shaped, fine-boned, glowing with a golden tan and a flush of sun across her cheeks and nose. A tangled mass of white gold ringlets tumbled over her shoulders, half hiding a scattering of colorful butterflies tattooed on her upper arm and shoulder.

Then he gazed at her eyes, and oh, man. They were the dazzling mixed blue-greens of the Caribbean, and he was diving in, losing himself in their depths.

Vaguely he was aware of the diner woman saying, "So you'll have the strawberry pie, miss?"

He blinked and dragged himself back before he drowned.

The blonde's delicate tongue-tip came out and flicked naturally pink lips, and again lust slammed through him. She shook her head and said wistfully, "Just a chamomile tea, thanks. So, are you Marianne?"

"That's right, hon. This is my place. One chamomile coming up."

Chamomile tea? That jarred him out of his reverie. Might as well drink lawn clippings in hot water; it'd taste as good. Alicia, his biological mother, had been big on the stuff. And why didn't the blonde order the pie she'd sounded so enthusiastic about? Was she one of those constant dieters?

She sure didn't need to be. He'd seen her legs through that filmy flower-patterned blue skirt. Above it, her faded blue tank top revealed toned shoulders and arms. Full little breasts, unconfined by a bra.

Pink-tipped nipples. Not brown. Somehow, he knew that.

Shit, what was wrong with him?

Besides a growing erection that made him glad his cargo shorts were loose and his tank untucked. He'd been in tropical places where women walked around almost naked and not had so strong a reaction. Okay, he was a man of science. He could analyze this phenomenon logically. It was a simple combination of a bodily need that had gone too long unsatisfied and a woman who was a lovely physical specimen. Perfectly understandable, even if disconcerting.

When he returned his gaze to her face, she urged, "Have the pie." Ocean-colored eyes dancing, she added, "Maybe if

I'm really, really nice to you, you'll let me have a taste." Her tongue flicked out again.

Blood rushed to his groin as he imagined that pink tongue lapping his shaft. The blonde would be appalled if she had any idea what he was thinking.

Unless . . . His friend and colleague Adrienne—whom he'd known since grad school—said women found him attractive, though he never noticed it himself. The blonde couldn't be flirting, could she? No. No possible way. She could have any man she wanted, so why would she want a science geek like him?

The diner woman put a small china teapot and a mug in front of her and she said, "Thanks, Marianne."

"I'll have the pie," he choked out.

"Sure you will," Marianne said with a knowing grin. She glanced at the blonde. "Whipped cream?"

"Is there any other way?"

He imagined the blonde painting his cock in whipped cream and licking it all off, and wanted to bury his face in his hands and groan. Since he'd first seen her, he'd been . . . bewitched. Except, there was no such thing as bewitchment in scientific reality. This was very unsettling. He rather desperately fingered the scientific journal he'd brought in with him. If he buried himself in its pages, he'd be on safe ground.

"You'd rather read than talk to me?" she teased. "My feelings are hurt."

"Uh . . ." He glanced back at her.

Her impish grin revealed perfect white teeth. "If we're going to share . . ." She paused.

He held his breath. Share? What man wouldn't want to share any damned thing with this woman?

"Pie," she finished, "I figure we should introduce ourselves." She held out a slim hand with short, unpainted nails and several unusual rings. "Jenna Fallon."

"Mark Chambers." He took her hand warily. Sure enough, when she shook firmly, he felt a sexy sensation. A cross between a glow and a tingle spread up his arm. He hurriedly let go, picked up his coffee mug, and took a sip, trying to regain his equilibrium. "You live around here, Jenna?" Likely so, since she'd been on foot.

She shook her head, curls dancing, revealing a couple of simple stud earrings in each ear, then settling. "I'm from Canada. Been living in Santa Cruz, working on a peregrine falcon survey that's run out of UC Santa Cruz."

"Great," he said with relief. She was into the environment like him. A colleague, not a woman. Well, of course she was a woman, but he was okay when he dealt with them as colleagues. He was actually okay in bed, too; sex was one of the activities that deserved to be done well, and his partners always seemed happy. It was the in-between stuff, the social part, that gave him problems.

Carefully, she poured a disgustingly weak greenish brew from the pot into her mug, sipped, and smiled. Eyes bright, she said, "It's part of a really successful conservation project. Did you know the falcons are an endangered species in California? In 1970, they only found two nesting pairs. Now, after a captive breeding program, there are over two hundred and fifty."

On firm conversational ground now, he said, "Yeah, the DDT and other pesticides almost did them in. Thank God those have been banned, and the captive breeding programs worked." He studied her. "Bet it was a challenge to track them down. They have a habit of nesting in remote areas."

When her eyes widened in surprise, he said, "I'm a marine biologist, and I've learned a fair bit about marine birds. Oddly enough, I've been in Santa Cruz too. Working on a research project at UCSC's Long Marine Lab."

"Seriously? Isn't this wild? We never met in Santa Cruz,

yet we both happen to walk into Marianne's Diner at the same moment." She grinned. "The universe is pretty amazing."

"Yes, it is." A place of science and of still-to-be understood mysteries. A place mankind seemed hell-bent on destroying. He knew people often found him rigid, but he had no patience for those who didn't give a damn about this incredible world.

Marianne refilled his coffee and put a plate in front of him. He barely glanced at it, except to note two forks, until Jenna enthused, "Now, that's a work of art."

He took another look. Flaky-looking crust, plump red strawberries suspended in glaze, a mound of whipped cream. Not bad at all.

Jenna told the other woman, "Neal at the service station sent me your way, and I'm sure glad." She picked up a fork, then gazed up at Mark with wide, expectant eyes.

How could he say no to those eyes? "Go ahead. I have a feeling I'd have trouble stopping you." He only spoke the truth, but she grinned as if he'd said something amusing.

She carved off a sizable chunk—an entire, huge berry, a portion of crust, and a hefty dollop of cream, and opened those pink lips wide to take it in. Her eyes slid shut, and she tilted her head back, humming approval as she chewed, taking forever to consume that one bite. The sounds she made and the blissful expression on her face reminded him of slow, very satisfying lovemaking.

His cock throbbed and he swallowed hard, wanting what she was having.

Finally she opened her eyes and beamed at Marianne. "Perfection." Then she frowned down at the plate and up at Mark. "Aren't you having any?"

Pie, she meant pie. "I was . . ." *Watching you get orgasmic.* "Uh, waiting for you to taste-test."

"It's delicious." She dug in her fork again. "Here."

Next thing he knew, that laden fork was in front of his lips. Startled, he opened and let her slide the hefty bite into his mouth.

"Close your eyes," she said. "Things taste better that way."

Yeah, if he kept staring at her beautiful, animated face, he wouldn't taste a thing, so he obeyed even though he felt weirdly vulnerable about shutting his eyes while she gazed so expectantly at him.

Normally, when he ate, his mind was on work not on food, but now he concentrated as he chewed. Ripe, juicy fruit, the sweetness of the glaze, a rich, buttery taste to the pastry, and unsweetened cream with a hint of vanilla. Each flavor was distinct and the way they blended together was . . . perfect.

And don't miss a sexy game of
TRUTH OR DEMON by Kathy Love,
coming next month!

What the hell?

Killian blinked up at the unfamiliar ceiling—a dingy white ceiling. Not the crisp, new, white ceiling at home. Nor was he in his own bed. This one was decidedly feminine, covered in a ruffled bedspread plastered with pink and red cabbage roses. Nothing like his black silk sheets.

He glanced to the right to see an antique nightstand with a lamp that looked as if it came from a yard sale circa 1959 sat on top in its full flowered and beaded glory. An Agatha Christie was opened, facedown on the doily-covered surface. Several medication bottles were lined up beside that.

Great, not only was he in a strange bed, but it appeared to be that of an elderly woman.

He glanced to his left, hoping he'd see something that would make sense to him. He definitely needed an explanation for this predicament—and why he didn't seem to recall how he got there. But instead of some clue, he found someone staring back at him.

The ugliest, mangiest cat he'd ever seen. It stared at him with its one good eye. An eerie yellow eye. While the other was adhered together into a crusted black line. Its long, white hair—or at least he thought it was white—had a matted, gray tinge like it had rolled in ashes. Damp ashes.

Maybe Killian was still in Hell. But he suspected that even demons would throw this thing back.

Keeping his movements slow and subtle, Killian levered himself up onto his elbows, concerned even the slightest move would to set the beast into attack mode.

The cat hissed, its back arching and his tail, once broken or maybe just as naturally ugly as the rest of it, shot up like a tattered flag at half-mast. It hissed again, louder, its lips curling back to reveal a splintered fang and some serious tartar build up.

Killian braced himself for what appeared to be an inevitable fur-flying assault, but instead the feline monster darted over the chair and disappeared under the bed, surprisingly fast for such a massive creature.

"Great," he said, peering over the edge. Now he felt like he was stuck in some horror movie where the monster under the bed would lunge out and grab him as soon as he set a foot on the floor.

He fell back against the mattress. The scent of musty pillow masked only slightly by some kind of stale, powdery perfume billowed up around him.

Where the hell was he?

He lay there, searching his brain, but nothing came back to him. His last memory was getting off work and going home. But he was clearly no longer in Hell. This place was very definitely the dwelling of a human. Humans had a very different energy than demons.

Had he gone home with some human woman for a little nocturnal fun? Not his usual behavior, but not unheard of either.

He glanced around the room with its flowered walls and damask curtains. A pink housecoat was draped over a rocking chair in the corner.

He cringed at the sight. And not unless he'd suddenly developed a taste for the geriatric set.

"At least let it have been some hot granddaughter," he said aloud. The monster under the bed hissed in response. Probably not a good sign.

He remained there for a moment longer, then decided he couldn't stay trapped in this sea of frills and flowers indefinitely. He had to figure out where he was—and more importantly why.

He sat up, steeling himself for his next move. Then in one swift action, he swung his feet over the edge of the bed and gave himself a hard push against the mattress, vaulting a good three feet across the floor.

The dust ruffle quivered, then a paw with claws unsheathed shot out and smacked around, hoping to connect and maim. Finding nothing, it snapped back under the bed's depths. The bed skirt fluttered, then fell still.

"Ha," he called out to the animal, feeling smug. Then he just felt silly. He was a demon who managed to outsmart a cat. Yeah, that was something to get cocky over. Especially since he was a demon who had somehow managed to forget where the hell he was.

He stepped out of the bedroom into a small hallway. Directly in front of him was a bathroom that revealed more flowers on the shower curtain and on the matching towels hanging on a brass rack. Even the toilet seat cover had a big rose on it.

To his right was another bedroom. A dresser, a nightstand and brass bed—and of course more flowers.

He frowned. Would he really hook up with a human who was this obsessed with floral prints—very bold floral prints? He didn't think so, he was admittedly shallow, but anything seemed possible at this point.

He wandered to a living room with its swag draperies and ancient-looking velvet furniture. Ben-Gay, hand lotion, Aleve, a crystal bowl filled with mints and a box of tissues were arranged on another doily-covered table beside a tatty-looking recliner. A crocheted afghan was draped over the back.

"Let there be a granddaughter . . . let there be a granddaughter," he muttered, even though he'd seen not a single sign of youth so far.

He crossed the room to a fireplace, looking at the framed photos crowded along the mantel. Only one woman kept reappearing in the pictures and she didn't look to be a day younger than eighty. But he didn't recognize her. In fact none of the people in the pictures jogged his memory.

"Maybe I don't want to remember," he said, grimacing down at a picture of a group of elderly woman on what appeared to be adult-sized tricycles beside some beach.

Then his own shirt sleeve caught his attention—or more accurately his cuff link, deep red garnets set in a charm of a ferry boat. The symbol of his position and job in Hell.

He set down the picture and inspected himself. He was still dressed in his standard work uniform, a white shirt with a tab collar, a black vest and black trousers. He'd taken off his greatcoat sometime during the evening, but he was relieved to see all the rest of his clothing was intact.

A good sign nothing happened, but it still didn't give him any hint as to where he was or how he got there.

"Just get out of here," he told himself. He could just easily contemplate this bizarre situation in the luxury of his own place.

He closed his eyes, picturing his ultra-modern dwelling with its clean lines and stark colors. Not a single flower to be found anywhere. He visualized the living room with its black leather furniture. The bedroom with its king-sized bed and dark red walls. He especially visualized his black granite bar and the bottle of Glenfiddich Scotch Whisky.

A nice glass or two of fifty-year-old scotch and a little Xbox 360 on his big screen television seemed exactly like what he needed after all this strangeness. There was nothing like expensive liquor and Modern Warfare 2 to get him calmed down. Then maybe he'd recall his lost evening.

Let there be a hot granddaughter, he added again.

Then with his creature comforts affixed in his mind, he willed himself away from this odd apartment and back to his own world . . .

Except nothing happened.

No whirring sound, no sense of whisking through space and time. No—nothing.

He opened his eyes to find himself still surrounded by flowers and the scent of old age.

Pulling in a deep breath, he closed his eyes again, and really focused. But this time he noticed something he hadn't the first time. A sort of weighted feeling as if manacles were around his ankles keeping him in this dimension.

He released the breath he didn't even realize he held pent up in his lungs. What was going on? Why shouldn't he be able to dematerialize out of the human realm?

Buth then he realized *shouldn't* wasn't the right word. He felt like he *couldn't*. No, that wasn't exactly the right word either.

For the first time since waking up in this place, a sensation akin to panic constricted his chest. He forced himself to ignore the feeling, chanting over and over in his head that there was a reasonable explanation for all of this.

"Just go to a bar here," he muttered to himself. "Have a stiff drink here—and relax."

Things were bound to make sense if he just calmed down. How could he expect to think clearly surrounded by floral chaos.

Just then the "cat" from this morning, leapt up onto the recliner, the springs creaking under its massive bulk, It peered at him from its one good eye, then hissed.

"Yeah. I'm outta here."

He left the living room, striding toward a door at the end of another small hallway. It had to be the exit. But when he reached the door, he stopped. Everything within him told him to just grab the doorknob, turn it and leave, but again something stopped him. Told him he had to stay right here.

"Just go," he growled.

But he couldn't bring himself to move. That was until he heard the rattle of the doorknob, jiggling as if someone was inserting a key from the other side.

Killian glanced around, trying to decide what to do. He noticed the kitchen to his right and side-stepped into the narrow little room, leaning against an avocado-colored refrigerator as he listened. He heard the whoosh and creak of the door opening.

"Where is he?" a female voice said. A young female voice. The granddaughter?

"He's got to still be here," another female voice said.

Hmm, he hadn't considered there might have been more than one granddaughter. That certainly made things more interesting—and worth remembering.

Killian decided there was no point in hiding. After all, they were expecting him to be there, at least he thought they were talking about him, and they were the ones who could likely offer him the information he wanted.

He stepped out of the kitchen to see three young girls. And *girls* was definitely the operative word.

Dear Lucifer, was there *any* middle ground here?

As soon as they saw him, in almost comical unison, the girls screamed. And with the familiarity of that piercing sound, all his lost memories rushed back. The screaming girls, the flying snack foods, the thwack to the head.

Killian raised a hand, frowning down at his, for all practical purposes, abductors. Surprisingly, his gesture silenced them.

"Why did you bring me here?"

If his memories of the night before were any indication, he

needed to get answer as quickly as possible, before another candlestick-wielding woman appeared.

He shot a quick look over his shoulder, just for good measure.

The girl with a smattering of freckles across her nose and dark brown eyes moved out of the doorway, waving to the other two to join her. The other dark-haired girl joined her inside the apartment. Only the cherubic blond hesitated behind them. But finally, and clearly against her better judgment, she moved, although Killian noticed she didn't release the doorknob.

Ready for a speedy escape. Smart girl. He was not in a good mood. And he was a demon. Never a great combination.

"Who are you? And why did you bring me here?" he demanded.

The girls all shifted, nervous.

Then to his surprise, the freckle-faced one straightened to her full height—maybe a whopping 5'2"—and met his gaze directly.

"I'm Daisy."

Killian tried not to make a face. Of course, *more* flowers.

"This is Madison." Daisy said, gesturing to first one girl, then the other. "And Emma."

Madison surprised him by meeting his eyes too. She sported that ennui that all kids seemed to master as soon as their age hit double digits. Killian was tempted to point out to her she hadn't looked quite so bored just moments earlier when she was squealing, but he remained silent. Emma still clutched the doorknob, managing none of her friends' cool boredom. Quite the opposite. As soon as his gaze moved to her, she tensed as if she was ready to dart—or pass out. Her blue eyes widened and seemed to eat up half her face.

A twinge of sympathy pulled at him. He ignored it.

"I was the one who conjured you," Daisy said, her expression neither blasé nor frightened. This girl was simply direct and calm.

A girl with a mission.

"We all conjured you," Madison corrected, giving Daisy a pointed look.

"Yes." Daisy acknowledged her friend's look, but remained undaunted. "We all did. But we conjured you to fulfill my wish."

"Which we should have negotiated," Madison muttered, collapsing against the wall in a perfected slouch of disgust.

Daisy didn't even glance to her friend. She stayed focused on him. "We called you to—"

"Do something impossible," Madison interjected.

This time Daisy did shoot a censorious look at her friend. Then she said, "No. It might be a little tricky but not impossible."

Madison rolled her eyes. Emma swayed. Apparently passing out was still an option for the silent friend.

"What is this tricky—possibly impossible task?" Killian asked, growing tired of the teenage bickering.

This wasn't his usual thing. Hell, he'd never been conjured before, and he had very little experience with teenagers. But even with his admittedly limited experience, he wasn't prepared for what the earnest girl in front of him said next.

"I want you to find my sister a boyfriend."

Keep an eye out for Sylvia Day's
PRIDE AND PLEASURE,

available now from Brava!

"And what is it you hope to produce by procuring a suitor?"

"I am not in want of stud service, sir. Only a depraved mind would leap to that conclusion."

"Stud service . . ."

"Is that not what you are thinking?"

A wicked smile came to his lips. Eliza was certain her heart skipped a beat at the sight of it. "It wasn't, no."

Wanting to conclude this meeting as swiftly as possible, she rushed forward. "Do you have someone who can assist me or not?"

Bond snorted softly, but the derisive sound seemed to be directed inward and not at her. "From the top, if you would please, Miss Martin. Why do you need protection?"

"I have recently found myself to be a repeated victim of various unfortunate—and suspicious—events."

Eliza expected him to laugh or perhaps give her a doubtful look. He did neither. Instead, she watched a transformation sweep over him. As fiercely focused as he'd been since his arrival, he became more so when presented with the problem. She found herself appreciating him for more than his good looks.

He leaned slightly forward. "What manner of events?"

"I was pushed into the Serpentine. My saddle was tampered with. A snake was loosed in my bedroom—"

"I understand it was a Runner who referred you to Mr. Lynd, who in turn referred you to me."

"Yes. I hired a Runner for a month, but Mr. Bell discovered nothing. No attacks occurred while he was engaged."

"Who would want to injure you, and why?"

She offered him a slight smile, a small show of gratitude for the gravity he was displaying. Anthony Bell had come highly recommended, but he'd never taken her seriously. In fact, he had been amused by her tales and she'd never felt he was dedicated to the task of discovery. "Truthfully, I am not certain whether they truly intend bodily harm, or if they simply want to goad me into marriage as a way to establish some permanent security. I see no reason to any of it."

"Are you wealthy, Miss Martin? Or certain to be?"

"Yes. Which is why I doubt they sincerely aim to cause me grievous injury—I am worth more alive. But there are some who believe it isn't safe for me in my uncle's household. They claim he is an insufficient guardian, that he is touched, and ready for Bedlam. As if any individual capable of compassion would put a stray dog in such a place, let alone a beloved relative."

"Poppycock," the earl scoffed. "I am fit as a fiddle, in mind and body."

"You are, my lord," Eliza agreed, smiling fondly at him. "I have made it clear to all and sundry that Lord Melville will likely live to be one hundred years of age."

"And you hope that adding me to your stable of suitors will accomplish what, precisely?" Bond asked. "Deter the culprit?"

"I hope that by adding *one of your associates,*" she corrected, "I can avoid further incidents over the next six weeks of the Season. In addition, if my new suitor is perceived to be a threat, perhaps the scoundrel will turn his malicious attentions toward him. Then, perhaps, we can catch the fiend. Truly, I should like to know by what methods of deduction he formulated this plan and what he hoped to gain by it."

Bond settled back into his seat and appeared deep in thought.

"I would never suggest such a hazardous role for someone untrained," she said quickly. "But a thief-taker, a man accustomed to associating with criminals and other unfortunates . . . I should think those who engage in your profession would be more than a match for a nefarious fortune hunter."

"I see."

Beside her, her uncle murmured to himself, working out puzzles and equations in his mind. Like herself, he was most comfortable with events and reactions that could be quantified or predicted with some surety. Dealing with issues defying reason was too taxing.

"What type of individual would you consider ideal to play this role of suitor, protector, and investigator?" Bond asked finally.

"He should be quiet, even-tempered, and a proficient dancer."

Scowling, he queried, "How do dullness and the ability to dance signify in catching a possible murderer?"

"I did not say 'dull,' Mr. Bond. Kindly do not attribute words to me that I have not spoken. In order to be acknowledged as a true rival for my attentions, he should be someone whom everyone will believe I would be attracted to."

"You are not attracted to handsome men?"

"Mr. Bond, I dislike being rude. However, you leave me no recourse. The fact is, you clearly are not the sort of man whose temperament is compatible with matrimony."

"I am quite relieved to hear a female recognize that," he drawled.

"How could anyone doubt it?" She made a sweeping gesture with her hand. "I can more easily picture you in a sword fight or fisticuffs than I can see you enjoying an afternoon of croquet, after-dinner chess, or a quiet evening at home with family and friends. I am an intellectual, sir. And while I don't mean to imply a lack of mental acuity, you are obviously built for more physically strenuous pursuits."

"I see."

"Why, one had only to look at you to ascertain you aren't like the others at all! It would be evident straightaway that I would never consider a man such as you with even remote seriousness. It is quite obvious you and I do not suit in the most fundamental of ways, and everyone knows I am too observant to fail to see that. Quite frankly, sir, your are not my type of male."

The look he gave her was wry but without the smugness that would have made it irritating. He conveyed solid self-confidence free of conceit. She was dismayed to find herself strongly attracted to the quality.

He would be troublesome. Eliza did not like trouble overmuch.

He glanced at the earl. "Please forgive me, my lord, but I must speak bluntly in regard to this subject. Most especially because this is a matter concerning Miss Martin's physical well-being."

"Quite right," Melville agreed. "Straight to the point, I always say. Time is too precious to waste on inanities."

"Agreed." Bond's gaze returned to Eliza and he smled. "Miss Martin, forgive me, but I must point out that your inexperience is limiting your understanding of the situation."

"Inexperience with what?"

"Men. More precisely, fortune-hunting men."

"I would have you know," she retorted, "that over the course of six Seasons I have had more than enough experience with gentlemen in want of funds."

"Then why," he drawled, "are you unaware that they are successful for reasons far removed from social suitability?"

Eliza blinked. "I beg your pardon?"

"Women do not marry fortune hunters because they can dance and sit quietly. They marry them for their appearance and physical prowess—two attributes you have already established I have."

"I do not see—"

"Evidently, you do not, so I shall explain." His smile continued to grow. "Fortune hunters who flourish do not strive to satisfy a woman's intellectual needs. Those can be met through friends and acquaintances. They do not seek to provide the type of companionship one enjoys in social settings or with a game table between them. Again, there are others who can do so."

"Mr. Bond—"

"No, they strive to satisfy in the only position that is theirs alone, a position some men make no effort to excel in. So rare is this particular skill, that many a woman will disregard other considerations in favor of it."

"Please, say no—"

"Fornication," his lordship muttered, before returning to his conversation with himself.

Eliza shot to her feet. "My lord!"

As courtesy dictated, both her uncle and Mr. Bond rose along with her.

"I prefer to call it 'seduction,' " Bond said, his eyes laughing.

"I call it ridiculous," she rejoined, hands on her hips. "In the grand scheme of life, do you collect how little time a person spends abed when compared to other activities?"

His gaze dropped to her hips. The smile became a full-blown grin. "That truly depends on who else is occupying said bed."

"Dear heavens." Eliza shivered at the look Jasper Bond was giving her. It was . . . expectant. By some unknown, god-forsaken means she had managed to prod the man's damnable masculine pride into action.

"Give me a sennight," he suggested. "One week to prove both my point and my competency. If, at the end, you are not swayed by one or the other, I will accept no payment for services rendered."

"Excellent proposition," his lordship said. "No possibility of loss."

"Not true," Eliza contended. "How will I explain Mr. Bond's speedy departure?"

"Let us make it a fortnight, then," Bond amended.

"You fail to understand the problem. I am not an actor, sir. It will be evident to one and all that I am far from 'seduced.' "

The tone of his grin changed, aided by a hot flicker in his dark eyes. "Leave that aspect of the plan to me. After all, that's what I am being paid for."

"And if you fail? Once you resign, not only will I be forced to make excuses for you, I will have to bring in another thief-taker to act in your stead. The whole affair will be entirely too suspicious."

"Have you had the same pool of suitors for six years, Miss Martin?"

"That isn't—"

"Did you not just state the many reasons why you feel I am not an appropriate suitor for you? Can you not simply reiterate those points in response to any inquiries regarding my departure?"

"You are overly persistent, Mr. Bond."

"Quite," he nodded, "which is why I will discover who is responsible for the unfortunate events besetting you and what they'd hoped to gain."

She crossed her arms. "I am not convinced."

"Trust me. It is fortuitous, indeed, that Mr. Lynd brought us together. If I do not apprehend the culprit, I daresay he cannot be caught." His hand fisted around the top of his cane. "Client satisfaction is a point of pride, Miss Martin. By the time I am done, I guarantee you will be eminently gratified by my performance."